her deb...
CWA John Creas...
Branford Boase Award...
the Year at the National Book...
country, to speak to crowds at the...
of young people. *For Holly* is her thi...

Praise for Tanya Byrne:

'This book creeps up on you as more of the story is revealed . . . I became fascinated with the girls' relationship, constantly trying to guess how things would end up – but I'm impressed to say I got it wrong' *Woman* magazine

'Reminiscent of *The Catcher in the Rye*, this psychological jigsaw of a novel will appeal to your dark side. A troubling, demanding but addictive story' *Glamour*

'Dark but addictive' *Look*

'A tense, emotionally complex study of love and hate' *The Sunday Times*

'Punchy and raw . . . the engrossing and fast-paced narrative proves Byrne to be a consummate storyteller' *Red*

'An addictive, thrilling read' *Cosmopolitan*

'Intrigue and brilliant writing . . . a first rate debut' *Sun*

'Byrne is a talented writer with attitude and a fresh, original voice' *Daily Mail*

'Gripping' *Telegraph*

'Intriguing and utterly addictive' *Woman's Own*

'Gorgeously dark and twisted . . . impossible to put down' *Image*

'Compelling and clever. We loved' *Company*

'Intriguing and compelling' Sophie Hannah

By Tanya Byrne

Heart-Shaped Bruise
Follow Me Down
For Holly

FOR HOLLY

TANYA BYRNE

headline

First published in 2015 in paperback by
HEADLINE PUBLISHING GROUP

1

Cataloguing in Publication Data is available from the British Library

ISBN 978 1 4722 1438 6

Typeset in Goudy by Avon DataSet Ltd, Bidford-on-Avon, Warwickshire

Printed and bound in Great Britain by Clays Ltd, St Ives plc

Headline's policy is to use papers that are natural, renewable and recyclable
products and made from wood grown in well-managed forests and other
controlled sources. The logging and manufacturing processes are expected to
conform to the environmental regulations of the country of origin.

HEADLINE PUBLISHING GROUP
An Hachette UK Company
Carmelite House
50 Victoria Embankment
London EC4Y 0DZ

www.headline.co.uk
www.hachette.co.uk

For Nathan
Thank you for not stealing my thunder

There are only four people who know this story. Five including me.

You're the sixth.

As always, there are two sides to this: the one everyone knows and ours.

The one everyone knows is well documented so if you don't believe me, and I wouldn't blame you if you didn't, then you're welcome to find out for yourself. But either way you're not going to be able to avoid it because that's how you'll be defined from now on, as the girl who was at Gare du Nord. People will tell you how brave you are – that you're a fighter – and you'll have to just thank them with a smile and agree that you're lucky, even though you feel anything but.

That's why I don't tell anyone I was there, because I don't want to hear them say how glad they are that they weren't. I overhear people talking about it sometimes, about how they should have been there but slept through their alarm. I don't know why you'd want to lie about something like that, but I guess that's what people do when these things happen. They want to be a part of it, sign their name to it. If I believed half the stuff I've heard then most of Paris was there. I doubt they're all lying, but even so, it's the way they say it that makes me want to be sick, like they're special. Not lucky but *special*, as though they were spared because they're a good wife or brother or friend. That's rubbish. I need you to know that. Don't think for a second that you were there because you're none of those things. Sometimes you just sleep through your alarm. That's it. You can call it luck or fate or whatever helps you sleep at night, but no one is that special.

No one.

Then there's what happened to us. I hear the date all the time – 31 August – but I don't think about what happened at Gare du Nord, I think about you. About what I did. That's why I don't talk about it, because I can't, because you shouldn't have been there and that's my fault. I don't even know how to begin to say sorry for that, but I'm going to try.

I don't know how much you remember about that morning. Not much, probably. I don't remember all of it, either, just pieces. It's a bit like when you break a glass and you think you've swept it all up, but weeks later, you step on a shard and cut yourself. I remember the big bits that everyone knows, the stuff that was on the news, but it's the little things that hurt, the things no one knows. The email I almost sent at 4 a.m. telling you not to come. How much I worried about what to wear as if I cared what you thought of me. That's why I was running late, not because I'm special, but because I didn't know what to wear. So I wasn't even there when it happened – I was in a cab waiting to turn onto rue de Dunkerque – and while I was close enough to Gare du Nord to see it all play out, I didn't see enough to be of interest to the pack of journalists who descended on the city soon after, picking through the debris with wolfish hunger as they tried to find the right angle to secure the next day's front page.

I hope I don't sound disappointed about that because I'm not. I have thought about it, though, because I should have been there. If I got my shit together that morning I would have been standing under the Arrivals board when it happened, waiting for your train to pull in. That would have made the front page, I'm sure. Young, sweet Lola Durand, only seventeen and still smarting from the loss of my mother. You know what it's like to lose someone you love so I think you get how much I hate referring to my mother's death as *a loss*, as though she was a pair of sunglasses I left in the back of a cab. Taken is more apt. Stolen. Not that there's a word big enough – or loud enough – to describe it. But that's what the newspapers would have said, I'm sure. I've even thought about which photograph they would have used. Probably the one my father keeps in his wallet, me smiling loosely, potential burning through my school uniform.

But I wasn't there that morning. I'm lucky, Dad says. Maybe in a few years, when I don't have to fly to Paris because I'm too scared to get the train or when I can sleep through the night without being woken by the sudden snap of smashing glass I'll be able to smile when he says that.

Until then I don't feel lucky at all.

4

Sorry. I had to stop. I didn't think this would be so hard. Or maybe I did, which is why I've avoided talking about it. Either way, I hope you can read my writing. It isn't the neatest, but it's been a while since I've used a pen and paper to write anything other than a list. I wonder what the woman at the table next to mine thinks I'm writing. She keeps glancing at me so maybe she's seen my nose stud and black nail varnish and thinks I'm a writer. Everyone in Paris is a writer, a writer or a poet. I don't know what it is about this city, whether it's the coffee or that when it rains everything looks slightly smudged, like a watercolour, but everyone here has a story they want to tell. I'm no different, I suppose, even if you're the only one who's going to hear it.

I'm going to assume that you don't remember much about that morning, but you must remember how hot it was, the hottest day on record since 1976. It was horrendous, had been for *months*. It started Easter weekend and got steadily hotter so that by the time I arrived in Paris in June, the makeshift beach on the banks of the Seine was already open, a month earlier than usual. It was raining when I left London so I was startled to step off the train and feel the sun spilling through the glass roof. Startled then furious, its brightness in direct defiance of my mood.

I won't bore you with the saga that is me and my father. Here are the CliffsNotes: My mother died on Christmas Eve and in the New Year Dad said that he wanted to move home to France and accepted a job at Hôpital Lariboisière. Three months after that, at the end of March to be precise, he married Agatha. I don't know what more to say. I don't understand it and I probably never will. I'll try to watch what I say about Agatha, though, because you need to make up your own mind about her, but I'm not her biggest fan. But that was the deal: I could stay in London with my grandmother and finish my A-levels on the proviso that I spend the summer with Dad. I didn't want to, but I was so desperate to stay at home that I would have agreed to anything. Besides, I assumed he'd be too distracted with his new job and new wife to remember, but he did, and as cross as I was I must admit, I was quietly relieved not to be forgotten.

The weather was a blessing at first; the perfect excuse to escape the apartment and the stiff pleasantries Dad, Agatha and I exchanged every morning between sips of tea. 'A proper summer for a change,' he kept saying with a knowing smile, as though the city was a second-hand car he was trying to sell me. I should have known then what he was up to, but I was too busy gorging on the sunshine to question his motives.

This is your first time in Paris, right? Before the summer I'd only been here a few times myself. My father's from Carcassonne, in the South, so I've only been here for the odd weekend, usually when I've charmed Dad into letting me tag along to whatever medical conference he's speaking at. This is the first time I've been here in the summer, though. The city looks so different. It usually has a greyish hue, but in the sun, the buildings look scrubbed white and the sky's *huge*, this bright, unbroken blue that reminds me how tiny I am.

At first, I loved it. I ate ice cream and drank pastis and sat in parks reading magazines until I fell asleep (probably because of the pastis, which, no matter how much I water it down, is still lethal). It was so perfect that I almost forgot that I didn't want to be here. When the sun was at its hottest it reminded me of Barbados, of ambling around Brighton Farmer's Market, my dress sticking to my back as my grandmother sniffed mangoes and chatted to the woman filleting fish. It's a heat you can't fight, that you just have to give in to, and Paris did. The whole city slowed, everyone surrendering to the weight of the sun. There wasn't a bus worth running for, an occasion worth venturing out at midday for. The roads became sluggish, scooters not darting up and down them with the same urgency. I know there wasn't one in London, but by July there was a water shortage here, which left the city smelling like the inside of a broken fridge. The fountains and sprinklers were turned off, leaving window boxes to wither and lawns to scorch.

Before long it was too hot to sit outside, which is the only joy of such vicious weather, so people began to lose their patience. I did, too. I had no idea it would get to me so much. After all, I usually divide my summers between my family in Carcassonne and Barbados, so it's not like I'm not used to the heat. But there's a vast difference between falling asleep on a beach and having to get the Metro when it's so hot you can't summon the energy to hold onto the handrail.

It made the city feel even more unwelcoming, but in the end, the heat was what united me with the Parisians. I'd roll my eyes at the person sitting opposite me on the bus as I fanned myself with the copy of *20 minutes* I'd found on my seat or agree with the waiter that the weather was insufferable when he brought my pastis. *'Il pleuvra bientôt,'* everyone kept saying. But it didn't rain and the heat got thicker and thicker until it seemed to inhabit the city. I could feel it curling around me, licking at my skin when I walked down the street. Even inside you could feel the nearness of it, following you from room to room like a cat demanding to be fed.

At least in Barbados, in the shade of my aunt's porch, the breeze soothed the sting of the sun. But here, I feel hemmed in, the buildings inching closer and closer every day. And there's always someone in the way, a kid spilling Coke onto the already sticky pavement or someone trying to jump the queue at Carrefour. I get it now, why much of Paris is on *les vacances* from mid-July, but then I was surprised when some of the cafés began to close as well, tired of the complaints about the lack of air conditioning and the people who took up tables for hours so they could take off their shoes and rub sun cream into their burnt arms until the sun began its retreat.

Those who could headed South. We usually do, too, but even there it was unbearable. It was too hot for my grandparents, who headed to Toronto to spend the summer with my uncle and his family. So Dad suggested that when my boyfriend, Pan, got here (a condition he was forced to agree to if he wanted me to come) we go to Marseille instead. He said we could rent a boat and sail to Cassis, which sounded blissful until I realised 'we' included Agatha and I refused, reasoning that Paris in the summer couldn't be more claustrophobic than being stuck on a boat with her for five days.

It got even hotter after that, as if to spite me, so by the end of July, the city began to wilt, the news reporting melting roads and fights in supermarkets over the last bag of ice. I started to walk everywhere. Not that it was easier, but it was better than enduring the stuffiness of the Metro or the white and turquoise buses that chug around the city belching out even more heat. So when July melted into August – not long before I got in touch with you, actually – I was tired of it, exhausted by the perpetual stickiness that cold showers only offered a brief respite from.

One particularly heinous day, I caught myself praying for rain. I never thought I'd miss London's grey skies, but I did. And I missed silly things like socks and jeans and wearing my hair down. But most of all, I missed sleep. Eight hours of sweet, deep sleep swaddled in dry sheets.

That morning – the one I was meeting you at Gare du Nord – I shouldn't have been late. I was actually awake before my alarm went off and watched the sun rise between the gap in the curtains until it cast a hot white line across my bedroom floor. I'm not a morning person, I admit – I usually have to be lured out of bed with the promise of tea and a lift to college – so if it hadn't been so hot I might have questioned why I was awake, if the heavy ache in my bones that pinned me to the bed was a sign. It wasn't, of course, but when things like this happen I guess it's human nature to look for something – anything – to explain it. Not just because I need closure, but to understand why I did it so that I can say something other than sorry.

I think that's why I'm writing this. Dad told me to talk to you and I tried. I did. I even tried writing it down, which is why the first few pages of this notebook have been torn out, in case you were wondering where they were. I talked to you about everything I could think of, about the rain and the bird that comes to sit on your windowsill who I've named Dave and the nurse who prays for you even though Agatha's told her not to. But I kept coming back to this, to what I did. I don't understand it and I need to because I never want to do something like it again.

That sounds selfish – this is about you not me – but it would be easy to let this make me harder. I'm trying not to, but I don't always succeed. That isn't an excuse, rather an admission, because there's a reason why I am the way I am. Maybe one day, when you're better, you'll let me tell you about that, too, but I think you already know. Hearts aren't bones, are they? When they break they don't knit back together, they stay broken. We just have to be careful what we use to fill the crack. That's not to say I can't change, because in my weaker moments, usually at night when I can't sleep and I can't remember what I'm so angry about, I let myself wonder if I knew what was going to happen that morning. After all, my restlessness was due to more than just the heat. I couldn't sleep because I was having second thoughts, wasn't I? That's why I wrote that email at 4 a.m., telling you not to come. But I couldn't get the words right and by 8 a.m. it was too late, your train had already left.

So I know there was no sign, no nudge from the Universe warning me that something was going to happen. I was so slow that morning – dropping my toothbrush in the sink twice then forgetting to wash the conditioner out of my hair – because I was exhausted. I don't even know why I thought there was a sign. I don't believe in stuff like that any more. There's no such thing, only what we tell ourselves after these things happen so we don't feel so useless. But the truth is, if I hadn't done those things – dropped my toothbrush in the sink and not washed the conditioner out of my hair – I wouldn't have been late and I would have been at Gare du Nord as well.

11

I've never found money in the street or won anything except for a swimming ribbon when I was four just for getting in the pool, so I've never considered myself particularly lucky. Especially that morning when I left the apartment much later than I intended so I was not only forced to take the Metro, but to run to catch it. By then it was 11.30 a.m. so the rue de Rennes was cluttered with tourists, most of whom were seeking shelter under the awnings of the few cafés that were still open. I could see from their red faces that they'd been caught out by the sun, no doubt thrilled when they first arrived until they were battered down by it, like the rest of us.

I don't know how they could have been unprepared. It was all anyone talked about for weeks – the heatwave. People were dying. Parliament had been recalled from summer break. Planes couldn't take off, their wheels stuck in the tarmac. All of this when the sun should have been dimming as everyone's thoughts turned towards autumn, to jumpers and chestnut soup and going back to school. It was the last day of August so I was thinking about college, too, about being back in grey, grumpy London where I could wear a leather jacket without fainting.

Don't ask me why I wore a leather jacket that morning. Another moment of madness, I guess. I could feel the collar sticking to the back of my neck as I ran towards Saint-Sulpice with all the grace of a newborn colt in my unlaced DMs. I was about to take it off when I neared the Metro and saw something was wrong. There was a gaggle of tourists gathered at the top of the stairs, frowning at their maps, and I remember muttering, 'No, no, no,' when I realised it was shut.

If I let myself, I'd say that was a sign, too, but at the time I didn't think anything of it, assuming it was down to another track fire because of the heat as I tried to hail a cab. I don't know why I didn't keep going and take the Metro from Saint-Germain-des-Prés instead, but when I checked my watch and realised that your train was arriving in twelve minutes, panic got the better of me. It shouldn't, but it makes me feel better in a way, making such a silly decision. Cabs are scarce enough that no Parisian would bother trying to hail one, especially on a Sunday. That's what makes me feel better, not that it meant that I wasn't at Gare du Nord when it happened, but that I'm still not a Parisian. I feel like one sometimes, when I'm giving someone directions or trying to find another charm for my bracelet at *La Perlerie*. And I don't know when that happened, when the city began to feel like a pair of shoes I'd worn in.

My grandmother says it's because I'm fearless. You're my age so I think you get that. Do you even know how brave it was to come here by yourself? At least I had my father, even if I wasn't talking to him. So maybe we are fearless. Fearless not in the fighting dragons sort of way, but in that way you can only be when you're seventeen and scared of everything and nothing, all at once. But I like to think Paris has something to do with it as well. Quiet, charming Paris that

13

you can't help but fall in love with, like a boy you know will break your heart. And just like falling in love with those boys, falling in love with the city was something that just happened, even though I refused to unpack. I think that's what surprised me more than anything, how the fridge in the apartment began to fill up with the fig yogurts I couldn't stop eating. And I kept buying stuff for my room. Flowers and candles and postcards that I stuck around the frame of my mirror, next to the photos of me and Pan. Old ones I'd bought from a stall on the Left Bank which, when translated, weren't that interesting, but looked so romantic, the ink faded to grey so it looked like the words would eventually disappear altogether.

I'll deny it if my father ever asks because I don't want him to know that he was right – I do love Paris – but somewhere between arriving in a huff in June and that sunny August morning in Saint-Sulpice, Paris had become, not home exactly, but it didn't feel like I was on holiday any more, either. I even felt a shiver of pride the first time someone recognised my sing-songy accent and asked if I was from Carcassonne as well. Even so, I was still a tourist, because there I was, running up rue du Vieux-Colombier trying to nab a cab before it pulled onto rue de Rennes.

It didn't make a difference, though. I remember feeling the collar of my jacket sticking to the back of my neck again as I stopped on the corner and looked up the street, hoping to see one with its light on. The day before it had peaked at forty-one degrees and it already felt that hot, the backs of my knees wet with sweat, so I cursed myself for wearing a leather jacket. But as I said, that's another reason why I was late, because I couldn't decide what to wear and changed several times before settling on a dress and the jacket for no other reason than I didn't have time to change again. But when I caught my reflection in a shop window, I winced, the black and white striped dress I was wearing hopelessly twee. I don't know why I cared what you thought, but I looked like someone from a French textbook. I may as well have been wearing a beret and had a string of onions around my neck. Perhaps if I'd unpacked I would have had more options, but if I had, I would have got to Saint-Sulpice before it closed. Nineteen minutes and my story would end here.

But I didn't unpack and I eventually got a cab. I was so relieved that I had to suck in a breath before I could ask the driver to take me to Gare du Nord. If he noticed how flustered I was, he didn't say anything, just pulled away from the kerb with a sigh, as though I was asking something unreasonable of him. That made my panic dissolve immediately and I reciprocated with an equally petulant sigh, demanding that he turn the radio off because it was giving me a headache. It wasn't, but I was anxious enough about meeting you, and the fiery discussion about that evening's Paris Saint-Germain game was more of an irritation than a distraction.

The driver obliged with a grunt, which made my jaw clench as I shrugged off my jacket and asked if he had air con. When he ignored me I felt a stab of homesickness thinking about the London cabbies with their shaved heads and Chelsea tattoos, complaining about the weather and the idiot in front of them who won't overtake the bus. Dad always indulges them, agreeing about the suicidal cyclists and rolling his eyes when it rains, as though that never happens in England. And he says goodbye to them with such genuine affection, as though they've formed a bond in the ten-minute drive from the train station to our house, before giving them a tip. He never used to tip – the French rarely do – but apparently when he found out that he should, he was mortified, overtipping everyone as though he's trying to make up for lost time.

He still does, which baffles waiters when he tells them to keep the change, especially in the quieter cafés that the tourists don't stray far enough to find, where old men chain-smoke and sip a cup of coffee all afternoon while their dogs nap at their feet. 'They're paid enough,' the woman at the next table told him once, her face tightening as though Dad had done it to embarrass her. That made me sit up, despite ignoring him through much of dinner, stabbing at my pasta with a fork and answering each of his questions about my day with a pained sigh.

As soon as the woman looked away, something in me tensed. I can't lie, being angry with my father doesn't come as easily as it used to. It did when he first told me that he'd married Agatha (not that he was going to marry her, but that he already had) and the Earth slipped off its axis.

16

I actually felt it – the shift – as the anger roared through me, burning away everything until it was all I could feel. So for a moment, it was a relief to feel something other than the hole Mum's death had left because I was beginning to wonder if I would ever feel anything other than the absence of her. I think you understand that, too. I think you know what it's like to sit on the edge of the bath and cry over the smell of your mother's dressing gown.

I was sure Dad did stuff like that as well, but apparently not. So for weeks after he told me, my cheeks stung whenever someone mentioned him. They still do. I wasn't even answering my phone to him so I laughed when he insisted that I spend the summer with him. But Pan made me promise to try, reminding me that I'd already lost one parent so I couldn't lose another.

So I tried. And while things are slightly better between us (I at least acknowledge he exists now) I still have to leave the room whenever Agatha says something to make him laugh. Even the nearness of him makes me angry, especially when I forget and go to hug him goodnight and catch myself, my hands balled into fists as I back away. Or when I open the fridge to find that he's bought fig yogurt. The little, quiet things he does that make my resolve buckle, and I can't let it, because it feels too much like I'm forgetting my mother as well.

It's exhausting, though. You'll know what I mean when you meet him, but my father isn't an easy man to be angry with. The truth is, he doesn't have a bad bone in his body.

He goes to church every Sunday and volunteers for Médecins Sans Frontières and never – ever – raises his voice to me, even when I'm being sullen and surly and seventeen. So when that woman in the café was rude to him, as mad as I was, some overprotective gene in me took over and I 'accidentally' knocked my glass of Diet Coke off the table onto her Hermes bag. It made him gasp then laugh suddenly, so suddenly that he blushed and covered his mouth with his hand, as though he didn't know that he'd done it out loud.

That's what I was thinking about that morning when I was in the back of the cab telling myself that the driver didn't deserve a tip. I was thinking about Dad, who hides his under the receipt now, as if it's something he should be ashamed of, and the muscles in my shoulders softened. Especially when I saw the photograph hanging from the rear-view mirror.

Of all the things to remember about that day, it's that photo, the one with a baby on one side and a woman on the other that kept flipping back and forth, like the two sides of the driver's heart. I bet you have something like that, too, something that makes you cry when you think about it. I imagine him sometimes, going home and holding his wife, relearning the smell of her perfume and how perfectly his hand fits on the small of her back as he kisses his son on the forehead. I wonder if it changed him like it did me – like it did both of us – if he made sure that he was home for dinner every night and brought her flowers on a Friday. It must have, for a couple of weeks, at least, until they stopped talking about it on the news.

That's the only thing I remember in definite detail, that photograph. I don't trust that everything else is my own in case it's something I heard on the news. But that's the trouble with things like this; there are so many different versions of what happened that it's hard to hold onto your own. Things still come back to me, though, usually when I least expect it. I'll be waiting for the kettle to boil and I'll remember the rip in the leather of the back seat and how I ran my finger over it while the cab sat in traffic. Or I'll walk past someone in the street and smell the driver's aftershave – something cheap, musky – and it will turn my stomach inside out like an umbrella in a gust of wind. But I keep going back to that photo, to how even that gruff, curmudgeonly old man loved and was loved and it's almost enough to make me believe in anything.

It calmed me down, actually, watching the photograph spin, and when my breathing had settled and my heart stopped beating hard enough that I could hear it in my ears, I took a tissue out of my bag and dabbed at my throat and hairline as I rolled down the window. Not that it helped, the air outside so thick I was sure I could take bites out of it if I tried. But then the cab stopped next to a bus stop and I heard an old lady complaining to another about waiting twenty minutes. *'Cette chaleur est insupportable,'* she sighed, fanning herself with one of those red paper fans you get in China Town. *'Il pleuvra bientôt,'* the other lady sighed back and that calmed me down as well, the familiar sounds of the city. You'll get to know them, too. Chatter and coffee cups on saucers. Paris even has a smell, the warm, briny smell of the Seine sweetened by crêpes browning on hot plates at the carts on every corner.

Listening to the women chat was enough to settle my nerves, at least until a scooter shot past, filling the back of the cab with the smell of petrol. It was so strong that I could taste the *ting* of it as I checked my watch again. '*Allez! Allez!*' I gasped when I saw what time it was. '*Le train de mes amis arrive dans deux minutes.*' I hope you don't mind that I referred to you as that – *mes amis*. You probably do, but I didn't know what else to call you. Not that the driver was listening as he gesticulated wildly and asked me what I wanted him to do. '*Vous voulez que je vole?*'

The French are charming like that; you ask a perfectly reasonable question and they come back with something ridiculous. So I was about to tell him that, yes, I did want him to fly, when I noticed how close we were. We weren't in traffic at all, rather waiting at a red light to turn down rue de Dunkerque, the familiar shape of Gare du Nord ahead of us. That's when Pan rang, the sound of my phone making me jump. I don't know how he knew, but he did, and I know what you're thinking, that I should have answered, but I didn't. I wish I could tell you why, that I had an explanation that makes me look less like an asshole, but I don't. It's only looking back on it now that I can see that I was too far gone to even listen to Pan any more. I wonder sometimes what would have happened if I had answered. There was nothing he could have done – your train was already pulling into Gare du Nord – but I have such an unshakeable faith in him and his ability to save me from anything that I'm sure he could have done something.

But I didn't answer.

'Okay,' I told the driver with a sigh, the backs of my knees starting to sweat again as I realised that I wasn't going to get to the station to meet you in time. Why did you have to lose your phone? Not that it would have made a difference – you needed to get out, not stay put and wait for me – but I needed to do something, so I decided to walk. '*Je vais marcher,*' I told him with another sigh, and it was such a relief to get out of the heat of the cab that I didn't hear what the driver muttered when I handed him €30 and told him to keep the change.

I was running between two cars when I heard the BOOM and scraped my leg on an exhaust pipe. I didn't even feel it, but I think that's what I scraped my leg on. And I didn't hear anything either, but that's what I say when people ask because that's what explosions sound like, right? BOOM. That's what they want to hear and I'm happy to oblige because it's easier that way, to think of it as a story. A campfire tale about a headless horseman that will make them shiver.

Really, it wasn't as dramatic as that. Outside, I mean. I can't even imagine what it was like for you. But outside it sounded more like someone had kicked a door shut. But it was enough to make me look up. I couldn't see anything, though, everything still and perfectly in place. I even noticed how blue the sky was, then it wasn't as the station came apart at the seams.

When things like that happen in films, it's chaos, people run and scream and push each other out of the way, but I don't remember anything like that. It must have been like that inside, but outside I just remember everyone turning to look towards Gare du Nord. And I remember glass, thousands and thousands of pieces of glass flying into the air as the roof exploded.

It was so beautiful that I couldn't help but stare as each piece caught the sunlight. That's when I saw the first thread of smoke, like a crack in the middle of the sky. As soon as I saw it, I heard everything – glass breaking and metal buckling – and it was so loud – so very, very loud – as though the sky was tearing in two. Maybe it was, because the sky went from blue to black as I heard an aching roar of thunder. Then it was dark, the broken glass like stars, falling, falling until I could feel them on my cheeks. My instinct was to cover my face with my hands, but after a moment or two I realised that it wasn't glass.

It was rain.

You know that part, don't you? Or you will. You want to know why I lied, right? Why I made you meet me at Gare du Nord. This is the hard part because I don't know why. That's not what you want to hear, but I don't know what else to say. So I hold my hands up. What I did was awful and I have no idea how to make it up to you. The sad thing is, I don't think there is anything I can say. Sometimes we break things and they stay broken and I think this is one of those things. I still want to explain, though, if you'll let me. I understand if you don't want to hear it, but if you've read this far, maybe you do.

Looking back on it now, I guess it was inevitable. Not what happened to you, but that I'd do something stupid. I know it's unfair to ask for your sympathy, but you know what it's like to lose someone you love. You know what it does to you. That isn't an excuse, but I honestly don't know what I was thinking. All I can say is that if I'd been in my right mind I wouldn't have done it, and I know that I wasn't in my right mind because what I did to you was the last in a string of increasingly destructive decisions. It started with me refusing to move to Paris with my father then ignoring him (my only recourse when he refused to talk about why he'd married Agatha), and when that wasn't enough, I started to skip school and go to Sainsbury's, sneak cans of cider into the pockets of my blazer and drink them in the park. Typical teenage behaviour, I suppose, but I wasn't with my mates, I was drinking on my own at 2 p.m. on a Wednesday afternoon, like the other alcoholics.

No one noticed, though, and if they did, they didn't say anything, no doubt terrified that I'd start crying about my dead mother. Pan did, of course. He held my hair when I was being sick at a party, and when I called him to tell him that I'd had another nightmare, ten minutes later he'd knock on the back door and I'd sneak him up to my room. For weeks it was the only way I could sleep, the two of us tangled up in my bed, our heads on the same pillow. But then I was in Paris and he wasn't there and my father was, and well, you know the rest.

I still don't know how it got to this point, though, how I went from skipping school to *this*. I've been thinking about it and it started just before I got in touch with you. I was caught putting a lipstick in my bag at Sephora (another sensible decision) and after waiting almost an hour in the manager's office for my father to get me, I began to wonder if he was coming at all. I know now that he'd switched his phone off because he was in church so it wasn't my punishment, being made to wait, but despite huffing and tutting about it, my stomach clenched every time I thought the door was going to open. Not because I was scared, I just didn't want him to look at me in that way he did whenever he was called upon to retrieve me from whatever office I'd been sent to.

He used to be mildly amused by my antics. He would tell me off, of course, shaking his head when I ripped my dress climbing a tree or that time I freed the frogs from the science lab at school, but it was always with a shiver of a smile and a half-hearted wag of his finger. Now he looks at me like he doesn't recognise me. I don't know what he sees when he looks at me, but I know it isn't the giggly, ringletted girl who used to pick out his tie every morning, and I get that because I don't recognise myself, either. I think you

24

get that, too, growing up in care. Love isn't what we think it is, is it? It isn't in our blood. Just because we're related to someone and share the same colour eyes as them, doesn't mean we share that too. The way you love your family wavers in the same way it does with anyone else. It may feel different – not as hot, as eager – but it's just as fallible. I know that I'm not supposed to say that out loud, but you know what I mean, don't you? You know that our families can't love us all the time. Sometimes we do something we can't take back, like I have. And sometimes we don't have to do anything at all – like you – we're just born into a family who doesn't know how to love us the right way.

It's not that my father doesn't try – he does – but I'm a difficult person to love. The sad thing is, despite pushing him away at every turn, that's my biggest fear, that one day he'll stop trying, because I don't believe him when he says that there's nothing I can do to stop him loving me. He stopped loving my mother, didn't he? So one day I'll cross that line he insists isn't there (if I haven't already) and that will be it. There's nothing worse than someone you love seeing you for who you really are. Not for who they *think* you are, but all the things you hate about yourself, the things you can't change. The scrapes and scabs and scars you don't want anyone else to see.

So maybe that's what I was trying to do when I took that lipstick: to show him before he found out for himself. Whatever my reasons, it had been forty-eight minutes and he still wasn't there. I knew how long it had been because I made a point of checking my watch with a bored sigh every few minutes, a tactic that doesn't really work on the French given that surliness is their default setting. So I resorted to glaring at the security guard who was standing between me and the door to the office in case I made a run for it. I had no intention of doing so. I may have been stupid enough to get caught shoplifting, but I wasn't stupid enough to think I could outrun him in flip-flops. 'You gotta know when you're licked,' my mother used to say. I was certainly that, my nerves knotting as I thought about what Dad was going to say when he got there. Ignoring Agatha and standing him up for dinner was one thing; shoplifting was quite another.

'*Voulez-vous jouer je vois, je vois, devine quoi?*' I asked the security guard, because that's how I deal with tense situations: sarcasm. Not that there was much to play I-Spy with in the tiny office. The shop floor was glossy and light, everything black and white, making the rows of eyeshadows look even brighter, but in there it was miserable, the walls covered in notices about the store opening times and the Sephora summer party. There was a photo of Gaspard Ulliel taped to the side of the filing cabinet and even though he looked slightly jaundiced because it had been printed off on a cheap printer, I couldn't help but smile. Do you know Gaspard Ulliel? He's the guy in the Chanel ads. I had a debilitating crush on him when I was twelve after seeing a film he was in with Audrey Tautou. I made my father take me with him to two of his conferences that year, sure that I'd bump into Gaspard in Shakespeare and Company as we reached for the same copy of *Twilight*.

I didn't, of course, so it's funny that I ended up in Paris after I'd begged my parents to move here. Careful what you wish for, I thought as I gestured at the window. *'Pourriez-vous ouvrir la fenêtre?'* I asked the security guard, and when he ignored me, I sighed and crossed my arms. The window wasn't very big so opening it wouldn't have made much difference, but I was so hot that I could feel a bead of sweat rolling down my back.

'S'il vous plaît. J'ai tellement chaud.' I fanned myself with my hand to make the point, but he just continued to rock back and forth on his heels. 'Fine,' I muttered, reaching for one of the Clarins pamphlets on the desk in front of me and fanning myself with it instead.

'Ne touches à rien!' he hissed, snatching it from me.

'Ah! Je crève de chaleur!' I huffed when he put it back on the desk.

I was melting. Even the skin between my fingers was sweating. This was the middle of August (a couple of weeks before I got in touch with you, in fact), so Paris was well and truly in the grip of the heatwave. I rarely burn but my shoulders were red just from the short walk from Agatha's apartment. Actually, it should have been a short walk – it usually took ten minutes – but in the heat it took nearly twenty. Funnily enough, that's how I ended up in Sephora, because I remembered it had air conditioning. I'd taken my flip-flops off when I walked in and pressed my feet to the cool tiles. It earned me a filthy look from one of the assistants (which, with hindsight, is probably why she was watching me so closely) but it felt so good it was difficult to care.

'*Vous devez avoir chaud aussi?*' I pushed, but if the security guard was hot, he didn't admit it. He just lifted his chin to look at the door as it finally swung open. The manager, a thin woman with a sharp fringe and hair dyed the colour of pumpkin pulp, came in first, swiftly followed by my father who looked at me like I thought he would, like he didn't recognise me.

The manager didn't introduce herself again, just gestured at Dad to sit in the chair next to mine. Clémence, I think her name was. Or Clémentine. It doesn't matter now. It all happened so quickly – walking out of the shop and getting as far as the corner of Boulevard Saint-Germain and Boulevard Saint-Michel before realising I wasn't alone – that I wasn't listening, anyway.

'*Merci, Rollo.*' The manager nodded at the security guard, who took a step back, his hands behind his back and his legs apart as if he was waiting for her to say, 'At ease.' He was clearly relishing the drama of it all. But then apprehending a shoplifter in the street must have made a nice change from directing customers towards the Dior stand.

'*Ton père,*' she began, sitting on the edge of the desk in front of us. She hesitated, looking between me and Dad, and when the skin between her neatly plucked eyebrows creased, my fingers curled around the arms of the chair.

'*Oui, il est mon père,*' I snapped, my cheeks stinging like they do every time someone says something like that. I should be used to it by now, but it's got worse since Mum died. Me and Dad made more sense when she was alive, but without her we don't look like we belong together. If people paid attention, they'd see that we have the same chin, the same colour hair. But most people can't see beyond the fact that his skin is white and mine isn't. Last week a waiter assumed that I was his girlfriend and I was so upset that I couldn't finish my pizza.

'It's okay,' Dad said softly, putting his hand on my arm, but I pulled away.

'No it isn't,' I said, glaring at her.

'*Je suis désolée,*' she said with a smile that told me that she wasn't sorry at all. But I didn't dignify it with a response, just turned my face to look out the window, but when I saw a man in chef's whites across the street, smoking a cigarette, I had to look away again. I don't know if you smoke, but it's a new thing for me, craving cigarettes. It's like being hungry but ten times worse. It's distracting enough – dizzying enough – at the best of times, but in the heat of the office with the manager looking at me, I bit down so hard on my bottom lip I tasted blood.

If Pan had been there he wouldn't have been smug enough to say, *I told you so,* but he would have been pretty smug, because smoking was another of my A+ decisions.

An act of rebellion against my doctor father which had become something I'd started to do when he wasn't there. Looking back on it now, I should have known then, when it started getting hard to tell what was rebellion and what wasn't any more.

'Ton père,' she went on, 'a présenté ses excuses et il m'a expliqué ce qui c'est passé.'

I rolled my eyes because I knew exactly what Dad's apology involved. *Grief makes you do things that you wouldn't normally do*. That's what he usually says.

Not that he'd ever had to apologise for anything like this.

'Jesus,' I said under my breath. 'It was just a bloody lipstick.'

If the manager understood, she didn't respond. 'Donc, je ne vais pas appeler la police.' She held up a finger and arched an eyebrow at me. 'Mais il faut que tu ne reviennes pas dans ce magasin. Tu n'es pas la bienvenue chez Sephora. Tu comprends, Lola?'

'Oui, madame,' Dad said, letting go of a breath as I sucked mine in. I know I should have been equally relieved that she wasn't calling the police, but being banned from Sephora was a punishment I hadn't considered.

She stood up and gestured at the security guard.

'Merci, madame,' Dad said, ushering me out of the office before I could say anything to make her change her mind.

The security guard took great pleasure in escorting us out. There was a long moment of silence as we walked through the shop floor and everyone stopped and stared. When we passed the tills, I heard someone ask what I'd done but didn't hear the reply as I caught the eye of an assistant, who shook her head miserably, as though I'd pissed in her handbag, not tried to shoplift a €10 lipstick. But I just smiled, tempted to knock over the Benefit display on my way out.

Dad must have seen me veering towards it, though, because he grabbed my elbow and tugged me away. 'Don't even think about it, Lola,' he said under his breath, but I ignored him as I stopped and smiled sweetly at the assistant handing out wire baskets by the door.

'*J'aime votre rouge à lèvres. Vous l'avez acheté ici?*'

She looked at me for a moment, utterly bewildered, before Dad pulled me away.

'*À bientôt!*' I sang and, just in case he wasn't pissed off with me already, I smiled again at the assistant, pointed at my mouth and said, '*C'est quelle marque, votre rouge à lèvres?*'

'Lola,' he said through his teeth, pulling me away.

'What? I was just asking if she got her lipstick here.'

When he let go of my elbow, I waited for him to let rip. I knew he wouldn't shout at me because my father is almost the polar opposite of me. Where I stomp and swear and slam doors my father remains unreasonably calm. So I already knew what he was going to say. First, he'd ask why I felt the need to shoplift, and when I shrugged, he'd ask to see my purse, his jaw clenching when he found that I had more than enough to pay for the lipstick. Then he'd remind me that I was applying to universities soon and lecture me about how getting into Edinburgh would be hard enough, let alone with a criminal record, which would be the perfect time to tell him that I wasn't going to university, I was going travelling with Pan.

Not that I'd planned it, of course.

But he ignored me, which wasn't nearly as satisfying, I admit. So I just rolled my eyes as he paced towards the kerb. A couple had to stop to let him pass, but he didn't notice as he held his arm out to the approaching cab. It didn't pull over, though, and when it turned onto rue Hautefeuille, he threw his hands up. '*Et alors?*' he called after it. '*Je suis invisible?*'

'The apartment's only up the road. Let's walk,' I said with a sigh, taking my cigarettes out of my bag. When I looked up, I half expected him to snatch them from me, but he was gone.

I know I'm seventeen and far too old to worry about losing sight of my father, but when I couldn't see him in the tangle of tourists ambling towards me up Boulevard Saint-Germain, I held my breath like I did when I was six and I got lost in the Natural History Museum. It was my own fault for running off when I caught my first glimpse of the whale hovering ahead of me like a great blue madeleine, but after straining over the barrier for several minutes, trying to touch it, I turned to my father for help only to find that he wasn't there. I think that was the first time he wasn't and I erupted into tears, something I rarely did, even that time I ripped my dress falling out of a tree. I was immediately surrounded by worried mothers who patted my head and wiped my cheeks with their fingers. But that only made me more hysterical, convinced that my father was gone and I would have to go home with one of those women, as though the Natural History Museum was some sort of swap shop for unwanted children. But then I saw my father running towards me and as soon as he was close enough, I launched myself at him and didn't let go. Even on the train home, I sat in his lap, my cheek pressed to his scratchy wool scarf.

Eleven years later and I felt that same punch of panic when I couldn't see him, and it's moments like that when I don't feel grown up at all, despite my nose stud and black nail varnish and the secret cigarettes I smoke in cafés where the waiters know my name. But I think that's a good thing, because it means I can't be that bad, doesn't it? Remember that, the next time you're mad at me. Think of me standing outside Sephora, trying not to cry, and remember that I'm still human, even if I don't act that way sometimes.

It took a moment, but when a woman in a white sundress further down the street turned onto rue Hautefeuille I finally saw him. I hesitated, unsure if he wanted me to follow, but did anyway, almost knocking over a man in my haste to catch up. '*Pardon!*' I gasped, wriggling away when his hot hands cupped my elbows. By then Dad was striding past the Faculté de Médecine and as I stood on the corner of rue Hautefeuille, waiting to cross the road, I held my breath again as I watched him pass without glancing at it. He studied at Paris V, so every time he passes it he smiles. Every time. And that scared me more than anything, more than what he was going to say when I caught up with him – or worse, what he *wasn't* going to say, as if I wasn't worth arguing about any more – that he was so mad he couldn't smile at his favourite building in Paris.

Did your foster parents do stuff like that? Did they have songs that made them grin when they came on the radio or a park that would make them hold hands every time they drove past it? I'm sure they did. I used to think that smile – the way he smiles when he passes the Faculté de Médecine – was a happy one, but as I watched him walk further and further from me, I caught myself wondering if it was more wistful than fond. After all, if he hadn't helped his friend move back to London the summer after they graduated, he would never have fallen in love with his friend's new housemate, the girl with the big laugh and a smile just like mine.

It's ridiculous to think that he regrets meeting my mother, Pan says. But every time he does, I remind him that the first thing Dad did when she died was move back to France, and when Pan doesn't respond, the thought roots in a little deeper. That's the worst thing. Do you do that, too? Question everything? I know I shouldn't but I do. The smiles that may not be smiles. The things Dad won't say any more, like Mum's name. He used to say it with such softness – Alicia – as if he was scared of breaking it. Now he just refers to her as *your mother*.

Perhaps it hurts too much. That's what Pan says. I laugh when he does and I don't know when that happened, when it became easier to think the worst of my father than to accept that he doesn't know what he's doing, either, because he has to. He's the grown-up. He knows everything. He knows how clouds are made and the capital of Oman and the square root of seven. If he doesn't know how to deal with this then how the hell am I supposed to?

'Dad!' I called after him, but when he didn't stop, my instinct was to run. Luckily, I had the sense to look up before I crossed the road, the pack of cigarettes falling from my hand as I jumped back onto the kerb, narrowly avoiding a grubby white van as it careened around the corner on two wheels. The driver stopped when he saw me and threw his hands up. '*Regardez!*' he yelled, pointing at his eye. I scowled and bent down to pick up my cigarettes then pointed the box at the van's indicators. '*Indiquez! Je ne suis pas devin!*' He shook his head, muttering something I couldn't hear as he carried on down rue Hautefeuille, just as fast.

I did the same, muttering something I won't repeat as I crossed the road. By the time I did, Dad was nearing Odéon station, so I started to run again, my fingers curling around the cigarette box, almost crushing it. I hoped he wouldn't disappear into the Metro before I could catch up with him. I don't know about you, but I'm not really into exercise. Pan plays football and basketball and will try anything if

35

asked, such is his need to be surrounded by people. I prefer more solitary pursuits, like reading and napping, both of which I'm very good at and don't call upon me to run. So why I went after my father – in forty-degree heat, no less – I don't know. Usually I would have sulked in the nearest café until I'd calmed down enough to go back to the apartment, but there I was, running up Boulevard Saint-Germain. I hadn't run like that since Pan tried to kiss me when we were twelve. That hadn't ended well (which probably explains my aversion to running) and concluded with me tripping and scuffing my knee. Or maybe it did end well, because when Pan helped me off the pavement with a worried frown, it was the first time he'd been anything other than the annoying boy next door and I found myself wondering if kissing him wouldn't be so bad.

Dad didn't go into the Metro and I was breathless with relief, my satchel banging against my hip as I struggled to catch up. He must have been breathless as well, because when I got closer I could see the cloud of sweat spreading across the back of his shirt. He was usually so composed. Even at my mother's funeral, he shook everyone's hand with a smooth smile, the dark skin under his eyes the only thing that betrayed him. So to see him like that made me run even faster.

Tourists were drifting out of Starbucks. I watched them stop to blink up at the sun as I passed and felt a pinch of envy at how contented they looked, the afternoon a red carpet that rolled out in front of them as they consulted their maps and sipped frappuccinos. I was so hot that I almost grabbed one of them, sizing up the kid walking towards me before deciding that I didn't need to add 'mugging children' to my list of misdemeanours for the day.

'Dad, wait!' I called after him, my lungs straining with the effort of keeping up, but he didn't stop. So I called after him again, but just as I was close enough to reach for his sleeve, I almost went flying. It took me a moment to realise that I'd tripped on a dog lead and I was mortified. '*Oh, pardon!*' I said to the man waiting at the bus stop, but he shook his head as he tugged the tiny dog away. It yapped hysterically at my ankles and I almost tripped on my flip-flops again as I carried on up the road. By then, Dad was passing the cinema. He stepped onto the kerb to avoid the queue for the two-fifteen matinee and I finally caught up.

'Dad,' I said, panting madly as I ran alongside him.

He didn't look at me. 'Lola, don't.'

'Don't what?'

'I can't.'

'Can't what?'

He stopped and spun on his heels to face me. 'Lola, stop repeating everything I say.'

It made me stop, too. 'Fine.' I shrugged. 'I'll leave you alone, then.' When he finally looked at me, he was so angry that I had to look away, putting the cigarette box back in my bag so he wouldn't see my chin quiver. When I looked up again, he was shaking his head.

'You don't get to be the one who's mad here, Lola.'

37

'But you said—'

'Not here,' he said through gritted teeth, looking around. 'Not in the street.'

Of course not there. It was never the right time. My dad isn't a shouter. My mum didn't care – she'd kiss her teeth and tell me off in church if she had to – but my dad's more the wait-until-we-get-home type. It's always *Not now, Lola* or *Later, Lola*, as if there's a right time to talk about these things. Maybe there is. I never seem to know when that is, though. I'm always crying in restaurants after a spoonful of crème brûlée because it was Mum's favourite or when a waiter mistakes me for Dad's girlfriend. But that's the thing with emotions, isn't it? They're messy, inconvenient things that you can't swallow back or tuck in your pocket until you get home.

At least I can't.

My father can. I wish I knew how, because the grief was like an iceberg that crashed into my heart the night my mother died and I've been drowning ever since. But maybe I do know how, because that's Dad, isn't it? He has a smile for everyone. The same smile he uses at the hospital when he's consoling a worried patient or distracting a child before they have a CT scan. The one that doesn't quite reach his eyes. It's not disingenuous, he's just been pretending to smile for so long that I'm pretty sure he doesn't know how to any more. Just like he doesn't know what to say when I'm crying in a restaurant over crème brûlée because he can't understand anything that can't be stitched up or cut

38

out. He doesn't believe in time or space or hope, he believes in science – in medicine – and there's no cure for a sad teenage girl. There used to be. There used to be tickles and mint choc chip ice cream, but that isn't enough any more.

It isn't enough.

Sorry, Laurent kicked me out of the café because they're closing. Where was I? Okay. Yes. Dad and I walked the rest of the way in silence. I dragged my feet until we finally approached the door that leads to the apartment, partly because I was trying to avoid the inevitable bollocking he was going to give me, but mainly because, as I said, I'm still a six-year-old.

I always refer to it as *the apartment*, but it's Agatha's apartment. When Dad told me that they'd got married, that Friday he surprised me after college and I ran – actually *ran* – when I saw him waiting for me with a bunch of sunflowers, foolishly assuming he was there for me, I laughed when he said that he was moving into her apartment. 'Why don't you buy a house? You can afford it,' I'd said, plucking a petal off one of the sunflowers so I didn't have to look at him. He laughed, too, and when I saw Agatha's apartment, I realised why. Hopefully, you'll see for yourself. I'm sure you'll be as stunned as I was. I was expecting a flat not unlike the one my grandmother lived in before she moved in with us. (Me, actually. There is no more us, is there?) Somewhere with thin walls and windows that steam up when the heating's on. But it's a huge, bright space that takes up the top two floors of an imposing Haussmann building opposite Les Deux Magots.

It was a joy at first, the sanctuary of my vast bedroom with its parquet floors and tall windows, not that I gave either of them the satisfaction of showing it. My room at home is nothing like that. It isn't small, but there are studio flats that aren't as big as my room in Agatha's apartment. The first time I saw it, I almost dropped my suitcase when the door opened to reveal an enormous room painted *Ladurée* green. There was a piano in the corner and I would have thought Agatha was trying to butter me up if the rest of the apartment hadn't been equally exquisite.

As I said, you'll see for yourself, but I love it. I've never told anyone that – not even Pan – because it feels too much like a betrayal, but it's beyond beautiful, like something from a magazine. My favourite room is the library. I don't know what I would have done without it this summer. I've spent hours in there, lying on the brown suede sofa flicking through Agatha's *Vogues*. She has every issue since the first one she bought when she was fourteen. 'The year Anna Wintour took over,' she says as though it's a burning point in history. But then to her it is.

Would she be Agatha Abbot now if she hadn't bought it?

The magazines take up the best part of a wall. I know what you're thinking, but even I wouldn't be so cruel as to damage one of them (which I want noted for the record, by the way). I do like to rearrange them sometimes, though, which is much more satisfying than it should be, given that eventually each issue finds itself back in its rightful place. But knowing that I've ruffled Agatha enough to make her spend an hour putting them all back is enough for me.

'I'll take the stairs,' I told Dad when the door swung shut behind us. It was petty, I know (which is why I said it), but I couldn't take the lift. The thought of being in a confined space with him, even for a few minutes, when he was so upset with me made my stomach ache.

Do you ever get used to it, do you think? To your parents being mad at you? Maybe when you're thirty and you have kids of your own that disappointed look they give you doesn't sting so much. Maybe it's because Dad doesn't get angry. He gets passive aggressive, which is infuriating when all I want to do is yell, but he always gives me a chance to explain, even if he disagrees with everything I say. Even the first time he caught me and Pan kissing in my room and I thought he was going to have a stroke, he listened to what we had to say before he called Pan's mum.

But now he wouldn't even look at me.

'Fine,' he said, pulling the gate of the elevator so hard I felt the clang of it in my teeth.

The elevator, an ancient brass and wrought-iron contraption which was the first thing that made me smile the morning I arrived in Paris, runs up and down the middle of the building. The staircase wraps around it, so if I'd looked, I would have seen Dad through the cage when he passed. But I didn't, my nose in the air as I walked up the

43

stairs, my hand leaving palm prints on the rail. As pretty as it is, the elevator takes an age, so I might have made it up to the fifth floor before him if I hadn't bumped into Madame Morin. She was carrying Babette, her cake-coloured Pomeranian, who shivered gleefully when I stopped to scratch her behind the ear.

'*Bonjour, Lola,*' Madame Morin said, kissing me on both cheeks. She smelt as she always did of Chanel N°5 and the cigarettes she tried to hide with it. '*Comment allez-vous aujourd'hui?*'

'*J'ai trop chaud,*' I muttered and Madame Morin chuckled lightly.

'*Il pleuvra bientôt,*' she said with a wave as she continued on down the stairs.

'Please God,' I muttered as I continued up them.

By the time I got to the second floor, I'd never hated Agatha more, as if she'd chosen to live on the fifth floor to spite me. It certainly felt like it as I hauled myself up to the next one, no longer able to remember my reasoning for not taking the lift.

Mercifully, despite my bedroom smelling like the inside of a gym bag, when I finally walked into the apartment, it smelt as it always does, of Agatha's perfume. That's something else you'll learn. That smell is in every room, on every cushion. I even smell it on my sheets sometimes. It's unique to her, apparently, a scent blended by a perfumer on the Left Bank. (Three parts jasmine to two parts pure evil, I assume.) I once overheard her telling Dad it would make the perfect eighteenth birthday present and, um, no. At €30,000 a pop, I'd rather have a Mini Cooper convertible, thank you very much, Agatha.

I don't know why the apartment smelt of her perfume, though, especially with the windows open. Surely it should have smelt like the rest of the city, like it was dying. The high ceilings and stripped floors helped, I suppose, as did the vases of white freesias in every room. Still, I don't know why Agatha bothered. Opening the windows offered no relief, just let the noise of the street in, but she refused to ruin the aesthetic of the apartment by having anything as ugly as a fan. Not that she's fazed by the weather. Sweating is far too human a reaction to allow herself.

I'll be honest, I was tempted to head straight for my room. I probably should have, but I just wanted to get it over and done with, let Dad say what he had to say, because he and Agatha were going to a Médecins Sans Frontières fundraiser that evening and knowing him, if we left it until morning, he'd just pretend like nothing had happened. Especially with Pan arriving; he wouldn't talk about it with Pan there and it'd just become another of those things we're furious about but never mention. There's already too many of those, so I found him in the kitchen, the sleeves of his shirt rolled up to his elbows as he washed his hands in the sink. He didn't notice me – or perhaps he ignored me – so I walked over to the fridge and when I opened it to find that he'd restocked my fig yogurt I couldn't maintain my strop.

That was until he told me to go to my room.

'What?' I almost laughed, my fingers curling around the handle of the fridge as I turned to look at him, but he didn't look up and kept scrubbing his hands as if he was going into surgery.

'Go to your room, Lola.'

'Dad, it's not even three o'clock,' I reminded him, taking out a bottle of water.

He turned the tap off and reached for a towel. 'I don't care. Go to your room.'

When he turned to face me, I frowned and kicked the fridge door shut. 'Dad, I'm not ten.'

'Stop acting like it, then.'

'How am I acting like I'm ten? Ten-year-olds shoplift sweets, not make-up.'

'Case in point,' he said when I rolled my eyes, so I rolled them again.

'Whatever,' I sighed, too tired to think of a wittier response.

'You sound like a ten-year-old, too.'

'You're the one who doesn't want to talk about it.'

'I don't want to talk *now*, Lola.'

'When, then?'

He hooked his finger into his tie, loosening it enough to undo the top button of his shirt, then closed his eyes and let go of a breath. 'I think we both need to calm down, Lola.'

'Fine.' I put the bottle of water on the island between us.

'Let me know when's convenient for you.'

'That's not fair,' he called after me as I turned to walk out of the kitchen.

'I'll call your assistant, Sabine, see if she can fit me in. *Sixteen thirty to sixteen forty-five: Berate daughter.*'

He called after me again, but I didn't miss a step, heading for the spiral staircase in the hall, my flip-flops slapping against each step as I walked up it. But when I got upstairs, I didn't go to my bedroom; I stood at the top of them. I shouldn't have tested him, I know, because that's all we seem to do now – set tests for one another that we inevitably fail – but all I could think was, *Don't do it, Dad*, as I peered down the stairs. But sure enough, he passed underneath.

I wasn't surprised to see him heading for Agatha's studio, but I can't tell you how much it hurt that he could talk to her but not me. Even as I'm writing this I know that's my fault because I push him away then blame him when he doesn't come back, but we weren't always like this, you know.

I wasn't always like this.

But there he was, going to tell her what I'd done, and I wanted to run after him, take him by the front of his shirt and shake him, tell him to talk to me. *Tell me.* But I waited a moment then crept back down the stairs, my heart in my throat as I saw him reach the end of the hall.

You'll see what I mean when you go there, but the apartment, much like Agatha, is impossibly neat. The hall runs the length of the apartment, from the front door right down the middle. Each of the rooms open onto it, the kitchen and dining room on one side and the salon and library on the other, with the spiral staircase in the middle, curling up to the top floor like a corkscrew. Hidden at the end of the hall, to the right of the stone Buddha (Agatha's a Buddhist, apparently, something I've yet to see any evidence of, unless being cool to the point of sociopathy is being Buddhist) and set back slightly from the other rooms so you can't see the door, is Agatha's studio. Even though I've told you where it is, you still won't see it unless you walk to the end of the hall, which, I suppose, is the point, because it's the one room she's asked me not to go into. A rule I broke the first opportunity I got, you won't be surprised to hear.

I've seen the apartment several times in *Vogue*, on those lazy afternoons lying on the sofa in the library reading about urban florals and how to repair winter-damaged skin. The first time I turned the page to see her face, it was such a shock, I closed the magazine. I have no idea why, given that her clothes were in almost every issue. I guess I don't make the connection between Agatha Abbot the fashion designer and the Agatha who married my father any more. But there she was. And she was in another issue, and another, until I realised it was an annual thing.

An afternoon with Agatha Abbot.

She looked the same each time: immaculate in black, her blond hair tied in a chignon and her trademark mother of pearl glasses perched on the end of her nose. I don't know why I read each interview. Boredom, perhaps. Curiosity, definitely. Not that I knew any more about her afterwards. I knew about her collections, about how little she misses England and why she declined the offer to design Kate Middleton's wedding dress. ('I have no desire to wear a wedding dress so why would I want to make one?') But I still didn't know *who* she was. This strange woman my father married who seemed to exist in direct defiance of my mother. Pan says it can't be a coincidence, that they're complete opposites. Where my mother never stood still, always arguing with someone on the radio or gulping down a mug of coffee while she ironed her skirt because she was late for work, Agatha is careful, her eyebrow saying all she wants to most of the time. They even look completely different, Agatha tall and thin where my mother was nothing but soft curves and a froth of liquorice-coloured curls she was never quite able to control.

I'll show you a photo of her, if you like. You can compare it to the ones of Agatha in *Vogue*, sitting neatly on the settee in the salon or standing on the balcony, her chin raised as she looks out over Paris as if it's all hers. She never lets them into her studio, though. I had no idea it was so notorious. Did you? It's a place few people see, even her most demanding clients, who she visits at home or in their suite at the Four Seasons if she has to meet them at all. Most of the time her assistant, Sylvie, is sent to fetch measurements and requirements while Agatha does whatever she does in her studio. I hear people whispering sometimes, when she throws one of her dinner parties. '*Où est-il?*' they'll say, peering down the hall, and I'm tempted to point to the end. I don't know why I haven't, but then she's never once been in my room, never berated me for the clothes spilling out of my suitcase or the licked yogurt lids I leave everywhere, so as much as I don't understand her, I at least understand that.

That she needs a room of her own.

Having said that, I have been in there, the morning after I arrived while she was at the shop discussing the Christmas window display. I know I shouldn't have, but if you meet her, you'll understand. Agatha is *infuriating*. I've been living with her for four months now and I still have no idea who she is. She makes perfume but wears one made for her by someone else and designs clothes but only wears black. Why, I don't know. I asked her once and all she said was, 'Because it's easier.' And that, right there, is Agatha in a nutshell. She gives you nothing.

Absolutely nothing.

So that's why I went into her studio, not to be nosy, but because I hoped it would help me understand her better. The rest of the apartment is so rich – red leather and black lacquer and gold touching everything from the picture frames to the birds painted on the Chinese screens in every room – that I was surprised at how white it was. It was shocking, making each glimpse of the rooftops through the naked windows look like paintings in a gallery.

I don't know about you, but I don't much care about fashion. Okay. That isn't strictly true. I'm seventeen, of course I care what I wear, but in that hopeless hipster second-hand coat and DMs kind of way. I couldn't care less about labels. (She says, bragging about her DMs.) But even I was in awe. It was a bit like a sweet shop, reams of gold braid and coloured ribbon on the table in the middle and what I'm guessing was once an apothecary cabinet now filled with buttons.

I really hope you get to see it. As bright as it is, the studio was still obviously Agatha's. Everything had its place. Her sketches were masking-taped to the drafting table, the rolls of fabric propped against one wall, like a clump of silk bamboo. Even the buttons were sorted neatly, drawer-by-drawer. The clothes she designs are just as precise. Neat and elegant – flawless, I would say, if I was feeling generous – but always with a detail that stops them being predictable. A jacket lined with an unexpected print or a dress cut at an angle to expose a skirt of feathers.

If that isn't Agatha, I don't know what is. Hopefully, you'll find out for yourself, but just when you think you know her, she'll mention a summer in Ibiza with Kate Moss and you'll realise that you don't know her at all. I was sure I'd leave Paris no closer to finding out. Not that I wanted to. I just wanted to know what it was about her that made Dad forget so easily. That made him want to smile and laugh and live when most days I feel like I'm still sitting in that green plastic chair at St Thomas', waiting for someone to tell me that my mother is going to be okay.

After Dad told me that he'd married Agatha, I didn't say anything for a long time and sat there, cradling the sunflowers he'd given me. It wasn't surliness, rather shock, because we were supposed to be in it together, you know? He's the only one who knows what it was like in that waiting room while Mum was in surgery, the only one who knows what it was like to walk back into the house without her. He took three plates out for dinner, like I did, and couldn't look at the bouquets of flowers that kept arriving, as though a dozen white lilies could possibly ease the ache of the grief pulling us apart, bone-by-bone.

It made me feel better when I couldn't get out of bed or when I ignored my phone because I was sick of saying that I was fine, that he was somewhere, doing the same thing. But he wasn't. He'd moved on, fallen in love and got married. Started a whole new life without me. So when he asked me if I wanted to meet Agatha, I said no because when I looked at him, I still saw Mum, saw both of them, saw Dad taking his hand off her shoulder to cover her eyes when they posed for a photograph and Mum making him dance at weddings even though he didn't want to.

It was Pan who persuaded me to meet her, reasoning that it wasn't something I could avoid forever despite my attempts to argue otherwise. Mercifully, when they first came to London together, she didn't stay at our house, but it meant that Dad didn't either, which is what did it for me. It didn't matter what Agatha said or did after that; she would always be the one Dad chose over me.

They stayed at the Savoy and I was summoned for afternoon tea like an out of town relative they felt obliged to see but would rather not invite to their house. Dad wore a suit. Agatha wore black. I wore DMs and the khaki Army and Navy parka Pan had written Y.A.L.A on the back of with white paint. With hindsight, I should have dressed more appropriately. After all, I was nervous enough as it was, I didn't need to be stared at as well, but I know what my father wanted – what he always wants – for me to be a good little girl, to sit neatly in my prettiest dress and be charming so I wouldn't scare his new wife. I had no intention of doing any such thing, so when he saw me swagger into the Thames Foyer, my curly hair everywhere, he went rigid. Agatha, however, looked mildly amused. She's always been entertained by me, but especially so that afternoon when everyone turned to look at me as I walked over to where they were sitting.

'Hey,' I said with a sullen sigh, not making eye contact with either of them. My father kissed me on both cheeks, but Agatha didn't. She didn't do anything in fact, just looked at me in that way she does. You'll see what I mean when you meet her. Agatha has this way of looking at you like she sees everything. The ladder in your tights and the chip in your nail varnish. She sees it all, but she doesn't say a thing, just smiles as if to say, *I see*.

What my father sees in her, I don't know. But there has to be something, right? Because there he was, walking into her studio. I waited a second then followed, hissing at my flip-flops to hush as I tiptoed towards it. I hid behind the Buddha at the end of the hall, my heart jumping onto my tongue when Sylvie scuttled out, no doubt despatched to make tea or deliver new sketches to the atelier. I knew that I couldn't be seen thanks to the swell of the Buddha's stomach, but I held my breath anyway, pressing my back to the wall as I said a little prayer that Sylvie wouldn't look back as she walked towards the front door. Thankfully, she didn't, just scooped up a pile of envelopes from the side table and hurried out.

I let go of the breath then, walking around the Buddha to press my ear against the door to the studio. It took a second or two for my heart to settle enough to hear anything, and when it did, I heard Agatha's voice first. 'Pan gets here tomorrow. He always calms her down.'

My cheeks burned and yeah, I know – I know – that I'm irrationally overprotective of Pan, but it's the way she said it, so casually, as if she knows me. Knows him. Do you have someone like Pan? If you do then you'll know why it was all I could do not to go in there. But before I could, I heard my father say, 'Yes, but shoplifting, Agatha. This can't go on. I can't do this any more.'

Do you remember when I said that there's nothing worse than someone you love seeing you for who you really are? Well, if there's a moment that I became this – *me*, the me who once thought of you as collateral damage – it was then, because he didn't have to look at me, I heard it in his voice.

I can't do this any more. Not pain or disappointment or even pity, but defeat.

This is going to sound so fucked up, but you're lucky you grew up in care. If you haven't already lobbed this notebook across the room then I'm sure you want to, but think about it: what's worse? Having no parents or losing them? At least you'll never know what it's like to have your call rejected or to eat alone in a restaurant because your dad's been paged. And you'll never be a surly teenager who slams her door and sneaks her boyfriend in at night and shoplifts lipsticks because her dad's so done with her that he can't even be bothered to try any more.

I hope you never know what it is for someone you love to give up on you.

It was a struggle to stand up after that so I didn't catch what they were saying until I heard Agatha: 'If she's doing this to get our attention, Simon, she's succeeded.'

Our.

Agatha and I only speak when we have to, so hearing her crisp English accent is always a shock, especially after being in Paris so long, but I felt the word sink into me like a splinter.

'What are we going to do, Simon?'

We.

'We have to do something.'

We.

'She can't go back to London.'

It wasn't until I felt a sting in my palms that I realised

my fingers were balled so tightly my nails were cutting into them. I made myself stop but it didn't help, every muscle in my body clenching, all at once, when I heard Dad say, 'I know.'

What little control I had over myself abandoned me then as I charged into the studio. Agatha didn't flinch, just sat at the drafting table, her glasses folded in her hand. I half expected her to throw her head back and laugh like a pantomime villain when I flew in, but she did what she always does when I have one of my outbursts and tilted her head at me, more curious than startled at the peculiar teenage girl who always seems to be crying.

My father was surprised, though, and spun around to face me, his cheeks pink. 'Lola.'

'What do you mean, I can't go back to London?'

I took a step towards him, but he took one back and turned to look at Agatha. They exchanged a glance and suddenly I was fourteen again and asking Michelle Ansah why she'd invited everyone in our year to her birthday party but me. The look she gave Sandra Holt before they dissolved into giggles was the same one Dad gave Agatha – like they were closing a door in my face – and I had to get out of there.

I heard my father call after me, but I didn't stop and he didn't follow.

I know I shouldn't have run off like that. What would you have done? Most people would have stayed and dealt with it, I suppose. But that's the trouble with me and my father; we never seem to be in the same place at the same time any more. When I want to talk he doesn't and when he wants to talk I don't. I think we're doing it on purpose now.

I ended up hiding in my favourite café – the one I'm in now – on rue des Beaux-Arts, far enough away from Ladurée that the tourists never find it so the café is somewhere I've only ever told Pan about. I knew Dad wouldn't find me there, either (if he was even looking, of course). Not that it's a secret. I can take you there if you like. The weather's too miserable for it now, but have you tried *diabolo menthe*? If you haven't then you must have seen people drinking it. It's bright green – Night Nurse green – and Laurent, the waiter here, makes the best ones. Seriously. The first time he brought me one (when he saw me struggling to finish my pastis) I thought it would taste like Night Nurse, too, but it's delicious. It's made out of mint syrup and lemonade and I'm pretty sure that the smell of mint will always remind me of this summer.

I don't know why I haven't told Dad about this café, but every time he asks me where I'm going when I'm leaving the apartment, I lie. That sounds so stupid, but as I said, we weren't always like this. There was a time I told him everything. I laugh when I think about it now, how I used to save up my stories until he got home from the hospital so that I could regale him with tales of correcting my teacher and my epic battle in the garden with Pan with the swords we'd used up all the tin foil making.

Daddy's Girl, my mother used to call me when I fell and cried out for him. If I was, I'm not any more, because every time I see him smile at Agatha my chest feels like an empty cupboard. That's what I mean when I say that you're lucky, because it's a terrible thing to look at your father and realise that you don't need him any more. Maybe that's growing up. Maybe that's why I cried that day at the Natural History Museum when I was six, because I knew that he wouldn't always be there. He isn't. That sounds harsh, but I think you can relate to that more than anyone. That's definitely growing up. It feels like it, anyway. It's not that I don't miss him when I'm in London. I do – of course I do – but not like I miss my mother, with that same unreachable ache that makes me cry in restaurants sometimes. It isn't fair, I know, because the loss is incomparable, but in a way I've lost my father as well. The father I knew, anyway. The one who loved my mother.

But if he and I don't look right without her, then maybe we don't make sense without her, either. Dad's good at practical things like cut knees and reattaching doll limbs and Mum was good at everything else. She was the one who slept in my bed when I had a nightmare and reminded me it wasn't the end of the world when I failed a test. Between them I had everything I needed and now . . . Well, let's just say that the €20 Dad gives me every time he can't make dinner because he's been called in to the hospital isn't nearly enough.

I'm laughing because you don't know how many people tell me how lucky I am to be living in Paris with an Agatha Abbot handbag in every colour. You probably look at my life and think it's perfect compared to yours. I guess it is. But nothing's perfect. No one's perfect, either. Especially me. I don't need to tell you that, but I need you to remember this: if I really wanted to hurt my father, I'd tell him the truth. I'd tell him that it feels like I've lost him, too.

The irony is, he *wants* to know – about my life, about what university I want to go to and what I'm saving up for – even if he's unprepared for a response other than, 'Fine, Papa,' when he asks how I am. So I know it worries him, the things I keep from him. He hates that my bedroom door is always closed now, hates how I shut my laptop when he walks in without knocking. I've seen the way he looks at me. He no doubt assumes the worst, torturing himself thinking about what me and Pan are doing. But what he should really worry about are the cafés I don't tell him about and the books he doesn't know I've read and the lists I write on whatever I can find, on napkins and beer mats and flattened out cigarette boxes: lists of all the things I want to do, places I want to go, cities I've never even mentioned.

If he ever read them he wouldn't believe I wrote them.

Do you think that's what growing up is? Not so much growing up, rather *out* and away from the person your parents want you to be. I buy my own clothes now and I don't need him to drive me everywhere like I used to and that's worse than whatever he lies awake worrying about – if me and Pan are sleeping together, if we're being careful, if I'll ever be able to be in the same room as Agatha for more than a few minutes – because I'm becoming someone else, someone who likes to eat peanut butter straight from the jar and wear pink lipstick despite his aversion to both. And I like to drink red wine with lunch, something else I discovered in this café. Not that he'd be angry about it, the French are much more liberal about these things, but I still don't want him to know that we have that in common, that we both like red wine. And it's these moments, when I won't give him the smallest morsel of information, that I wonder if we've gone too far in opposing directions.

That's something else he should worry about, I thought as I picked at the salad Laurent brought me, if we're ever going to find our way back. The thought made me drink my wine too quickly and I shouldn't have ordered another, but Laurent never asks for ID (another reason this café is so dear to me). I drank that too quickly as well, my head spinning when I stood up. *'Je vais m'asseoir à l'extérieur,'* I told him when I ordered another, pointing at the door.

Sitting outside was foolish – Dad might have seen me – but it had been an hour and, I reasoned, if he was going to find me, he would have by then. Besides, I needed some air, my scalp sweating from sitting in the stuffy café. Laurent must have known because he didn't bring me another glass of wine, he brought me a carafe of water and my unfinished salad. *'Mangez, Lola,'* he told me with a frown not unlike Pan's. Eating didn't make me feel better, though, and neither did smoking, but it marked the time, each cigarette another five minutes wasted. Ten if I took my time. Besides, what else was I going to do? I didn't have a plan when I stormed out, only to put as much distance between me and Dad as possible, which left another three hours to waste before he and Agatha left for the Médecins Sans Frontières fundraiser.

'Ça va, Lola?' Laurent asked when he came outside to collect my plate. I nodded, stunned that this man – this stranger, really – knew me well enough to ask if I was okay. *'Quand est-ce que Pan arrive?'*

I brightened at the thought of Pan's visit. *'Demain.'*

'Ah. Voici le sourire!'

I didn't realise until he said it that I was smiling. I touched my cheeks with my hands, giggling to myself as he walked back into the café. The thought of seeing Pan again, of bringing him here for lunch the next day, made me dizzy. I knew it would be strange, sharing the city with

61

him after spending so much of the summer alone. That made me dizzy as well, the thought of showing him around, introducing him to each café and park bench as if they were my friends.

I wondered if it – Paris – would be different with him there. After all, I'd spent the summer perfecting that dance with Dad and Agatha – out when they were in, in when they were out – to the point that having to waste three hours was nothing. Three hours was lunch; a walk to Parc Monceau and back. It amazes me how gleefully I waste time now. I can lose a day wandering around the Marais eating wedges of poppy-seed strudel, an afternoon watching a film at La Pagode, an hour trying to work out if a €5 pair of Ray-Bans in Guerrisol are fake.

At first I was miserable, the days unbearably long. I would run down the battery of my phone calling Pan to ask about the most inane things – what he was having for lunch, what the weather was like in London – and texting him photos of everything I'd seen that day so it would feel like we'd seen them together. That was the hardest thing: being there without him. There's something kind of tragic about being alone in Paris, where it feels as though everyone is in love.

I used to cry sometimes or I'd find myself at Gare du Nord, looking up at the Departures board. But then I found this café. Laurent didn't say, *'Vous-êtes seule?'* the first time I went in, and didn't make a point of removing the other wine glass and napkin when I sat down, which was a relief because it was awful, at first, eating alone. Have you ever done it? I never had before I got here. Not even a coffee. I couldn't do it for weeks, preferring to buy something and eat it in a park than go into a café by myself. But I grew weary of baguettes and crêpes then one afternoon I passed this café. A woman was sitting on one of the benches outside, smoking a cigarette with great panache, and I couldn't help but stop. She didn't have a magazine and wasn't tapping at her phone; she was just sitting there, enjoying a cigarette and a coffee, and I thought, how brave.

So I went in.

I've been in every day since and I feel so comfortable here that I don't need a magazine or my phone, either. I'm content to chat to Laurent while he wipes down the tables and tease him about the Specials that haven't changed in weeks. But as brave as that feels sometimes, I was still glad that Pan was coming because it isn't right to be that happy on your own.

I hadn't thought about it before now, but there's something kind of tragic about that as well. I'm not telling you all of this so that you feel sorry for me, but I need you to know how alone I was because I think you get that. I think you understand the things you'll do when you're sad and lonely and there's no one there to stop you.

'Où maintenant?' Laurent asked when I went inside to pay the bill.

I didn't know where I was going, so I just shrugged. 'Qui sait, Laurent?'

'*Excusez-moi, mademoiselle,*' someone said as I turned to leave. When I looked back, a tall guy with cornrows stood up and tugged his headphones down so they hung around his neck, the tinny sound of a song I recognised bleeding through them. '*Je m'appelle Didier.*' He reached over the table he was standing behind and handed me a neon green flyer for an exhibition.

The café's so close to the National School of Fine Arts (or ENSBA as everyone here calls it) that artists were always coming in to hand out flyers for their exhibitions. Didier's – an illustration of Ronald McDonald leading a string of children towards the edge of a cliff – was much like the others I'd been given; everyone in Paris determined to be the next Banksy, it seems. It reminded me of a sticker I'd seen earlier. I don't usually notice them, dotted on the lamp posts and bins around here, but it was stuck to the window of Café de Flore. That sort of thing was overlooked here – maybe even in Montmartre – but not on the rue de Rennes. *Absolument pas!* Saint-Germain is the little black dress of Paris. It's classic. Elegant. The tourists come to drink coffee and buy €30 boxes of *macarons* so as not to think about anything as taxing as politics. So when I looked down at the flyer, I couldn't help but smile as I wondered if he'd put the sticker there.

I knew the gallery; I'd seen another exhibition there. That wasn't my thing, either, but at least it was different, the walls papered with pages of *Le Monde*, the headlines replaced with lyrics. GOD SAVE THE QUEEN and

EMANCIPATE YOURSELF FROM MENTAL SLAVERY.

Didier must have sensed I was wavering, because he grinned. '*Il y aura de la bière.*'

I smiled but I don't know why; I don't even like beer. But when his smile widened and he pointed at his table and asked me to stay for a coffee, I regretted it.

I considered it. I know some people would have. Perhaps I should have given that, apart from Laurent, I haven't made any friends in Paris. It would have been nice to waste the hours until Dad and Agatha left for the fundraiser drinking coffee and talking about Shepard Fairey. But there was something about the way he looked at me from under his eyelashes, like Pan does, that made me realise it would be more than just a coffee.

'*Merci.*' I smiled and fanned myself with my hand. '*Mais j'ai besoin d'un peu d'air.*'

'*Il pleuvra bientôt,*' Laurent called after me as I headed for the door.

I rolled my eyes and reminded him that he'd said that every day for the last month as I walked out, deciding to head to Square-Gabriel Pierné to sit on one of the book-shaped benches under the shadow of the trees. But as I was walking up rue Bonaparte, I saw the sign for Didier's exhibition in the window of Espace Seven and stopped. If this was a film, I told myself, taking my phone out of my bag, I'd go and we'd fall in love. 'Everyone's in love when they're in Paris,' Agatha said with a wave of her hand when I told her I wasn't interested in a summer

65

romance. 'You'll fall in love, too,' she added as though it was something only tourists did, like visiting the Eiffel Tower.

'I'm leaving you,' I told Pan when he answered.

He didn't miss a beat. 'Who for this time?'

'His name's Didier.'

'He sounds like an asshole.'

'He's an artist.'

'Definitely an asshole.'

'Oi. I could have been his muse!'

'You don't shut up long enough to be anyone's muse.'

I tried not to laugh, but couldn't help it. 'You excited about tomorrow?'

'Of course, but I can't imagine how it's hotter there than here.' He groaned. 'I'm dying.'

'Didn't you just get back from India?'

'It was only thirty-three degrees when I left.'

'*Only* thirty-three degrees.'

'It was *forty* in Paris yesterday.'

'Pack your booty shorts, baby.'

'Already have.'

'You've already packed?'

'Yep. I'm looking at my bag right now.'

I took the phone away from my ear to check the time and when I realised it was only three o'clock in London I'd never loved him more. 'You're such a dork.'

'Dork trumps asshole.'

It definitely does.

'What've you been up to today? Pushed Agatha down a flight of stairs?'

I heard a rustle through the phone and when I imagined him lying back on his bed with his hand behind his head, I felt a sudden stab of homesickness. I missed his room. Missed the green walls and his M.I.A. posters and his stripy duvet cover that always smells of those purple washing tablets that his mother uses. I even missed his stupid comic books that I'm not allowed to touch after an incident with a mug of tea that I tried – and failed – to blame on his cat.

I wondered what he was doing, listening for the scratch of his pencil through the phone. Pan's a doodler. (He's an artist, actually, but he'd never refer to himself as one.) That's my first memory of him, sitting at his kitchen table, the tip of his tongue poking out of the corner of his mouth and a green crayon in his fist. We were six and his family had just moved in next door. My mother wasn't the pop-round-with-a-chicken-casserole type, so she brought a box of tea and the menu from the Chinese restaurant at the top of the road. Pan's mother looked a little bewildered, especially when Mum told her to try the crispy seaweed, but she invited us in anyway.

Mum had told me that they had children so I was beside myself with anticipation. You're an only child too so I think you get that. You'll also get how disappointed I was when we walked past the living room and glanced in to see Pan's twin sisters, Thush and Karm, tottering unsteadily around his brother, Sen, as he sat on the floor in front of the

67

television, watching *Bob the Builder*. Mum says I huffed when I saw how young they were, which I deny, but if I did it was because I was cross at her for getting my hopes up. But then we followed Pan's mother into the kitchen and that's when I saw him at the table and my little heart fluttered.

He didn't want to play football, though, he wanted to colour in. I thought we'd never be friends, but now he's the one who plays football and I'm the one pulling him away from his conversation with the guy selling the *Big Issue* outside the station. I don't know when that happened – when he became the sociable one, the one who's mates with everyone while the only friend I've made here is a forty-year-old waiter – but that's one thing that hasn't changed, his doodling. I don't even think he knows he's doing it any more. It used to bother me, especially when I was trying to tell him something. We'd be on the bus and I'd be telling him about whatever Michelle Ansah and I were feuding about that week and I'd catch him drawing an alien on the back of the seat in front of us. I used to think he wasn't listening but he was. That's what Pan's like; he'll make you miss the beginning of a film because he's chatting to the guy selling the *Big Issue*, but he can tell you what you were wearing that night.

Now I like to watch him sketch, his brow furrowed and his hand in his long hair to keep it out of his eyes. Even his parents are used to it. He used to drive them nuts when he was a kid. I'd hear his mother yelling at him through the walls and smile, wondering if she'd found the door he'd drawn on the skirting board in his bedroom or the tree on the side of the shed. I bit down on my bottom lip as I thought about it, about him lying in the middle of his bed, looking at the brown leather bag he brought back from Chennai a few years ago that seems to serve him for every trip he takes, whether it's two days or a month. I missed him, too. Not just the way his nose wrinkles when he laughs and how he lets me plait his hair when we're watching a film, but the nearness of him, the space he takes up in my life. How he knows not to touch my hair when we're watching a film and carries my bag home from college, even when I tell him I'm fine, and listens to my ferocious rants about Agatha then, when I stop for breath, asks me to give her a chance. I've never told him this, but he makes me a better person, and without him something was off balance.

I was off balance.

That's what's been missing, I thought, as I looked at the poster for Didier's exhibition. Pan. Do you wear a watch? You know how if you forget to put it on in the morning everything feels off for the whole day? That's what it was like, being in Paris without him.

So I didn't tell him what happened that afternoon, about what I'd done at Sephora and Dad making me stay, and I should have, because I always tell him everything – or at least I used to – but it wasn't something I could tell him over the phone, was it?

'I'd better get home. I'm supposed to be grounded.'

He went quiet but as I was about to ask him if he was okay, I realised what I'd said.

Home.

It's just a word, isn't it? *Home.* You get that, don't you? I don't know how many foster homes you've been in – Dad says it was a lot – but you must have done that after a while, called wherever you were home. It doesn't mean anything, does it?

It's just a word.

I wanted to tell Pan that, list all the reasons why I hated being in Paris and couldn't wait for him to get there. But I knew I'd make it worse. I can never say what I want to in these situations. I usually end up babbling and apologising clumsily (which is why I'm writing this down; I could never say all of this to your face), so I made myself put my phone back in my bag. He'll be here tomorrow. That's what I told myself as I sat on my favourite bench by the Seine, the one near Pont Royal bridge. If you ever need some space – and you will – let me know and I'll tell you where it is because it's one of the few places in Paris that you can be alone. Not completely – I don't think you can ever be completely alone in a city like this, even if it feels as though you are sometimes – but most of the tourists don't realise the bench is there. Most people walk right past it, distracted by the stalls selling

71

old books or the antique shops on the other side of the road. Why look over the wall when you have that view of the Louvre across the river?

I guess that's why most people don't notice the steps leading down to the path. It's only used by cyclists and the odd local walking their dog, which meant that no one bothered me as I sat there, watching the boats swish by. I could hear each one approaching as the tour guide pointed out the art shop, Sennelier. Even if you're not into art, you should go in there. It's beautiful. They used to mix paint for Cézanne and Degas and invented the oil pastel for Pablo Picasso, apparently.

I'm chuckling because I sound like Wikipedia. That was another way I found to waste an afternoon when I first got here – I've taken the tour four times now – so I know the story off by heart. I know that Quai Voltaire was originally called Quai des Théatins but was renamed after Voltaire in ... Okay, I'm rubbish with dates. It was a *really* long time ago. But I do remember that the people with the green stalls on either side of the river are called *bouquinistes*. Isn't that such a lovely word? *Bouquiniste*. I thought they sold tourist tat at first but they sell all kinds of cool stuff. Not just books, but old magazines and fashion plates of ladies in huge silk dresses. That's where I got the postcards I've stuck around the mirror in my room, from a *bouquiniste* near Notre Dame. I don't know if you're into that sort of stuff, but even if you're not, you can't avoid it. That's what Paris is like: you approach a stall to buy a postcard and end up flicking through a hundred-year-old cookbook.

I probably sound like a right weirdo. I look like one, too, because I just chuckled again and Laurent asked me if I've lost it. Pan would rip the shit out of me if he read this. I don't answer my phone when *America's Top Model* is on and I'm doing boat tours and talking about oil pastels. I don't even like art. I can't remember the last time I went to an art gallery without being made to. Actually, I do; I took Pan to the Lichtenstein exhibition at the Tate Modern last year, but only because it was his birthday. I'd never waste a Saturday doing something like that. Pan does. He loves Sennelier and the story of Picasso's oil pastel. Thinking about it now, that's probably why I'm so drawn to it. I thought I was getting away from the tourists, but maybe I'm trying to get closer to him.

Whatever my reasons, all I know is that he'd think this was hilarious. I've never been bothered about art before. I'm more Damian Marley than Damien Hirst, he says, and I am. I never get what I'm meant to be looking at and don't know the right way to walk around a gallery. He does, but when I'm on my own I always seem to go against the tide, which isn't necessarily a bad thing, but I'm often the only one looking at a painting while everyone else moves on. So before I got here, it would *never* have occurred to me to spend a morning wandering around an art gallery – or on a boat tour. When I'm at home, I go shopping or lie on Pan's bed watching him sketch. But that's what Paris does to you. If you don't already know that, you'll see. You can't walk

73

into somewhere like the Musée d'Orsay and not fall in love with it. I can't lie, I still don't get half of it, but check out the fly toilet on level two. If that doesn't make you smile, nothing will.

God. What am I talking about? Shut up, Lola. I'm babbling, I know. Procrastinating, actually. How did I even get on to this? Oh yeah, the Musée d'Orsay. So after I said that word that means absolutely nothing, I considered walking down there, but it was nice by the river, waving back at the kids in their cotton sunhats and Crocs and watching the tour guides point out the green stalls. Before I could think it, I heard one of them say, 'The Seine is the only river in the world that runs between two bookshelves,' and I should have smiled, because I texted Pan with that the first time I took the tour. But before I could ask myself why the memory made my stomach hurt so much, I noticed someone on the boat taking a photo of me, as though I was another landmark.

Statue of sad girl, smoking.

He'll be here tomorrow, I thought again as I turned my face away.

Do you do that? Repeat things? A bit like a mantra, I suppose. Anyway, that's what I told myself every time I remembered what I'd said to Pan. *He'll be here tomorrow.* As though him getting there would somehow correct an imbalance in the universe. He'd get there and I wouldn't have to explain; he'd see for himself that nothing had changed.

74

That I hadn't changed.

I was so distracted by the thought that I didn't even notice that I'd smoked my way through a pack of cigarettes. I was disgusted with myself, so when I got back to the apartment, the first thing I wanted to do was to get into the shower and wash the smell of tobacco out of my hair. I didn't realise I wasn't alone until I heard someone behind me. I stopped, turning away from the spiral staircase expecting to find the housekeeper, Josette, asking if I was hungry.

But it was Agatha.

I almost dropped the bunch of roses I was holding.

'Agatha.'

'Josette,' she called out, taking off her glasses. When the housekeeper appeared at her side, Agatha said, '*Appelez Simon. Dites-lui que Lola est rentrée.*'

'Why?' I frowned when Josette turned and walked back into the kitchen. 'Where's Dad?'

'Out looking for you.'

'Looking for me?' I was so flustered it was all I could say. I'd spent most of the summer wandering the city until it got dark but Dad had never gone looking for me before.

'He was worried,' Agatha said with a small sigh. 'I told him it wasn't worth missing the fundraiser for. You're like a moody cat, Lola. You always come home when you're hungry.'

I felt it like a knee to the ribs but for once, I didn't take the bait.

75

'One more thing,' she said as I turned towards the staircase. 'I called BSP.'

I stopped and turned back to face her. 'BSP?'

'The British School of Paris. The headmaster is a dear friend.'

'What?'

I stared at her, but she went on. 'I've arranged for you to meet with him tomorrow.'

'Tomorrow?' My heart began to beat very, very slowly. 'But Pan's coming tomorrow.'

'He can come with us, if you like.'

I don't know how much damage you can do to someone with a bunch of roses, but if my father hadn't walked back into the apartment then, I would have given it a good go.

'Did you know about this?' I asked before he'd even taken his key out of the door.

'About what?'

'That *she*,' I pointed the roses at Agatha, 'arranged an interview at BSP tomorrow.'

When he didn't respond, I shook my head and turned to face the stairs again.

'Of course you did,' I hissed as I stomped up them, the staircase shivering with each step.

'Lola, listen.'

'Whatever, Dad. I'm going to my room,' I muttered, because I knew then why he'd gone looking for me. He wasn't worried about me, he wanted to talk. I almost laughed

76

because it was like that day I walked out of college to see him holding those sunflowers. I thought he was going to tell me that he was coming home, but he wanted to tell me about Agatha.

'Lola.'

'What?' I didn't mean to say it so aggressively, but that's the trouble with my father, he won't talk until he's ready, but when he is, he doesn't care if I am or not.

'Excuse me?' he said just as fiercely. I ignored him, charging down the corridor towards my room when I got to the top of the stairs. He followed. 'Lola, we need to talk about this.'

'To me? I thought you only talked to Agatha.'

I just read that back and I'd bang my head on the table if I wasn't sure Laurent would have me committed. I wish I wasn't so seventeen sometimes. But you must get like that too. The funny thing is, given how tense things have been since I've been in Paris, I think Dad would be surprised if he saw me chatting to Laurent or how easily I smile at the newsagent near Café de Flore every time I pass. It's funny, isn't it? How kind we are to strangers. How much we care what they think of us. I don't know when I stopped caring what my father thinks of me but it's been a long time since I smiled at him. I stop myself doing it now, like when you go to text a friend that you've fallen out with and remember that you can't. That's all I seem to do now, stop myself. Stop myself smiling. Stop myself hugging him goodnight.

Stop myself talking altogether.

It makes everything worse, though, because my father does not respond well to strops. I think he's always been slightly confounded by me. Mum said that when I was a baby, he used to ask me why I was crying, as though I could be reasoned with, and when I was old enough to climb over the gate at the bottom of the stairs he'd remind me that there was nothing upstairs that I hadn't seen already. So when I go monosyllabic on him, he doesn't know what to do, which is probably why I do it, because it's the only time he's honest with me, when he's angry. I guess it's because he's trying so hard not to lose his temper that he can't pretend as well. He can't just give me a stiff smile and say, *Not now, Lola*. And that's all I want, for him to tell me the truth because it can't hurt any more than overhearing him say, *I can't do this any more*.

'Did you get my messages?' he called after me, the slap of his shoes on the parquet floor as he followed me down the hall so loud that I couldn't hear my flip-flops anymore. But I didn't respond, and when I got to my bedroom, I tried to close the door behind me, but he stopped me, holding his arm out as he walked in after me. 'I left you three, Lola.'

'My phone died,' I lied, pacing over to the bed and tossing the bunch of roses onto it.

'Why didn't it go straight to voicemail, then?'

OH MY GOD. I want to scream thinking about it. You'll see, but that's my father *all over*. He either pretends like nothing has happened or he meets me head on. There is literally no in between. So I know what he wanted me to say – he wanted me to say, *Because I didn't want to talk to you, Dad* – but I refused to give him the satisfaction of being the one who'd been wronged.

'Lola, we need to talk about this.'

'There's nothing to talk about,' I told him, kicking off my flip-flops. One of them bounced across the room and landed under the stool by my dressing table. 'I'm not staying.'

'Lola—'

'No,' I interrupted, shrugging off my bag. It landed on the floor by my feet with a meaty thud. 'I'm not staying. I'm going back home with Pan next week. That was the deal.'

'Yes it was, Lola,' he said, following me across the room into the bathroom. I tried to shut the door on him again, but didn't succeed. 'Until I realised what a state you're in.'

'State?' I scoffed, walking over to the sink and turning on the cold tap.

'You reek of cigarettes.' He waited for me to deny it, but I ignored him, my nails gouging the soap as I reached over and snatched it out of the dish. 'And shoplifting, Lola,' he said, suddenly breathless, as though it pained him to say it. 'What on earth were you thinking?'

'It was *a lipstick*. Stop making out like I'm Myra Hindley or something.'

'That's my point. You think this is a joke.'

'Of course I don't. I just have some perspective.'

'I don't think you do any more.'

I knew that he was looking at me in the mirror over the

sink, but I didn't look up, washing my hands until all I could smell was rose from the soap I'd bought from Ebe, the Egyptian woman who sells them at Marché de Montreuil. It immediately made me feel better. It's funny how smells do that. The smell of Luster's Pink Holding Spray will always be comforting because it reminds me of Mum, and now, it seems, the smell of rose is as well because it reminds me of that afternoon at Marché de Montreuil and how I'd chatted to Ebe for half an hour as she got me to smell each soap. Not because it's a particularly happy memory (even if later I found a vintage Michael Jackson T-shirt for €5) but because it reminds me that I'll be all right on my own.

'Oh now you want to do this?' I turned off the tap and lifted my chin to look at him in the mirror but he looked away. 'Okay. So BSP. I have to say, I'm pleasantly surprised that you're not shipping me off to boarding school, Dad.'

'Lola.'

'Or to a nunnery.'

'Lola—'

I didn't let him finish. 'It doesn't matter. I'm not staying.'

'Lola, please,' he said as I reached for a towel. 'Can we just talk about this properly?'

'There's nothing to talk about.' I dried my hands and threw it on the counter next to the sink then pushed past him out of the bathroom. 'In fact,' I walked over to my suitcase and heaved it onto the bed, just avoiding the roses. 'I'll tell Pan not to come and go home tomorrow instead.'

'Lola, listen.'

I held my breath as he walked over to where I was standing because even though I wouldn't look at him, my fingers fluttering as I grabbed the pair of jeans that was spilling over the edge of the suitcase and shoved them back inside, I was listening. Listening and hoping that once – just once – he'd hold me and tell me that it was going to be okay. That he understood.

But he didn't, he just stood there watching me shove everything back into my suitcase so I had something to do with my hands that wasn't shoving him, because I really wanted to shove him. Shove him and ask why he didn't understand. But then I didn't even understand how I was feeling, so how was he supposed to? I should have told him that. I don't know why I didn't. I just remember stuffing my clothes into my suitcase and thinking that everything would be okay when I got home, back to my untidy house with its red front door and chilly bathroom, Mum's dressing gown still hanging on the door. Everything would make sense again when I was at home. I would feel the floorboards in my bedroom shift under my feet as I walked across it and hear the sparrows chattering in the quince tree in the garden, and when I knocked on my bedroom wall, Pan would knock back. That's all I wanted, I realised: to not be on my own any more.

I'm so tired of being on my own.

And with that, something in me finally gave way.

'Listen to what?' I didn't mean to shout, but it was like a neglected bath overflowing. I could feel the anger spilling through me, hot and fast, as I tried to catch my breath and couldn't. 'To what a state I'm in? Don't worry, Dad. I'm going, so you don't have to deal with it any more.'

I walked over to the chest of drawers, swatting away a tear with my hand before he could see. I hoped he'd take the hint and leave me alone because I knew there would be more. My chest hurt with the effort of holding them in.

But he followed. 'That's what I'm trying to say,' he said, walking with me across the room. I opened the top drawer so suddenly the whole chest tipped forward, but he put his hands out to stop it, catching a silver frame before it toppled off. 'I *want* to deal with it.' When I rolled my eyes, he stood the frame back on top with a pointed sigh. 'We can't keep ignoring this, Lola.'

'Isn't that what we do, Dad? Ignore everything.' I chuckled bitterly, snatching whatever was in the top drawer and pacing back to the bed. I hadn't unpacked, so whatever it was wasn't mine. I don't even remember what it was, just throwing it in my suitcase with my other stuff. 'Like how you absolutely, definitely did not cheat on Mum with Agatha.'

'Please, Lola.' I heard his voice get tighter. 'Not this again. I told you—'

'Yeah, yeah. Love at first sight, I know. Because she's so charming, isn't she?'

'Lola, enough.'

'No, I've had enough, Dad.' I spun around to face him,

my hands balled into fists. 'She's such a bitch, why can't you see it? *How* can't you see that?'

He put his hands on his hips. 'I said *enough*.'

'You've heard the way she talks to me!'

'You give as good as you get, Lola.'

It hurt so much that I had to turn my back on him because I was sure I was going to cry, but when I looked up, I could see him in the glass of the print over my bed, rubbing his forehead with his hand.

I don't know what he said after that, my heart so loud in my ears that I'm sure he could hear it too. My hands shook as I zipped up my suitcase, but as I was about to lift it off the bed, he put his hand over mine. The shock of it made me yank my hand away because I can't remember the last time he touched me. He does, of course – he puts his hand on the small of my back when he's guiding me out of a lift and kisses me lightly on both cheeks when he says hello – but I can't remember the last time he tried to comfort me. That was Mum's job. She was the hugger, the one who put her nose in my hair and told me that everything was going to be okay. Dad used to as well. He used to tickle me until I stopped crying then get me a bowl of mint choc chip ice cream. But then I turned ten and I was too old for it. Too old to climb trees. Too old to do cartwheels in a dress. Too old to sleep in Pan's bed. I still did all of those things, but I can't help but wonder sometimes if who I am now – if everything I am and say and wear – is in defiance of him.

Who would I be if he let me do what I want?

I don't even know.

'You need help, Lola,' he said, his hands up, as though I was an escaped bird he was trying to put back in a cage. 'Please let me help you.'

'How? By forcing me to stay here?'

'I'm not forcing you to do anything, Lola.'

'Good, because I'm going home tomorrow.'

'No, you're not.'

I laughed and it sounded wrong, as though I'd cursed in church. Even with the windows open, the sounds of the street drowning out the tick of the clock in the salon and Josette shuffling around the kitchen preparing dinner, the apartment was too quiet. Library quiet. I don't know. Maybe you'll like it. I don't know what your foster homes were like so maybe you'll appreciate the peace. I'm scared to breathe sometimes, though. Everything's so perfect – the white chairs that I wouldn't dare sit on and the neat rows of leather-bound books in the library that I wouldn't dare read – that it doesn't feel like home, you know? Not like my home, anyway, where the radio's always on and the washing machine's always churning and my grandmother's always on the phone to one of her friends from church, laughing about whatever Mrs Lloyd's done this week.

'You really think I'd be better off here, Dad?'

'Of course I do.'

'I'm *miserable* here.'

He arched an eyebrow as if to say, *Are you?*

But he didn't say it. 'Are you happier at home?'

'How would you know? You're not there.'

'Exactly. I think that's why you're so unhappy Lola, because I'm not there.'

I looked at him like he was mad. 'I'm unhappy because my mother just died.' I paused as I waited for something on his face to register what I'd said. A tremble in his chin, a sudden sadness in his eyes. Something – *anything* – to let me know that he still felt something. But his face didn't change and I shook my head. 'I'm sorry it's taking me so long to get over it.'

That did register, his cheeks going from pink to red. 'That's not what I meant, Lola.'

'What do you mean, then? What am I doing wrong?'

I think you understand that, like there's a way of making yourself feel better but you don't know what it is. There must be, because everyone else got over it much quicker than I did. Look at Dad, he got remarried while I was still crying over crème brûlée. Even my grandmother had started using Mum's shampoo as though it was a shame to waste it.

It's such a silly thing to get upset about, I know – shampoo – but it's too soon. I don't know. Maybe there's an expiration date on grief. It feels that way sometimes. It was a month for me. After that, if my homework was late, I was told off like everyone else. Even my friends are tired of it, palming me off on Pan at parties when I drink too much and start sobbing. I know it had been eight months (eight months, two weeks and five days, not that I was counting), but I wanted to shake them. You must have found it hard at school as well, everyone complaining about homework and not having a car or being able to afford a dress from ASOS that they'll probably only wear once. Stupid shit I used to complain about as well that doesn't matter any more. Oh boo hoo your cat died. Poor you. My mother was run down in the street by a drunk driver. Someone from the council had to scrub her blood off the pavement.

I want to stand on a table in the canteen sometimes and tell them that they don't have a fucking clue. But I can't, can I? They're the lucky ones. They get to enjoy this – life, being a teenager – while I lie awake at night thinking about how my mother died alone. But at least I had a childhood. You didn't have much of one, did you? So you get it, don't you? I really need you to get it, because my father doesn't.

'Of course you're not doing anything wrong, Lola,' he said suddenly.

I looked at him from under my eyelashes. 'So what are you trying to say, then?'

'That there are people who can help.'

'Like who? *You*?'

'That isn't fair.'

I wasn't trying to hurt him, but I knew I had when he shook his head and stared at me. But that's another thing about my father, even when he's ready to talk, he isn't ready to listen.

'But you're doing so well, Dad,' I said, and I shouldn't have – the look he gave me told me that much – but it was such a relief, finally saying it out loud, like plucking a splinter from my heart. 'Look at you.' I stepped back and looked at him with a bitter smile. 'I've never seen you so happy.'

There was a long moment of silence and I was sure that was it, that he'd tell me to get out, take me to Gare du Nord himself. But for the second time that day he caught me off guard and didn't say anything at all, and that was worse. If he yelled at me, I could dismiss it, laugh at him when he told me to go to my room and remind him that I was already in my room. But he didn't say a word and I know that if he hadn't given up on me before, he did then.

'Whatever, Dad.' The tops of my ears burned as I turned back to the bed and grabbed the handle of my suitcase. 'You were quite happy to leave me to come here. What's changed?'

'Is that what you think?' I heard him ask, but I wasn't brave enough to look at him. I didn't even lift my chin to look at his reflection in the print over the bed as I dragged my suitcase off it.

'What am I supposed to think?' I asked, turning to put it down on the floor between us.

'You think that I'm happy about this? About us being apart?'

He put his hands on his hips and waited and I know what he wanted me to say, that I'm fine with it, that it's for the best, me being in London. That's all he's wanted me to say since he married Agatha, how pleased I am for him, how he deserves to be happy. And it's not that I don't think he does, it's that him being okay reminds me that I'm not. So maybe there is something wrong with me. There must be, to do what I did to you. So if that's what you've been waiting for me to say, let me say it now: I'm fucked up. So fucked up, because there – in the middle of that huge green room with its postcards around the mirror and window boxes of pink geraniums that I secretly watered with Vittel because I didn't want them to die – I'd never felt more right, sure that he would come to me, close the distance between us and tell me that he loved me. But he didn't and I turned my face away as I felt another tear make its escape, because *that's* why we don't talk, because I won't say what he wants to hear and he never says what I need to hear.

He called after me as I paced back into the en suite and began indiscriminately grabbing at bottles. At one point I remember picking up something heavy, an obscenely expensive bottle of bubble bath that was already in the bathroom when I got there and weighed almost as much as my suitcase. I'd never even used it, but I still tried to stuff it into my wash bag with everything else because if I hadn't, I think I might have thrown it at him.

'Lola, *qu'est-ce que tu as? Qu'est-ce qui se passe dans ta tête?*' he said, so flustered that he reverted to French.

'I don't know, Dad. What's wrong with me?'

'You can't possibly think that I don't want you here.'

'All right, Dad. Whatever you say,' I muttered, pushing past him and heading for my suitcase.

'Lola, please. Talk to me.'

I was aware of him standing next to me but didn't look up as I unzipped it and tried to push my wash bag in. 'What do you want me to say?' I asked, giving the wash bag one last shove. It finally went in and I closed the zip with a satisfied huff before going in search of my flip-flops.

'Just be honest with me,' he said, following me over to the dressing table.

I chuckled sourly as I bent down to retrieve one of my flip-flops from under the stool. 'Since when did you want me to be honest?'

'I always have, Lola.'

'Fine.' I stopped and turned to face him. 'You want me to be honest? Okay.' I held my arms out. 'I'm really happy that you've moved on, Dad. I just wish you hadn't done it without me.'

He blinked at me, the skin between his eyebrows pinching. 'You can't possibly think I've done that.'

'Look at you, Dad. You're fine.'

'Fine? You think I'm fine?'

'Of course you are.'

I made myself look away when I realised that I was staring at the strange wedding band on his left hand. It was too bright, too gold. The one he used to wear – the one I know – was scuffed and out of shape from the time he forgot to tape it before a rugby game and broke his finger.

And I remember the feel of it – smooth and reassuringly cool so it stung just a little every time he made me take his hand when we crossed a road. I didn't know this ring. I'd never tried it on, never read the inscription, if there even was one. A *die illa et in aeterna* – forever and a day – the one he used to wear said. He didn't take it off very often, but when he did, he would rub his finger with his thumb as though the words had imprinted into his skin, like Braille.

They obviously didn't.

'I just need you to be not fine, just for a second,' I told him, holding up a finger as I paced to the other side of the room. 'So I don't feel like I'm going mad.'

'Will you stop walking away from me?'

'Sorry, you're the one who does that, aren't you?' I said, just loud enough that he could hear as I found my other flip-flop by the bedside table and put it on.

'Lola.'

He sounded so offended that it made me even madder.

'What?' I turned to face him again. 'What do you want me to say, Dad?'

'I don't want you to say anything. I want you to listen for once.'

'That's rich, coming from you.'

He ignored this. 'I am not fine.' He followed as I walked back to the dressing table and snatched my wide-toothed comb off it. 'And if you think I am it's because I've been in therapy for months.'

I hesitated, my hands stilling for a moment as I wondered why he hadn't told me this before. Was he ashamed of it? I unzipped my suitcase again and slipped the comb inside. *Is that why he always tells me to wait until we get home? Because he's ashamed of me too?*

Then he said, 'I think it would help you as well,' and he probably thought I ignored him because I disagreed, but I couldn't catch my breath as I realised that he *was* ashamed of me.

'You need to deal with this,' he told me as I walked over to the desk.

'I am,' I managed to say, avoiding his gaze when he came to stand next to me, watching as I bent down to unplug my laptop charger and wound it around my hand.

'How?' he asked, walking with me back to my suitcase. 'By shoplifting and getting drunk?' The shock of it almost made my legs give way. It must have been obvious because he added, 'Your grandmother's old, but she's not stupid.'

'You don't know what you're talking about.' It came out much more softly – more unsure – than I intended as I tried to swallow back the pearl of pain in my throat, but couldn't.

'I do, Lola.'

'How? You're not there.'

'But your grandmother is. She hears you sneaking in, falling all over the place.'

I was so shocked I laughed, in that wild, slightly hysterical way people do when they hear that someone's

91

died. 'Dad, please,' I said, cursing myself for the way the words wobbled again.

'She told me.'

'Told you what?'

'About the drinking, the staying out, not going to college.'

'No.' I went rigid with panic just as I had earlier that day when the security guard at Sephora stopped me and said, 'Excusez-moi, mademoiselle.'

'She can't take it, Lola.'

The pearl in my throat grew. 'You're lying.'

He was. I don't know who you imagine when I talk about my grandmother, but if it's an old lady with a walking stick, you couldn't be more wrong. My grandmother is fierce in every sense of the word. She wears a leopard print coat and gold nail varnish and I've seen her make teenage boys cry for talking back to her. So if she knew about that stuff, she would've told me. There's no way she would've heard me come home drunk and not kicked my arse.

No way.

'Why would I lie, Lola?'

'To make me stay.'

'It's true. She doesn't know what to do.'

'She doesn't have to do anything.'

'She's too old to be lying awake all night worrying about you.'

'She's fine, Dad,' I said, taking a step back to look at him, utterly baffled. He was making out like I was a delinquent or something. I was just doing normal teenage stuff, stuff all my friends did. You must have as well, come on. Like you've never bunked off school.

Everyone has.

'She's not, Lola.'

'I know what you're doing.' My hand shook as I pointed at him. 'And I won't let you.'

'Let me what?'

'Turn me against Nan.'

It was his turn to look baffled. 'Why would I do that?'

'To make me stay.'

'She thinks you need to.'

'No, she doesn't.'

'We've discussed it.'

'When?'

'Before I asked you to come here.'

'So she doesn't want me, either?' My voice broke as I said it, but it was such an effort to remain standing, the floor suddenly not as steady under my feet, that I didn't care.

'No.' He looked mortified. 'Not at all. She just wants you to get better.'

I looked down, waiting for him to give me the big speech he'd no doubt been rehearsing while he wandered around the city looking for me as I opened the zip on the front of my suitcase and shoved the laptop charger in. The speech about how I'd gone off the rails, how I needed some discipline, but he waited for me to look at him again. 'I

93

need you, Lola,' he said and I almost cried because it's just like my father to say what I need to hear eight months too late.

Eight months, two weeks and five days.

Not that I was counting.

The next morning I was up before Dad, which hasn't happened since . . . I don't think it ever has, actually. Even when I have an exam he's up before me, ready to test me on the periodic table.

With Oxygen so you can breathe and Fluorine for your pretty teeth.

For someone as mercurial as my father it's kind of comforting that he's such a creature of habit. He always gets up at the same time and showers at the same time, even drinks his coffee from the same mug. Thinking about it now, I guess it's strange. After all, his job is hardly a nine to five. Perhaps that's why. He can't control his time at the hospital but he can at home. It used to drive me insane, though, how predictable he is. But when Mum died, I found it comforting, even if all I did was lie in bed with the curtains shut while I listened to him making coffee in the kitchen or coming back after church with croissants and a copy of the *Sunday Times*. Normal things. Stuff he did before Mum died that reminded me what my life was like before then, because I'd forgotten.

In the fog of my grief it was those little things – the smell of coffee in the morning and croissants on a Sunday – that brought me back, like lights guiding me back to shore. So while I complain that her death didn't change him, that I've never seen him cry or heard him pacing around the house at night, unable to sleep, I'm glad he didn't change, because everything else did. For weeks I was sure I heard my mother coming home from work, the letterbox rattling as she slammed the front door, and woke up to the sound of her singing in the shower. There's always that moment when you wake up, isn't there? When you forget. I suppose it's easier, living in foster homes. Not *easy* – growing up in care can't have been easy – but easier to live in a house that your parents have never lived in. You don't have to look at the book they didn't finish on their bedside table or sit on the edge of the bath and weep as someone from Oxfam comes to collect their clothes. Those are the things I'll never get over. I still take three plates out for dinner and turn my music up so Mum will tell me to turn it down. She doesn't, of course, and neither does my grandmother, because she's letting me work my way through it, apparently. That's what Dad says.

Maybe it's writing it down or maybe it's just being here, away from the house for the first time since she died, but it's so obvious now that all of it – playing my music too loud and bunking off college and shoplifting, even what I did to you – was for attention. That isn't an excuse, I'm just saying that I wanted someone to notice, I guess. Notice that I wasn't okay. But they did. I wish I'd seen it at the time, the silly texts my friends sent me about *EastEnders* and the bars of chocolate they'd buy me for no reason. I thought they didn't care, but they just didn't know what to say, did they? That's what happens when you keep telling people you're fine: eventually they stop asking. I hope you never felt like that when you were in care – like a burden – but if you did then I think you get that, too, the things we say to make other people feel better.

But you get to a point when you can't do it any more, don't you? When you can't keep pretending that everything is okay and surrender to the fact it isn't. Which is what happened that morning – the morning after my row with Dad – I couldn't do it any more because that was it. If Dad was right and my grandmother didn't want me to go back to London then I'd lost everything.

Even my home.

All I had left was Pan, so that's why I was up, showered and dressed before Dad, why I packed everything I could fit in my satchel. Not too much in case it looked full, but enough for a few days, at least. Given that I can't go away for a weekend without taking a suitcase, it surprised me how ruthless I was, but it's remarkable how easy it is to decide what you can live without when you have to. Anything else I needed I could buy or borrow from Pan. I'd checked and knew I had €379.42 in my bank account, which wasn't much, but it was enough to keep us going until we found jobs. I've never worked before, have you? Dad won't let me. He says that spending my weekends perfecting the piano and volunteering at the Princess Alice

Hospice will look better on my UCAS application than a Saturday job at Boots. But I've always wanted to work in a café. I don't know why. That's the Paris I used to daydream about: me working in a café while Pan sells his sketches on the Left Bank, the pair of us living in a tiny studio with noisy neighbours and a view of the Eiffel Tower in the distance, like a candle in the middle of a birthday cake.

The thought made my right leg bounce as I sat on the edge of the bed and waited for my father to get up. I checked my watch and when I realised that he wouldn't be up for another five minutes, I went through my bag again before looking around the room one last time to see if there was anything I'd forgotten. There were lots of things – my laptop, my DMs, the Michael Jackson T-shirt I bought that day at Marché de Montreuil, the Chimamanda Ngozi Adichie book I'd been reading since I'd heard that Beyoncé song – but like I said, it surprised me how ruthless I was. You must be the same, moving from foster home to foster home. It's just stuff, right? It's replaceable. Apart from the things I needed – practical things like money and my passport – I had everything I cared about: the pink plastic ring Pan won in that two-penny arcade game when we were thirteen and the photo of my mother I carry everywhere, the one I took the last time we were in Barbados, the two of us pulling our best selfie faces.

I'm sure you have stuff like that, too.

Stuff you'd never leave behind.

I was checking my purse again to make sure I had my bank card when I heard a noise. It could have been Josette, putting the coffee on so it would be ready for Dad when he got up, but then I heard the pipes groan and realised that he was in the shower. It was like a starter pistol, my hands shaking as I slung my bag on my shoulder. It was so heavy I almost toppled over, so I lifted the strap over my head and let it fall across my chest as I crept towards the door, opening it carefully. I cursed the old brass handle as it tried to betray me, glaring at it before peering out. The sound of the shower was louder out there and as I glanced towards my father and Agatha's room at the other end of the hall, I realised that I was holding my breath. It made me feel fifteen again, sneaking into the house at 1 a.m. after falling asleep on Pan's sofa halfway through a film. It's been a while since I felt bad about something like that so I wouldn't usually be so discreet, but I knew that if my father saw me leaving the apartment at 7 a.m. he'd want to know where I was going. I had twelve minutes. After that he'd be out of the shower, and while the apartment was big enough that he might not hear me go, I wasn't willing to take the risk.

I tried not to run towards the stairs, my heart in my throat as I glanced back down the hall. Agatha, as always, was the fly in my ointment. She was less predictable than my father and even though I hadn't heard her, she might well already be up. I've gone down to the kitchen in the middle of the night to get a glass of water and seen the light on in her studio or looked into the salon as I passed, to see her sitting neatly on the canapé, flicking through a copy of *WWD*.

I'm not sure she even sleeps.

So I walked down the hall as though it was a frozen lake, my head spinning from holding my breath. I made myself stop and suck in a breath when I got to the spiral staircase then walked down it just as carefully, hoping that Josette wouldn't be waiting at the bottom to ask if I wanted coffee. She wasn't, but I could hear her humming in the kitchen, the steady tap of her knife striking the wooden chopping board the first thing to make me miss a step. I could laugh because of all the things to make me think twice about what I was doing; it wasn't the thought of her calling me for breakfast or Dad offering to get me out of bed when I didn't answer; it was the smell of mango and how worried my grandmother would be when Dad called to ask if I was there. But this wasn't enough to make me stay or stop me running down the stairs when I finally closed the front door behind me. I couldn't stop running then, not even when the concierge said good morning, my heart bouncing off my ribs as I ran out onto rue de Rennes.

By the time I got to the café, the strap of my satchel had left a ridge in my shoulder. It was a relief to put it down, Laurent's eyebrow arching when I dumped it on the floor next to my table. But he didn't say anything, nor did he ask why I was there so early, just let me help him put out the chairs then made me a crêpe that I was too nervous to eat.

Normally he'd tell me off, but he didn't say a word when I picked up my bag, just asked if he'd see me again. The way he looked at me, like he knew he wouldn't, was enough to make me dip my head as I walked out.

It was harder to leave there than the apartment. I'd miss it more, I realised as I walked away. Miss the way Laurent hisses at the radio whenever Marseille score and how he bribes me with eclairs to play the piano. I should have scratched my name under my table before I left, but if there's one thing I've learned it's that in the end, there's no time for these things. Of all the stupid shit I've done it's only the things I haven't done that I truly regret.

I had to wait for the bank to open. I made a point of going to the one on rue Bonaparte, not just because it was the closest, but so there would be no risk of bumping into Dad if he hadn't already headed out for the morning paper. The branch was tiny, though, so the teller looked a little bemused when he unlocked the door to find me waiting on the pavement. '*Allez-vous faire du shopping?*' he asked when he re-emerged behind the glass of the counter. I humoured him with a smile then asked to withdraw whatever was in my account. He chuckled. '*Allez-vous à Chanel?*'

When I made myself laugh too, it sounded so fake I hoped he didn't notice. If I didn't want him to, I probably should have stopped playing with the chain attached to the pen on the counter, but I couldn't stop thinking about what an epically stupid idea it was. The account was in my name, but I'm seventeen. What if I needed Dad's permission to withdraw that much money?

I usually go to the ATM so I had no idea how long these things took, but it seemed to take forever. I almost asked him if everything was okay but hid behind my hair, suddenly aware of the CCTV cameras pointed at me from every angle as I imagined a red light flashing somewhere. ALERT. ALERT. RUNAWAY TEENAGER. But just as I was about to tell him to forget it and ask for my card back, the till popped open and I was so relieved I felt giddy.

There it was: €379.42.

I don't think I've ever seen that much money all at once. I thought it would look like more, like those wedges of dirty notes in films, but each euro was immaculate – bright orange and blue and red – as though they'd just been printed. I felt like I did the first time I bought a pack of cigarettes when I was fourteen as the teller slid the envelope under the glass towards me, as though I'd pulled off a great heist. I tried not to snatch it, flashing him one last smile as I stuffed it in my bag and hurried out of the bank, my bag that little bit heavier. It had only just gone 9 a.m. but it was already viciously hot, a pearl of sweat running from my hair and down the nape of my neck as I stood outside the bank and contemplated how hideous the Metro would be, especially in rush hour. So when I saw a cab coming towards me down rue Bonaparte, I stuck my arm out.

The traffic was especially sluggish – even for a Monday morning – so I should have walked, but I was painfully aware of the envelope of cash in my bag, sure that would be the day I encountered one of the Paris pickpockets the guide books warn you about. The thought made my hands ball into fists in my lap as I realised that if someone took my bag I would have nothing. Everything I had – everything I wanted to keep, I should say – was in that bag. Without it I would have to stay in Paris, in Agatha's vast, hollow apartment, and I couldn't. I'd rather work in a café for the rest of my life, live on ramen noodles and wear €5 T-shirts. At least then it would be my life and if I fucked it up, the only person I'd be letting down was myself.

I know what you're thinking, that it's my fault, that none of this would have happened if I'd got my shit together and stopped blaming – and hurting – everyone I loved. I'm a coward, I know, running away like that. I see it now, but then I was so scared. I'd never felt that before, the way I felt as I sat in the back of that cab, holding my bag to my chest. Have you? Like you're completely and utterly on your own. Of course you have. That makes me feel worse, because here I am, asking for your sympathy, and you're probably thinking what a spiteful, entitled brat I am. You're right, but I've never been on my own. Even when I'm wandering around Paris, wasting afternoons on boat tours, I'm still not alone. There's a couple from Texas who stop and ask for directions to the Champs-Élysées or the customers in the café who clap when Laurent persuades me to play the piano. All I had was €379.42 and whatever I'd managed to fit into my bag. I couldn't borrow €20 from my father the next time I was broke or put something on Agatha's account at Le Bon Marché, and it was scary.

Good scary.

First kiss scary.

I wonder if you felt the same thing that morning you got on the train to Gare du Nord. I feel sick thinking about it, but I guess you did. I'm sorry. This is so messed up. You must have been so excited. I was, I realised, the thought of seeing Pan making me giddy again as the cab stopped at the zebra crossing on Pont Saint-Michel. I must have been smiling because a guy walking over the bridge smiled, too. It was only then that I noticed how busy it was, the brisk commuters in their neat suits replaced by tourists in baseball caps and shorts. When the cab started moving again and I looked down the Seine towards Notre Dame, that's another thing I wish I'd done: taken the boat tour one last time. Listened to the story about Picasso's oil pastel and waved at the people sitting on the benches on the banks. I felt even more giddy at the thought of doing all of that stuff again in a new city with Pan. Stumbling across cafés and benches and claiming them as our own.

'*C'est trop, ce bouchon!*' the driver exclaimed, throwing his hands up.

'*Ça ne fait rien,*' I told him, and it was fine. I wasn't in a rush. I hadn't been able to convince Pan to get the 5.40 a.m. (funnily enough) but he had agreed to get the 7.01 a.m., which meant I had nearly an hour before his train got in. So I wasn't bothered about the traffic; quite happy to sit in the quiet of the cab and say one last goodbye to the Seine, the only river in the world that runs between two bookshelves.

When the cab turned onto rue de Dunkerque and I saw the familiar shape of Gare du Nord ahead, I must have been smiling again, because the driver asked me where I was going. '*Je ne sais pas.*' I shrugged when he pulled over. He watched me warily as I climbed out and, with hindsight, it was a strange thing to say outside a train station, but I didn't know where I was going. That was the point. '*Partout,*' I added with another shrug, heaving my bag off the back seat and handing him €30. '*Partout?*' he frowned and I nodded, turning to look at Gare du Nord, at the statues peering down at me and the squares of glass around the clock that sparkled like tiles at the bottom of a swimming pool in the sun.

I could go everywhere, I realised as I walked in, stepping around the tourists struggling with their cases and the couples kissing goodbye, and headed for the ticket office. *Partout*, I told myself as I picked up one of each timetable and headed out into the station. I had half an hour until Pan's train got in so could have waited in a café nearby – even the one across the road with its English menu and weak coffee – but I found a spot away from the sun spilling through the glass roof where I could still see the Arrivals board and flicked through the timetables.

I checked the TGV one first, biting down on a smile when I realised that if we got the 4.41 p.m. from the Gare

104

de Lyon we would be in Rome by morning. It wasn't somewhere I was desperate to visit, but Pan was, and it would be the last place my father would think to look for us. New York, maybe, London, definitely, but it would never occur to him that I'd go to Rome, which was reason enough to go. But then I saw the timetable for Barcelona. If we got the 2.07 p.m. we'd be there before Dad even realised we were gone. My breathing shallowed at the thought. It would be too obvious, though. Pan loves Gaudí; he made *Sagrada Familia* out of clay for his Art GCSE. It's the first thing you see when you walk into our old school. I thought my heart would explode when we went back to get our results and I saw it. I made him stand next to it so I could take a photo. He poked his tongue out when he pointed at it, but I saw the way he smiled when we walked away.

I was so busy daydreaming about us wandering around Park Güell that I almost missed his train arriving. It was five minutes early, which was nothing to do with him, but it was so Pan to be early, as though he couldn't wait to see me, either, that I caught myself running again.

I don't know if you have a Pan (I hope so, everyone deserves a Pan – his laugh makes me laugh and when I kiss him, he tastes like the birthday cake I had on my seventeenth birthday, like the last time I remember being happy) but when I got to the platform, I couldn't see him. I had to resist the urge to push my way through the knot of people climbing off the train, but then a guy bent down to pick up his suitcase and I saw him walking towards me.

I couldn't move, my heart beating so hard I couldn't catch my breath, because finally – finally – something made sense in this strange, too hot city with its dog cemetery and catacombs of bones where the oldest bridge – Pont Neuf – actually means new bridge. Where I made sense, because there he was, someone who got my sense of humour and knew to tell me to shut up when I was being stroppy. That's what I mean when I say that everyone deserves a Pan.

Everyone deserves someone they don't have to explain themselves to.

Even me.

He looked different, in a T-shirt I'd never seen before, his hands scrubbed clean of the dots of paint his skin is always rough with. But then he smiled and it was so familiar – so marrow-deep familiar, like hearing a song you haven't heard for ages on the radio – that I ran towards him. I wasn't supposed to, I was supposed to wait at the top of the platform, but the guard didn't stop me, muttering something about young love as I ran past him. Pan laughed and staggered back when I got to him, dropping his bag when I launched myself at him. 'Hello, you,' he said as I buried my face in his neck. I wanted to say it back, but when he lifted me up so my feet left the platform, I couldn't speak as I breathed him in. He smelled the same, of Dove soap and those purple washing tablets his mother uses, and as I felt the tip of his nose in my hair, I hoped I smelt the same, too.

Of me.

Of home.

'I've missed your face,' he said with a sigh, as though we hadn't Skyped every day, and when he put me down, he took it in his hands and looked at me like he was trying to find something in my face that he recognised. I almost didn't recognise him, either, I realised as I lifted my eyelashes to look at him, his hair almost touching his shoulders and his skin darker from a month in Chennai with his family. But then his smile widened. 'Look at these,' he said, tapping my nose with his finger. I'd forgotten about the freckles that had bubbled up thanks to the sun and scrunched my nose at him. 'I haven't seen these since last summer.'

'What's this?' I tugged his hair. 'You've let yourself go without me.' I chuckled but didn't let go, my finger idly turning in one of the thick waves his hair dries into, my smile softening as I imagined his mother telling him off for leaving the house with wet hair, like she does every morning. It's those things I miss about home. Not just him and my grandmother and my bedroom with its white painted floorboards and the tulip chair I got from that charity shop on the King's Road and made him carry home on the train, but those other things, like how he always leaves the house with wet hair (and gets told off for it). Things I could never recreate somewhere else, even if I painted the floorboards white and found another tulip chair.

'Totally.' He leaned down and pressed a kiss to my mouth. It made my eyelids flutter because that hadn't changed, either, how he makes me feel, like I can't be as bad as I think I am. So when he pressed another kiss to my forehead then buried his nose in my hair again, I reached up and curled my fingers around his wrists as he curled his around my neck, his thumbs stroking the line of my jaw. And with that we were the only people in Gare du Nord, the tourists forgotten as we swayed slightly as though we were dancing to a song only we could hear.

When we eventually pulled apart, he gave me another quick kiss then took my bag from me. 'Damn, Lo,' he said, hoisting it onto his shoulder. 'What you got in here?'

In the rush of seeing him again, I'd forgotten my plan, and felt a fizz of excitement as I remembered the train timetables that I'd stuffed in my bag with everything else.

'Don't be mad, okay?' I said as he bent down to pick up his holdall. When he straightened, he eyed me suspiciously. 'Hear me out, okay?'

'I just bought a car, Lola. I don't have bail money.'

I waited for him to look at me again then grinned. 'Let's run away.'

I held my breath, sure that he'd roll his eyes – maybe even laugh – but his shoulders fell, clearly relieved that I hadn't murdered Agatha and stuffed her into my satchel.

'Where to this time?' he asked, his smile like a pin in my bravado.

'I'm serious,' I told him, turning to walk beside him as he headed down the platform.

'Yeah?'

'Yes.'

'Where are we going, then? Mexico?'

'I mean it, Pan.' I looked up at him with a frown when he slung his arm around my shoulders and kissed the top of my head. 'If we go now, we could be in Barcelona for dinner.'

'Barcelona?'

'There's a two o'clock train from Gare de Lyon.' That made his smile slip, the skin between his eyebrows wrinkling as he realised that I wasn't joking. 'You've always wanted to go to Barcelona,' I reminded him, slipping my arm around his waist and letting my head fall onto his shoulder. 'Imagine it. We could live on paella and San Miguel. Sleep on the beach. You love tapas.'

'*You* love tapas,' he said, steering me away before I tripped on someone's rolling suitcase.

'Well you love San Miguel.'

'Excuse you. I'm a good Muslim boy. I never drink.'

'Yeah. Yeah.' I chuckled, my heart skipping as we approached the Departures board.

He glanced at it, too. 'Barcelona, eh? Why not?' He pulled me to him and kissed the top of my head again. 'If your dad doesn't mind. Have you told him?'

Pan knows me too well.

'Haven't you always wanted to go to Barcelona?' I reminded him because I didn't know what else to say, something in me sagging at the thought of telling him what had happened with Dad, about not going back to London. I

109

couldn't tell him there, in the station, the back of his T-shirt creased from sitting on the train for so long, could I? Okay, I could have and it was selfish, I know, but I just wanted that moment, a moment when it was just him and me, when I didn't have to think about Dad and Agatha and what I could do next to wedge myself between them. I felt like Andy Dufresne sometimes, picking away with my rock hammer hoping to see light – some space between them – and I was exhausted. I wanted to be the me I was when I was with Pan again. I miss that me. The me that forces him to dance to Taylor Swift and laughs until I cry when he tickles me.

It's funny how being with someone else reminds you who you really are.

But then he shrugged and said, 'I guess,' and the moment passed as I felt a kick of panic.

'What about Marseille, then?' I said, breathless at the thought of going back to the apartment and Dad pretending like nothing had happened. (Or worse, telling Pan that I'd be staying in Paris.) 'Remember when we stopped there for the day on our way to my grandparents' last year?' I looked up at him again and smiled slowly. 'Remember how blue the water was?'

'You said it was the colour of Sour Blue Raspberries.'

'What's wrong with Sour Blue Raspberries?'

'They're nasty, Lola.'

'You like Marmite.' I looked away and feigned disgust. 'Your opinion is invalid.'

'Says the girl who likes Taylor Swift.'

'I like one song!' I untangled myself from him and poked him in the side with my finger.

He sniggered, clearly unrepentant. 'That's how it starts, Lo.'

'Seriously, Pan.' I stopped walking and stood in front of him so he had to stop as well.

'Lola.'

'Please. Just think about it.'

He rolled his eyes and walked around me. 'We can't run away.'

'Why not? It'll be so much fun. We can hire a boat,' I told him, following him and walking backwards in front of him until he stopped again.

'A boat?'

'Yes. We can sail to Cassis.'

'You're going to sail a boat? *You?*'

'Don't say it like that! It can't be that hard.' He laughed and I shoved him. 'Why not?'

'Lola, you can't walk in flip-flops without tripping up.'

'We'll swim if we have to.'

'Swim?'

'Yes!'

'Okay.'

'We can find out if the water tastes like Sour Blue Raspberries as well.'

He looked unconvinced, shaking his head as he walked around me again.

'Come on, Pan,' I called after him as he headed for the exit. 'Let's just go.'

He didn't stop, though, and when I caught up with him, he sighed and slung his arm around me, pulling me to him again. 'And what are we going to do in Cassis?'

'Whatever we want.' I tried not to grin because I knew I had him. 'We don't even have to go to Cassis. We can go anywhere. I have three hundred and fifty euros and three pairs of knickers. The world is ours.'

'Three hundred and fifty euros and three pairs of knickers?'

He chuckled and when he stopped walking I did, too, getting on my tiptoes to wrap my arms around his neck. I peppered his face with kisses, hysterical at the thought of us falling asleep on a train and waking up somewhere else. I think that's what you wanted, too, when you got on that train to meet me. You wanted to start again, didn't you? Somewhere no one knew you, where you could be whoever you wanted to be. That's why I wanted to run away. I know you don't believe me, but I didn't want attention or even the satisfaction of hurting Dad as much as he hurt me when I overheard him saying that he couldn't do it any more. I wanted to find out who I am when no one's looking. When my grandmother isn't waiting for me to come home or Dad isn't apologising for whatever I've done this time. I could shave the sides of my head and Pan could let his grow as long as he wanted. He could paint all day while I played the piano in cafés at night to earn us our dinner and a bottle of red wine. But as I was about to thank him for going along with another of my ridiculous schemes, I heard someone say, '*Allez!*' and turned around to realise that we were at the front of the taxi queue. I glared at Pan, but he just nodded at the open car door.

'*Rue de Rennes, s'il vous plaît,*' I told the driver as I crawled into the back seat.

As soon as the cab pulled away, my stomach turned and I couldn't look at him as he wound down the window and took one last look at Gare du Nord. I'm a coward. I know I'm a coward. I should have told him. It's not like I could keep it a secret. Even if Dad or Agatha neglected to mention it, Pan would notice when I didn't go back to London with him.

He's clever like that.

So yeah, I'm a coward. I think you know that already, but that's how messed up I was back then. Besides, he should have heard it from me – he deserved to hear it from me – but I couldn't bear to say it out loud because then it would be real and even then, a couple of hours before my interview at BSP, I was still sure that I could change Dad's mind. So I did what I always do when I'm cornered, and sulked.

It's only been a couple of months, but you wouldn't believe how much the weather has changed. It's not freezing, but it's not warm enough to sit outside any more. I might have to go back into the café because the wind keeps ruffling through the pages of my notebook.

Sorry if you can't read my writing.

I say this every month, but Paris in October is my favourite. Everything is the colour of an old photograph, yellowy and washed out, the sky busy with clouds that bob merrily overhead and make me think of home and feeding the swans at Richmond Park. The leaves are starting to turn and that makes me think of home as well. October in Paris is nothing like it is in London. You'll see, I hope. At home it's drizzly and grim, the leaves browning as though they're rusting. But here the trees look more alive somehow, suddenly alight with red and orange, like they're on fire.

The morning I met Pan at the Gare du Nord Paris was on fire in a different way. It peaked at forty degrees that day, but it felt like much more in the cab. It's hard to breathe when I'm sitting next to him at the best of times, but with the sun bouncing off everything it touched – the street, the pavements, the windows of the cars around us – to flood the back of the cab, I couldn't catch my breath. I tried to shield myself from it with my hand but it was no use; the heat so strong I was sure I could feel it melting the pink plastic ring on my finger.

I already had a headache and it wasn't even 11 a.m. So when Pan nudged me as we passed a billboard for Agatha's new perfume on the rue du Louvre, I ignored him. It wasn't the most mature reaction, I admit, but my stomach turned again at the thought of walking back into the apartment, so I didn't need to think about Agatha. Still, I knew which billboard he'd seen. It follows me everywhere I go, Marion

Cotillard looking unbearably elegant in a black dress Agatha refuses to make again in case it becomes ubiquitous. (That's the word she used – ubiquitous. Who talks like that?) So I looked at the cyclist in front of us instead, frowning as he darted between the cars then peeled right down rue Saint-Honoré, making the car in front of us brake suddenly. The cab driver did, too, so suddenly that Pan and I jerked forward. But the driver didn't notice, just jabbed a finger at his head when the car in front of us started moving again.

'Ah, *putain idiot!*'

'*C'est la sélection naturelle,*' I told him with a bitter chuckle.

He didn't laugh back, just stared at me in the rear-view mirror. It was the first thing I'd said since giving him Agatha's address, so he'd no doubt assumed that neither Pan nor I spoke French, at least not enough French to understand what a *putain idiot* was.

'*Êtes-vous française?*' He looked at me in the rear-view mirror with a sceptical frown.

'*Mon père est français.*'

He nodded. '*Et celui-là est votre petit ami?*'

Pan had heard that enough to know that the driver had asked if he was my boyfriend and turned away from the window to roll his eyes. '*Malheureusement.*'

The cab driver laughed and I bit down on a smile, feigning indignation. 'Unfortunately?'

When I shoved him, Pan reached across for my hand.

As soon as our palms touched, my mood passed and I slid along the back seat towards him to press a kiss to his jaw. I know what you're thinking, but that's what we're like. We haven't agreed on a thing since the day we met and I wanted to play football and he wanted to colour in. He didn't give in to me that day and he hasn't since, so while I tut and moan and threaten to never speak to him again, I'm rarely mad at him for more than ten minutes. I hope that never changes. My friends worry about all sorts of things with their boyfriends – stuff you probably worry about, too, like whether they really love you, whether they're cheating on you, whether you should apply to the same universities as them – but I've never doubted those things with Pan. The only thing I worry about is that he'll hold it against me one day, the shitty things I do. I'm laughing because you're probably thinking that I should stop doing shitty things, then, and you're right, but I'm trying. If you don't already know why I'm telling you all of this, then this is me trying.

When we got to the apartment, Pan reached for my hand again as I climbed out of the cab to join him on the pavement. It instantly made me feel better until the door swung open and my heart started hammering. I half expected Dad to run out, asking where I'd been, but it was the concierge. He must have seen us pull up and came out to greet us, offering to take Pan's bag. Pan refused and when he shook his head the sun caught in his hair so he looked almost unreal – like the light was coming from him

– and I'd never loved him so much. Not love in a *Wow he's hot* way, but love somewhere in my bones, somewhere I couldn't see, but could feel making me stronger.

Better.

Braver.

Do you think that's what love is? Not what they say on the front of those cheesy Valentine's cards you see in petrol stations – *You complete me* – but is it when someone has seen you at your worst but still looks at you like you're the best thing that's ever happened to them? I think it might be.

I squeezed his hand, trying to ignore the urge to run and keep running, but when we got inside and his eyes widened, my nerves were forgotten as he tugged me towards the lift. 'It's like something from a film,' he said, grinning when the gate shut smoothly.

That's how I should have reacted when I first saw this place. I should have been excited – should have been in awe of the painted panel walls and gilt mirrors – but I just remember the unbearable *aching* silence as Dad and I rode the lift up to the fifth floor, me staring at the brass plate on the floor between our feet so I wouldn't have to make eye contact. Where Pan was delighted, his eyes lighting up when the cables groaned as the ancient lift stirred to life, I'd felt uncomfortable, ashamed of my scuffed Converse and the sound they'd made on the marble floor. I didn't belong there. Everything was so light – so delicate – from the chandeliers that sparkled like stardust to the orchid that sat on the corner of the concierge's desk, and there was me in worn out jeans, my hair *everywhere*.

Pan wasn't fazed, though. I'll never tell him this, but watching him made me fall in love with the apartment all over again. I think that's why I hadn't told him about it, because I was scared that if I described it to him, he'd know how much I wanted to belong there.

I'm laughing again because I've just remembered that we didn't knock, so I must have had my door key. I have no idea why. Of all the things I left behind that morning, my keys should have been the first. But that's another thing I'll never tell Pan: that I gave in so easily not because he was right, but because I knew I'd go back. Or at least I wanted to. Looking back on it now, maybe that's what all of it was about – my plan to run away – a theatrical way of showing him how much I didn't want to be there because it felt like too much of a betrayal that I did.

'Holy shit,' I heard him say under his breath when he followed me into the apartment.

'All right, isn't it?'

'All right?' he said, looking around as he followed me down the hall. 'It's Versailles.'

'Not quite.'

'Is this a—?' He stopped at the painting near the spiral staircase that made me dizzy if I looked at it for too long. 'It is. It's a Picasso.' He stared at me. 'Why are you making that face?'

'It's weird.'

118

He looked horrified. 'It's a Picasso, Lola.'

'So? It's still weird.'

I could sense that he was about to launch into a tirade convincing me otherwise so was most grateful when Josette poked her head out of the kitchen.

'*Bonjour, Josette. Ça va?*' I thumbed over my shoulder. '*C'est Pan.*'

He waved and smiled. '*Bonjour, Josette. Comment allez-vous?*'

'Hello, Pan,' she said in that way the French do when you try to speak French at them. 'Are you hungry?' She nodded at me. '*Dites-lui que j'ai acheté le thé qu'il aime.*'

I turned to Pan. 'She got you the tea you like.'

'*Merci beaucoup,*' he said clumsily and she shook her head.

'*Il est très beau,*' she said with a wicked smile.

'What did she say?' Pan asked when I told Josette to behave and pulled him away.

'You don't want to know,' I chuckled, taking his hand and leading him up the stairs.

My father was waiting at the top and the shock of it made me gasp.

'Hey, Dad,' I said, stepping back, almost sending poor Pan tumbling back down the stairs.

'You're here,' he said, flustered. 'Why didn't you tell me you were going to meet him?'

I almost laughed as I thought about sneaking out of the apartment a few hours before. If Pan had done as he was told for once, we'd have been having coffee and *chouquettes* at the Gare de Lyon while we waited for the 2.07 p.m. train to Barcelona Sants, and Dad had no idea.

'Hey, Simon,' Pan said, somewhere behind me.

Dad caught himself, putting on his best Professor Durand smile. 'Lovely to see you, Pan.'

'You too, Simon.'

'How was Chennai?' he asked, gesturing at us to follow him, and for once I was grateful for my father's painful politeness. My mother would have led with, *Do you know what your girlfriend's done now, Pan?*

We hadn't discussed sleeping arrangements, but I wasn't surprised when he led us to the end of the hall to the bedroom opposite his and Agatha's. The furthest from mine.

'Couldn't you find a room across the street, Dad?' I asked as we followed him in.

He ignored me, throwing his arm out at the room with a manic smile as though it was a prize on a game show. 'Will this do, Pan?'

Pan nodded, stunned. It was more or less the same size as my room, with two tall windows that opened onto balconets. I try to keep as much distance between myself and Agatha at all times, so I don't often stray to that end of the corridor. I'd only been in there once, my first morning in Paris when I'd refused to spend the day with my father, telling him to go to work, then wandered from room to room when I was finally alone. In fairness, I could see why they'd put Pan in that room. It was the most masculine, I guess. Where mine was shades of green and gold, like a

Ladurée box, everything in that room except for the parquet floor was painted white.

It was dominated by a huge bed that was also white, but my gaze went straight to the easel by the window. Pan saw it too and smiled loosely, but I sneered, unimpressed with Agatha's efforts to suck up. She'd done the same in my room, filled the wardrobe with clothes I'd refused to wear. (With hindsight, that's probably why I haven't unpacked, because I'm too scared to open the wardrobe in case I try on the leather jacket I know is in there.)

'It'll do, I suppose,' Pan said with a shrug.

Dad chuckled. 'I'll let you get settled in. If you need anything, shout.'

He made a point of leaving the door open and I was about to walk over and close it when Pan put his holdall down and nudged me.

'This is bigger than your nan's old flat.' When I ignored him and sat on the bed, he walked over and frowned at me. 'Where is she?'

'Who?'

'Agatha.'

'Why are you whispering?'

'This place makes me want to whisper.'

'Do you see what I mean now?'

'Yeah. It's very grown up.'

'At least that's one thing I don't have to worry about,' I thought out loud, falling back on the bed with a sigh and looking up at the ceiling, 'them having kids.'

As if on cue, Agatha swept in, heels clacking steadily on the parquet floor.

'Good morning, Pandiyan,' she said and every muscle in my body tensed, all at once.

'It's Pan,' I told her, sitting up and smoothing my hair down with my hands.

She didn't look at me. 'Welcome to Paris, Pandiyan.'

When she smiled the sun spilling through the window next to her hit her cheek so I could see all the edges of her face – her nose, her cheekbones, the stubborn sweep of her jaw. But that was Agatha; everything about her was severe, her nails, her heels, her cropped hair, a style she went for not long after meeting my father which had everyone in Paris cutting theirs too. Even her black shirt dress was sharply ironed and so immaculate I wondered if she'd sat down since she put it on. But then, always the contradiction, she'd foregone the red lipstick she usually wore in favour of a pale pink one that made her mouth look so soft she almost looked vulnerable.

Almost.

'I'm Agatha.' She stepped forward and held out her hand.

'It's a pleasure to meet you,' Pan said, shaking it carefully.

I rolled my eyes, but I got why he did that. You will too when you meet her. As formidable as she is, there's still something about her – some delicateness – that makes you think she's made of glass.

When he let go, she pressed her palms together and

lifted her chin to look at him. 'How was your journey? Not too horrendous, I hope. This heat is unbearable.'

'It was cool. *Literally*,' he sounded nervous, which was unlike Pan, his fingers fluttering as he swept his hair back with his hand. 'There was air conditioning on the train.'

Agatha looked pleased, as though she'd arranged it herself, then looked down at the leather holdall by his feet. 'Well, I'll let you get unpacked, Pandiyan.'

'He prefers Pan,' I said again. 'How is that so hard? Pan. P-A-N. Pan.'

She ignored me. 'If you need anything do let me know. I hear you've already met Josette.'

'Hello?' I held my arms out. 'Am I invisible?'

'Not in that, dear.' She smiled sweetly before turning towards Pan again as I looked down at my tie-dyed T-shirt. 'I'm not sure if the two of you have made plans—'

'We have.' I interrupted before she could tell him about my interview at BSP.

'It would be wonderful if you could join Simon and me for dinner this evening,' she said as if I hadn't spoken, and as grateful as I was that she hadn't told him, I still wanted to slap her.

'I. Um.' Pan looked between us, unsure what to say.

She looked at me, too, and smiled, her eyes alight with mischief because she knew I had no choice. 'When do you want us, Agatha?' I asked with a tired sigh.

'Whenever's convenient for you.'

'And convenient for us is?'

'Seven o'clock.'

'Fine.'

'Marvellous.' She turned smoothly on the balls of her feet and swept out again.

Pan waited for the sound of her heels to fade then turned to look at me. 'Well. She's. Um . . .' He didn't finish the thought, just put his hands on his hips.

'I know,' I muttered, falling back on the bed again.

You won't be surprised to hear that I didn't go to the interview at BSP; I stayed out all day with Pan, determined to make his first trip to Paris perfect. I'd been to Carcassonne, of course, but the first time I came here I was five. I don't remember all of it, but I do remember the first time I saw the Eiffel Tower, and the eclair I had at Angelina's, and I remember Mum and Dad taking me on the Ferris wheel at Place de la Concorde. It was snowing and apparently I said it was like being inside a snow globe. I don't remember that, but I do remember how it felt, like we were touching the sky.

That's all I wanted for Pan, to have a story like that to tell one day. So if I was determined for his trip to be special, that's why. Looking back on it now, though, I was doing exactly what Dad did when I got here and trying to sell the city to Pan as though it was a second-hand car. I dragged him from café to café and into every shop I thought he would like until I wore a hole in the bottom of my sandals. I don't know why I needed him to love it so much. Maybe I do, but at the time I thought it was because it was the first time I could enjoy the city without feeling guilty. I didn't have to feel bad for finding a second-hand bookshop, because he was there to leaf through the box of comics and ask me to translate the copy of *The Incal* he'd unearthed. So I could let myself enjoy the sunshine and the coffee and the long, lazy walks down roads I've been down so many times they're worn into my memory like lines down the spine of my favourite book. I could enjoy Paris, which suddenly wasn't as hot and huge and strange with him there.

I took him to the café first. 'Osamu Tezuka,' he gasped when we passed the bookshop next door, but I just smiled smugly and pulled him into the café, the book already in my bag to give him over lunch. Laurent cheered when he saw us, hugging me like an old friend who'd just got back from war before kissing Pan on both cheeks.

'Is this your table?' Pan asked as he ushered us towards the one in the corner.

'How did you guess?' I tilted my head at him then frowned as he sat opposite me and began running his hand under the table, his brow puckered. 'What are you doing?'

'Looking for your name.'

'Not yet,' I mouthed then gestured at him to sit next to me on the bench. 'In Paris couples sit next to one another.'

'Yeah?' he said with a loose smile, my knee automatically gravitating towards his when he sat next to me. 'When in Paris.'

He pressed his mouth to mine but before I could kiss him back, I heard Laurent whistle and pulled away as he put a cup of coffee on the table in front of us. '*Monsieur*,' he said, putting down a cup of tea as well and Pan blinked, clearly startled that he knew what he wanted, but before he could ask how, Laurent smiled. 'You're an artist, yes?'

It was my turn to be startled. I'd never heard Laurent speak English. Once, actually, when an American couple wandered in, clearly lost. 'Do you speak English?' one of them asked when Laurent came to take their order. 'No. I'm French,' he said and they didn't know what to say.

'*Oui. Je suis un artiste*,' Pan said awkwardly and Laurent beamed at the effort.

'If I give you some—' He stopped and held his thumb and forefinger a few inches apart to me. '*Comment dites-vous de la craie?*'

'Chalk.'

He nodded. 'If I give you some chalk will you decorate the board?'

He pointed to the board behind the bar and Pan smiled. '*Biensûr.*'

'*Un jour il sera peut-être quelque chose de valeur*,' Laurent said, patting him on the shoulder.

I agreed, smiling the way Dad used to at my parents' evenings as Laurent sauntered off, but Pan looked confused. 'He said maybe it will be worth something one day,' I translated, silencing his *I doubt it* chuckle with a kiss.

When I sat back, I saw Didier sitting by the window. He waved sheepishly and when I waved back, Pan looked across the café at him. 'Who's that?'

I flicked my hair with a bored sigh. 'The guy I'm leaving you for.'

'I like his T-shirt.'

I rolled my eyes and sipped my coffee. As glad as I am that Pan's not the sort of guy to punch someone for looking at me, he's too chilled for his own good sometimes.

'It's so weird,' I thought out loud, putting the coffee cup back on the saucer and licking my lips. 'I come in here every day and I've never seen him before, but that's two days in a row.'

'He came back for you.'

'How do you know?'

He kissed me again. ''Cos it's what I would have done.'

Okay. Here's the thing: remember when you were a kid and you walked home *really* slowly when you were in trouble because you knew that you were going to get told off when you got in? I'm shuddering just thinking about it, because while my father doesn't like to talk, you best believe my mother did. So I guess that's what I was doing that day with Pan, walking home really slowly.

Looking back on it now, that's another reason I took him to the café, not just because I wanted him to see it – a proper Parisian café that didn't have an English menu and Toulouse-Lautrec posters on the walls – but because I knew lunch would take *forever* and I'd have an excuse to put off telling him that Dad wanted me to stay. I was right. We were there almost three hours while Laurent brought us a variety of things we didn't order. I've learned to go with it since I tried to order a salad the first time I went in there and he told me that I needed an omelette. I've come to realise he's usually right, but for Pan who, despite coming with me to Carcassonne every summer since we were kids, won't eat anything more French than a Filet-O-Fish, it was painful.

'Why can't I have chips?' he whispered when Laurent brought us each a salad.

'Just eat it.'

He stabbed a cube of melon with his fork and held it up. 'Is this melon?'

'Yes.'

'In a salad?'

'You eat tomato if it's in a salad. Tomato's a fruit.'

'I don't eat salad.'

'You should eat salad. It's good for you.'

'I told you: I'm not giving in to this five-a-day propaganda.'

It went on like this for three hours. I can't remember the last time I laughed so much, especially when Laurent brought us a dish of sorbet and told Pan that it was made from *wee wee de sheep*. I told Pan a dozen times it was just pear sorbet, but he still refused to eat it, which made me laugh even more. So yeah, I know. I should have told him that Dad wasn't letting me go home, but I was enjoying how my muscles felt a little looser and the corners of my mouth didn't feel as rusty. So I couldn't tell him then, or as we walked to the Musée d'Orsay, not with him stopping at the window of every gallery along the way then insisting we cross the road to check out the *bouquinistes* by the river.

When I was distracted by a Mucha print, he bought me an old black-and-white postcard of Rambla de Canaletas in Barcelona. 'Soon,' he said with a kiss when he gave it to me, and I shivered because I don't know how he knew.

He hadn't seen my room yet – only the bits of it he'd seen on Skype – because I was so desperate to get out of the apartment that I told him I'd give him a tour later. So he hadn't seen the postcards I'd stuck around my mirror. I hadn't told him about them, either, too scared that he'd hear something in my voice, some softness that would betray me and let him know that I'd started adjusting the furniture and filling the vase on my dressing table with roses. So I don't know how he knew. But then he always does, which is why I hadn't told him. Not because I felt guilty but because when I did, he'd think I wanted to stay.

He knew something was wrong when I didn't thank him for the postcard, though, just hugged him until I'd blinked the tears away, but he didn't say anything. I didn't, either. And I didn't say anything when we got to the Musée d'Orsay because as soon as we walked in, his eyes widened the way they did that afternoon we found a gold ring while we were making mud pies in my garden. I did the same thing the first time I walked in there. I remember turning in a slow circle, the tourists moving around me as though I wasn't there, a pebble on the bed of a stream. The building used to be a railway station so it has a vast glass ceiling that you could never hope to touch and a grand, gold clock over the entrance that you only see if you turn back and look up at it. Like the one at Gare du Nord, it's surrounded by squares of glass, so that day it looked like the sun hanging high and proud in the sky. Pan took his phone out of his pocket to take a photo of it and I couldn't tell him then, could I? Or when he took my hand and led me around, stopping at paintings I'd never noticed and finding rooms I didn't even know were there.

I don't know why I didn't; I had so many chances. But he was so happy, pointing out that the glass of absinthe in one of Degas' paintings was the same colour as Laurent's *sorbet de pee pee* and laughing at the fly toilet on level two. I told myself that it was because I didn't want to ruin our day, but I know now that it was because I'd succeed in selling Paris to him, so if I told him, he'd *want* me to stay. So I left it until we were in the lift, heading up to Agatha's apartment.

'Dad won't let me go home,' I blurted out somewhere between the third and fourth floor.

Pan almost dropped the Musée d'Orsay guide he was flicking through. 'What?'

'He says I have to stay.'

I held my breath as I lifted my chin to look at him. He must have been holding his breath as well because he was as startled as I was when the lift arrived on the fifth floor with a bounce. I watched the door slide open then turned to look at him, willing him to say something, to tell me that it was going to be okay, like he always did, but he just blinked at me.

'When did this happen?'

'Last night.'

'And you didn't think to mention it?'

'When was I supposed to tell you?'

'I don't know, Lola,' he said, bending a Gauguin postcard in half as he shoved the book back into the plastic bag he was holding. 'At some point in the *six hours* we just spent together.'

'Well, I'm telling you now.'

'Five minutes before we have dinner with your father and Agatha.'

I ignored him, opening the gate with a huff.

'Where are you going?' He followed as I stomped out. 'We need to talk about this.'

'Talk about what?' I asked when I got to Agatha's front door, rooting through my bag for my key so I didn't have to look him in the eye. 'I'm not staying.'

'Do you want to?'

'What?' I looked up, horrified. 'Of course not!'

I wish I hadn't said it like that – so sharply – but it was as if he'd pinched me.

It calmed him down, though. 'Why's he so pissed, then?'

I blurted that out, too. 'I got caught shoplifting.'

He looked so disappointed, the shame of it made the back of my neck burn. 'Lola, you didn't.'

'I know.'

'You promised me the last time that you wouldn't do it again.'

'I know.'

'Stop saying I know!' he snapped and my heart leapt onto my tongue. 'Why, Lola?'

133

'I don't know.' The look he gave me told me that I was pushing it. 'I was bored.'

'*Bored?* If you're bored, Lola, read a book.' When I ignored him, he put his hands on his hips and tried to look me in the eye but I wouldn't let him. 'What'd you take?'

'Nothing.'

'Well, it must have been something.'

'Just a lipstick.'

'Yeah 'cos you don't have four hundred and twelve of those.'

'Not in that colour.'

'This isn't funny, Lola.'

'I've been banned from Sephora, Pan. There's no crueller punishment.'

'What did your dad say?' he asked, exhaling through his nose. 'Did he lose his shit?'

'What do you think?'

'Is that why you wanted to run away?' His shoulders fell when I nodded. 'It's all right.' He stopped to suck in a breath and when he nodded back I wondered if he was trying to convince himself, not me. 'It's all right. Don't worry. He'll have calmed down by the time we have to go home on Friday.'

'I dunno.'

He pulled me to him and kissed my forehead. 'You know what he's like.'

'I think he means it this time.'

134

'What do you mean?'

My gaze dipped to my toenails as I pressed my cheek to his chest. I'd painted them yellow, a colour I'd fallen hopelessly in love with because it looked like sunshine, then fell even more in love with when Agatha said it was vile. ('Why would you want to look as though you have jaundice?') The colour was called Fifteen Minutes, a Warhol reference I was sure Pan would love. I don't know when life became so hard. You get that, don't you? We're teenagers. Life should be about yellow nail varnish and kissing in cafés, shouldn't it?

When did everything become so hard?

'Lola, what happened?' He stepped back and looked down at me in time to catch a tear with his thumb. 'Why do you think he means it this time?'

'Nan doesn't want me to come back to London.'

He was quiet for so long that I made myself lift my chin to look at him. When I did, he frowned. 'What do you mean, she doesn't want you to come back to London? It's your home.'

'She says that I should be with Dad.'

'But you guys talked about that when he got the job at—'

He hesitated and I helped him out. 'Lariboisière.'

'Yeah.' He pointed at me and he looked so confused, like he does when he wakes up from a nap. 'You guys agreed that it made *no sense* to move here halfway through your A-levels.'

'I know.'

'Do they even do A-levels here?'

'I don't know.'

If he noticed that I looked down at my feet again, he didn't say anything. I know what you're thinking. I don't know why I lied, either. It's not like I could hide it from him, could I? Dad wouldn't tell me off in front of him, but Agatha was bound to say something about me missing my interview at BSP. She wouldn't sugar-coat it like I would have; she wouldn't kiss Pan's worried brow and tell him that everything was going to be okay. He deserved that much and I should have given it to him, but it was all I could do not to run and keep running.

'So why is he making you stay, Lo?'

'I don't know.'

As soon as I shrugged, he knew. 'What happened?' When I didn't answer him he put his hands on his hips. 'Lola, what happened?'

He waited for me to look at him but all I could do was bite down on my lip to distract myself from the fresh tears gathering at the corners of my eyes.

'Lola.'

'He thinks I need to see a counsellor,' I said at last, the words so loud in the empty hall.

'A counsellor?'

'Can you believe it?' I rolled my eyes, catching another tear with my knuckle.

'Because of your mum?'

I nodded.

'Does he know about the other stuff?'

I nodded again.

'So he knows that you have to retake the year?'

That hit me like a punch in the jaw. I'd forgotten about that.

'Of course not,' I scoffed. 'As if I'd still be breathing if he knew.'

'But your nan told him about the other stuff, yeah?'

I nodded carefully, trying not to dislodge any more tears.

'Oh, Lo,' he said softly, reaching for my hand, but I took a step back onto the doormat.

'Don't say it, okay?'

'Say what?' I couldn't look at him, but I knew he was frowning.

'I told you so,' I hissed, even though he would never say that.

Never.

'Lola.'

I crossed my arms and stared at him. 'Why are you being so calm?'

'What?'

'He's making me stay in Paris, Pan. Don't you care that we'll never see each other again?'

'Of course I do,' he said, but he wouldn't look at me and I felt something in me split open.

'You agree with him, don't you? You think I should stay.'

I could hear myself, I sounded hysterical but I couldn't stop. 'I knew it! So you don't want me, either?'

He grabbed my elbow as I charged towards the stairs. 'Lola, listen.'

'Let go!'

'Lola, listen to me.'

'No.'

'Look at me.'

I couldn't, my eyes out of focus, and I don't know whether it was the tears, the shock or a combination of the two, but I was suddenly very grateful that he wouldn't let go of my elbow.

'Lola, your mum died. You need to talk to someone about that.'

'I talk to you!'

'Of course you do but it's not helping, is it?'

It is! I wanted to tell him, but I couldn't catch my breath.

'Lola, you haven't been to college for a full week since your dad moved here.'

I have!

'And you're drinking every day now.'

I'm not!

'When was the last time you had a drink?'

I found my voice then. 'Are you serious, Pan?' I managed to pull away, narrowly avoiding the top step as I glared at him. 'You think I'm an alcoholic?'

'Of course not.' He looked appalled. 'I just think you're sad.'

138

I paced past him and stood outside Agatha's front door. 'I'm not sad, Pan.'

'If my mum died and my dad married someone else ten minutes later I'd be sad.'

'Don't tell me how I should feel, Pan.'

'I'm not because I haven't got a clue. *Clearly*.'

'So why are you having a go at me, then?'

I sounded pathetic, like a sniffly kid. I hated myself for it, but we'd never argued like that. Never. We bicker, but over silly shit like where to go for lunch and where to sit on a train. (I can't go backwards, a foible Pan will not accept.) But we're not one of those couples who yell at each other at a party on a Saturday night then get back together at college on Monday morning.

'I'm not having a go at you, Lola. Just *listen*.'

'To what? To how fucked up I am?'

'You're not fucked up, you just need help.'

'And this is helping? Yelling at me!'

'I don't know what to do, Lola!' He did yell then – actually, properly yelled – and it was enough to make me shake. 'Do you know how useless it makes me feel that I can't help you?'

'I don't need help!'

'You do! I miss you so much, Lola!'

I held my arms out. 'I'm right here, Pan!'

'No, I miss *you*, Lola! The Lola I used to make mud pies in your garden with, the one who can't sit going backwards on the train because it's like going back in time.' He smiled suddenly, softening at that. 'Today was the first time since I don't know when,' he stopped to let go of a breath and rub his forehead with his hand, 'when we didn't talk about what a bitch Agatha is.'

'She is a bitch, Pan.'

'This is what I mean! You're so angry!'

'And you don't think I have a reason to be?'

'Lola, you're not listening.' He threw his head back and groaned.

I waited for him to look at me again then arched an eyebrow. 'Listening to what?'

'What are you going to do about it?'

'About what?'

'About being angry.'

'I can't just turn it off, Pan.'

'Of course you can't, but it isn't going to magically disappear, either.'

'I know that!'

'Do you? You can't drink and cry and puke this out of you, Lola. You need to deal with it.'

'I know!'

'So why are you pushing everyone away? Your dad, your nan, me, your mates.'

'I am not!'

'Michelle says that she hasn't spoken to you since you got here.'

'When were you speaking to Michelle?'

'Look.' He closed his eyes. When he opened them again,

he looked exhausted. 'I don't know what you two are arguing about this week, but enough, Lola. She's worried about you.'

'No she isn't! Michelle Ansah only cares about herself!'

'Lola, you can't keep doing this. You need help.'

'I don't need help!' I balled my hands into fists and held them up. 'I just need time!'

'This isn't a cold, Lola. You're not going to get over it.'

'I know that!'

'And breaking your father and Agatha up isn't going to make things better, either.'

'It might!'

'This is *exactly* what I'm talking about! I don't know who this girl is.' He looked me up and down. 'This girl who steals lipsticks and bunks off college and doesn't answer her phone to her father,' he counted each thing off on his fingers, 'and drinks until she pukes and tells her grandmother to mind her own business when she asks her where she's going!'

That was it.

I see it now I've written it down.

That's when I should have stopped, done what he and Dad were saying and got help. If I had, none of this would have happened and you wouldn't have got hurt, and I'm so sorry. But Pan was right. I wasn't listening, but he was the only one who wasn't supposed to keep a tally of all the shitty things I'd done.

The only one.

The pain in my throat was too much to speak around so I could only point at him.

'Lola, listen,' he said, reaching for me, but I pulled away as the front door opened.

Agatha looked between us then smiled. 'Have you had a good day, kids?'

If you want to know how excruciating dinner was, just imagine your most embarrassing moment then picture it on YouTube . . . with 2,000,000 hits . . . and twenty comments saying, *Hey, I know that girl.* Maybe then you'll be able to understand how unbearable it was.

Dad was furious that I'd blown off my interview at BSP but he wouldn't tell me off in front of Pan, so he was practically vibrating with anger when I walked into the dining room. Agatha was thrilled, though. After interrupting our argument in the hall, she insisted Pan and I sit together. I needed as much space between him and me as possible, but I didn't want her to know that she'd got to me, so I went along with it, which amused her even more when she saw me inch my chair away from Pan's as soon as I sat down. When Pan inched his back towards mine, she tried to hide her smile behind her wine glass but I saw. And I saw how bright her eyes were when she looked at us. 'Oh to be seventeen and in love again,' she swooned.

'I'll settle for being forty-two and in love,' my father said with a dreamy smile, reaching across the table for her hand.

I almost puked on my plate.

Dinner with Mum and Dad was never like that. It was always a little chaotic, Eartha Kitt purring from the living room as we passed plates back and forth and picked pieces of chicken off the pile with our fingers. Dad would mock Mum's cooking ('What did this chicken do to offend you so, Alicia?') and she'd do impressions of him when he complained about something that had happened that day at the hospital. Dinner at Agatha's, however, was a much more formal affair. There was no Eartha Kitt, no paper towels or sticky bottles of Aunt May's pepper sauce. We ate in the dining room on china so thin I was worried to use my knife and the table so big I felt like I had to raise my voice sometimes. It was the opposite of the scuffed one in our kitchen at home – so small that our knees would knock together when we sat down – but at least it meant we were sitting comfortably apart, which was no bad thing. Especially when Dad and Agatha were like this, laughing lightly and exchanging smiles as they asked about our day.

Pan, oblivious to the aneurysm I was about to have as I stabbed at a hunk of aubergine with impotent rage, was as charming as ever, telling them about the little girl at the Musée d'Orsay who'd said he looked like Aladdin. My cheeks burned when Agatha tossed her head back and laughed, exposing the long line of her neck, her skin shockingly pale under the black of her dress, like something from an Anne Rice novel. I had to stop myself throwing my fork at her when she asked Pan if he was enjoying the meal. She'd made such a fuss about it – an aubergine and chickpea tagine! – ordering Josette to put the pot down in the middle of the table. My father is an unrepentant carnivore so it was the first time we hadn't had meat since I'd been there, which is kind of a big deal, I suppose, but I knew it was just another attempt to suck up to Pan. One he clearly appreciated, because when Josette lifted the lid off the tagine with a great flourish, he humoured Agatha with a cheer as I turned my nose up at the steaming mound of vegetables.

'I cannot eat another salad,' Agatha said with a sigh, holding her hands up. 'So your visit was the perfect excuse to try something new, Pandiyan.'

'Pan,' I muttered then sniffed the bowl of couscous Josette had handed me.

Agatha ignored me, of course, as though I had some form of Tourette's that made me say Pan at random intervals. 'Everything's vegetarian, Pandiyan,' she said with a proud smile.

He thanked her then quietly picked the raisins out of his couscous while Agatha regaled us with a story about a trip to Morocco with David Bowie that I might have actually listened to if I hadn't been so worried about Pan, who was struggling with a disc of apricot. He looked so miserable, no doubt wondering where the nearest Subway was, that my mood softened and I reached over when Agatha wasn't looking and relieved him of the apricot with my fork. He looked at me with a small smile, then reached for my hand under the table.

'Sylvie, what are you wearing?' Agatha said suddenly and we each looked up from our plates to find Agatha's assistant frozen in the doorway. She almost dropped the armful of sketches she was holding, the roll of fabric under her arm wobbling for a moment before she steadied it.

'*Pardon, Agatha?*'

It was a question but it sounded more like an apology.

'Go home and change. You can't go and see Madame Forbin in flip-flops.'

She parted her lips to protest as she looked down at her feet, no doubt desperate to remind Agatha of the heatwave and beg for mercy, but she thought better of it. '*Je suis désolée, Agatha.*'

When Sylvie scurried off Agatha turned to smile at Pan like nothing had happened. 'There are some wonderful halal restaurants in Montmartre, Pandiyan. You and Lola should spend the day there. That's where I lived when I first moved to Paris, in a tiny flat above a bakery.'

Pan was clearly bewildered but managed a nod. 'Didn't Monet have a studio there?'

'Yes.' She beamed. 'And Picasso.'

'And van Gogh,' my father added, pointing his wine glass at him.

'Oh my God, stop!' I said, curling my hand into a fist around my fork.

All three of them turned to look at me.

'Can we stop pretending that nothing is wrong?'

'What's wrong?' Agatha looked genuinely bewildered. 'Is it the tagine?'

'Fuck the tagine!'

'Lola.' Dad put down his wine glass and glared at me across the table.

'I'm not happy, okay?' I let go of Pan's hand. 'There, I said it.'

In the end it was remarkably easy, even if it had taken me eight months to admit.

'We know.' Dad and Agatha exchanged a glance and it was like being kicked.

'But if you think I'm going to be any happier here, you're out of your mind.'

Dad's gaze flicked to Pan then back to me. 'Can we talk about this later, Lola?'

'What's wrong with now?'

'We're eating.'

'I won't talk with my mouth full.'

His jaw clenched. 'Agatha has spent a lot of time planning this meal for Pan so his first evening in Paris would be special. Let's not spoil it, Lola.'

'She's right,' Agatha said with a sigh. 'We can't keep tiptoeing around this, Simon.'

I held my hand up. 'No one asked you, Cruella de Vil.'

'Lola,' Dad said, tugging the napkin out of his lap and throwing it on the table.

'It's nothing to do with her, Dad!'

'It's everything to do with me if you're going to be living here, Lola.'

I didn't look at her. 'Well, I don't *want* to live here so you don't have to worry.'

'But I think you have to. You need to be with your father.'

'No one cares what you think.' I felt everyone at the table tense, but before she could say anything, I held my hand up to her and frowned at Dad. 'Aren't you going to say anything?'

'I agree with Agatha.'

I rolled my eyes and sat back in my chair with my arms crossed. 'Of course you do!'

'I'm your father. You should be here with me, Lola.'

'She doesn't want me here, Dad!'

Agatha seemed surprised. 'Whatever gave you that idea?'

'What are you? Fifty?' Her gaze narrowed so fiercely you'd think I'd called her a whore. 'If you wanted kids, Agatha, you would have had them by now.'

Dad looked ready to erupt. 'Lola, please.'

'It's true!'

'Well,' Agatha said smoothly, reaching for her wine glass. 'That may be so, but it doesn't change the fact that you need to be here with your father.'

I slammed my fist on the table. The saltshaker shivered. 'Don't tell me what I need!'

'Lola.' Dad looked at Pan, then at me. 'Go to your room.'

'Gladly,' I said, glaring at Agatha as I pushed my chair

148

back and pointed at the pot in the middle of the table. 'And your tagine sucks!'

I heard her chuckle merrily as I stormed out.

Ten minutes later there was a tentative knock on my door. I knew it was Pan so I lifted my face off the pillow to say, 'Come in,' before letting it fall back again. I heard the squeak of his trainers on the parquet floor as he walked towards the bed then felt the mattress dip as he sat down.

'You okay?'

'Never better,' I said into the pillow, but it came out as a muffled grunt.

'I'm sorry I had a go at you earlier,' he said softly, rubbing my back with his hand.

''S'all right.'

I don't know how he understood, but he did, because he said, 'No it's not. I've just been so worried about you since your mum died and then you told me what your dad said—' He stopped and I heard him huff out a breath. 'In case it isn't obvious, I kind of like having you around.'

I rolled onto my back and looked at him. 'Ditto.'

'Today was—' He stopped to swipe his thumbs under my eyes then wiped them on his jeans. 'I can't remember the last time you laughed so much. That's why I got so upset.' When I frowned, he shrugged. 'I thought it was 'cos you're here. I thought that's why you're happy again.'

'No, you goob.' I nudged him with my knee. 'It's because *you're* here.'

He smiled loosely, the way he does when he's about to kiss me, and my heart fluttered at the promise of it. 'When he's calmed down,' he pressed his mouth to mine, 'we'll talk to him.'

'It's no use.'

'It's worth a try, isn't it?'

'Pan,' I propped myself up on my elbows and frowned at him, 'come on. You're going home on Friday. Enrolment at college starts *next week*.'

He shrugged and tucked his hair behind his ears. 'That's plenty of time.'

'But you've seen how pissed he is.'

'He listened to us when he got the job here and he will again.'

'No way.' I fell back on the bed again with a groan. 'When he finds out that I have to repeat the year he'll say that it's the perfect excuse to start again here.'

'We just need to come up with a plan. Your dad has a Vulcan regard for logic.'

'Why is he married to Agatha, then?'

'Because she makes a mean tagine.'

I pretended to shudder. 'That was your fault.'

He pretended to shudder, too. 'It was worse than that coconut cake your mum made.'

'The one with the hole?'

He nodded solemnly.

'That she tried to hide with icing?'

He nodded again.

150

'That's how we eat it at home,' I said, mimicking her Bajan accent.

'Even the birds wouldn't eat it.'

'That thing would have survived a nuclear holocaust.' I wiped my nose with the back of my hand then nudged him with my knee again. 'Remember the comic you drew about it?'

He threw his head back and laughed then looked at me, his gaze narrowing. 'Cruminator,' he said, putting on his best film trailer voice. 'Humanity's only chance to defeat Pienet.'

I laughed too and when I did, he grabbed my wrists and pulled me up into a hug.

'That's a nice sound,' he said into my hair.

'You're such a dork.'

'Dork trumps psycho stepmum.'

It definitely does.

If you ever get to meet Agatha – and I hope you do, because I think you want to – let me give you some advice: if you find yourself in a situation where you've called her Cruella de Vil, implied that she's fifty and/or cast aspersions on her hosting, just stay out of her way.

Seriously.

It's for the best.

That's exactly what Pan and I did; we hung out in his room for the rest of the evening with the windows – and door – open. It's funny how we were so far away but it felt

151

like we were at home, the two of us bickering over which film to watch and fighting over the pillows. I guess home is more than a house, somewhere with hiding places only you know about and your school photos on the walls. I suppose you know that more than anyone, how home is a feeling, too, not just of being safe, but being understood. After all, isn't that all any of us are trying to do with the books that we read and the strangers we smile at in the street, to be understood?

That's how Pan and I spent the rest of the week. Dad and Agatha left us to it, assuming we were making the most of our last few days together, and I told Pan that I was working on Dad and he believed me because I'd been on my best behaviour. I even made a show of going to the interview at BSP. I didn't tell Pan; he thought Dad, Agatha and I were having lunch to talk through our 'issues' and was proud of me. Dad was, too, his eyes wet as I sat between him and Agatha in the headmaster's office at BSP and charmed him into submission.

I was the most proud of me, though, if a little frightened by how easy it was. When I think how I used to tell my mother everything, from when I wanted to go on the pill to that Mars bar I stole from the newsagent that she made me take back the next day, it surprises me how easily I lied. It was like another language I'd perfected – like French – that I switched to without thinking. A means to an end, I kept telling myself. I just needed to get on the train with Pan and everything would be okay. After that what was Dad going to do? Come to London and drag me back by my hair?

Not to sound like a Scooby Doo villain, but I would have got away with it if it hadn't been for Agatha. She obviously knew me better than I thought, because the day we were meant to be leaving she appeared behind me as I rooted around under my bed looking for my satchel, which I'd packed the night before and hidden there so no one would see it.

'Looking for this?'

I stopped and pressed my forehead to the parquet floor.

When I emerged, fighting the urge to huff as I clambered to my feet and smoothed down my dress, I found her in the middle of my room holding my satchel up by the handle. My instinct was to march over and grab it, but I refused to give her the satisfaction. If it was anyone else I would have said something funny – delivered a Blair Waldorf worthy insult that would have made her face tighten – but I didn't trust my voice not to betray me so I shut up for once.

She lowered her arm. 'Aren't you going to say anything, Lola?'

'Agatha, please. You don't want me here any more than I want to be here.'

She didn't deny it. 'It's what your father wants.'

'What about what I want?'

'I don't care what you want.'

'Clearly.'

When I chuckled sourly she brought her other hand up to touch the string of pearls hanging from her collarbones. She didn't grab them – didn't fiddle with them – simply pressed her fingers to them as though she was checking they were still there. 'That's not what I meant.'

'What did you mean, then?'

'I meant that you're not in any state to make a decision like this.'

I arched an eyebrow at her. 'State?'

'We tried it your way and now it's time to—'

'*We?*' Each of my muscles clenched, all at once. 'There is no *we.*'

'There is now.'

I was glad I was crossing my arms because I don't know what I would have done otherwise.

'I'm going.' I tried so hard to keep the tremor out of my voice that I said it through my teeth. 'Whether it's today or tomorrow or next week, I will find a way to go home.'

'This is your home.'

'Never.' I stamped my foot, actually stamped my foot. 'This will *never* be my home.'

I took a step towards her, suddenly sick at the thought of our house, Mum's pink dressing gown hanging on the back of the bathroom door. Even though I'd learned to love Agatha's apartment, to lose afternoons in the library or on the balcony, my bare feet propped up on the wrought-iron railings as I ate *macarons* like Marie Antoinette, it could never feel like home. Home is somewhere you feel safe.

Somewhere there's a space for you.

'You can keep telling yourself that, Lola,' she said, walking over to the bed and putting my satchel on it. 'But this will be a lot less painful if you just grow up and accept it.'

She left the door open as she swept out and I charged over and slammed it shut so hard the picture frame on the wall next to it shivered. I knew my passport wouldn't be in my bag, but I still checked, sitting on the edge of my bed with a sigh when I realised that it wasn't. I couldn't go now – and she knew it – but before I could come up with a plan, there was a knock.

'Knock, knock,' Pan said, edging the door open and peering around it. 'Ready?'

'Yeah,' I said, because I didn't know what else to say. And I didn't know what to say in the elevator or on the walk to Saint-Sulpice or on the Metro. Even when we got to Gare du Nord, I smiled when he nudged me with his hip and reminded me that his mother was probably already making the pani puri for dinner. I didn't say a thing, not until we were approaching the escalator leading up to the departures lounge and stopped so suddenly the bloke behind us swore.

'What's wrong? Pan asked, tugging me out of his way. 'Did you forget your passport?' His hairline was silvered with sweat from being on the Metro, his collarbones, too, and I couldn't look at him as he frowned, my heart suddenly knocking against my ribs like a trapped bee.

'Yes.' I shook my head. 'I mean no.'

When I looked down at my yellow painted toenails, which he hadn't even noticed, he took me by the elbow and led me further away from the stream of people getting on the escalator. When he stopped, I knew that he was waiting for me to look up at him, but I couldn't.

'You're not coming, are you?'

I shook my head.

'Why didn't you tell me?'

'I was going to.'

'Were you?'

When I didn't answer, he let go of my elbow and stepped back. 'Just say it.'

It was my turn to frown. 'What?'

'That you want to stay.'

'Of course I don't!'

'Lola, please. I haven't seen you this happy in *months*.'

'Because *you're* here!'

He shook his head at me. 'Don't you think I can hear it in your voice every time you call?'

'Hear what?'

'You love it here.'

'I hate it, Pan. *Hate* it.' I reached for his hand and brought it up to my mouth to press a kiss to his palm. 'I just need more time.' He shook his head again but I pulled him closer and waited for him to meet my gaze. 'Enrolment is on

Tuesday. That's four days, Pan. Four days is a long time. We didn't even have that long when Dad got the job at Lariboisière.'

'That's the thing.' He sighed and closed his eyes. When he opened them again they were wet. 'When your dad got the job here we worked it out together. We spoke to your grandmother and went to him *together*.' He untangled his fingers from mine. 'We had a plan.'

'Pan—'

When I tried to reach for him again, he wouldn't let me. 'It used to be me and you against the world, and now.' He put his hands on his hips and scraped his teeth up his bottom lip. 'Now.'

He didn't finish the thought and the floor suddenly felt like a sponge beneath my feet.

'Pan, listen.'

'I don't know who you are any more, Lola.'

'I'm me.' I tugged on the front of his T-shirt so he'd look at me. 'I'm still me.'

'You're not the same since your mum died.'

'Of course I'm not the same!' I let go of his T-shirt, suddenly livid. 'My mother died!'

'I know, but it shouldn't be this bad.'

As soon as he said it, I know he regretted it because he wouldn't look at me, his bottom lip red raw from biting down on it. 'It shouldn't be this bad?' I tried not to lose my temper but I felt like a dog that had slipped its leash. 'What do you know, Pan?' I wanted to shove him. 'What have you lost? A goldfish? A fucking watch? You have no idea what it's like to lose a parent!'

I didn't realise I was shouting until he looked around at the people who'd stopped to stare at us. Usually I'd be mortified. I would have apologised, hidden behind my hair, but I didn't care as I felt something in me clench. It scared me because since Mum died, my heart's felt like a closed fist. When I'm with Pan it feels like an open hand, but that day it clamped shut and I knew then it was over. Perhaps I'd known all along. Looking back on it now, I see it was inevitable. For the first time since I'd walked into his kitchen to find him colouring, this was something he couldn't be part of. He could understand, but it wouldn't change him like it did me. The funny thing is, I think you get that more than he did, how sometimes something happens that's so big it doesn't just change everything, it changes you. Changes who you are. Something in your bones.

'I'm sorry, Pan!' I held my arms out. 'Am I embarrassing you?'

'Of course not. I just—'

I didn't let him finish. 'I'm sorry I'm not over my mother dying yet!'

'Lola, please.'

'No!' I pointed at him. 'You're as bad as Dad!'

'Lola, stop.' He reached for my hand and kissed the tips of my fingers. 'Listen. Just *listen*.'

'To what? To how you don't know me any more?' I tried

to pull away, but he wouldn't let go of my hand. 'If you don't know who I am, Pan, who does?'

'Lola, look at me.' When I did, his face softened. 'Your dad's right.'

'No!'

'You need help.'

'No!'

'Let him help you.'

'I don't need help. I just need time, Pan!'

'I agree.'

That surprised me. I stopped trying to wriggle away, but as soon as I lifted my eyelashes to look at him, I realised what he was saying and my legs suddenly didn't feel as steady.

'No.'

'Lola—'

'No!' I succeeded in pulling away and pointed at him again. 'Don't you fucking say it!'

'Lola—'

'Don't say what you're about to say!'

He pressed his hand to his chest and frowned miserably. 'Lola, I can't help you.'

'I don't need you to help me, I need you to tell me that everything's going to be okay!'

'I have. I've tried everything and it's not working. I don't know what else to do.'

'So you're throwing me away?'

'I'm not throwing you away! I'm giving you some space

to sort yourself out. You need to stay here, Lola. You *want* to stay here. You're only so determined to come back to London because of me, so I figured if I take myself out of the equation—'

'You *are* the equation, Pan!' I interrupted. 'You're the equation and the solution and the . . .' I wanted to slap him. Slap him and pull his hair and punch him in the heart. '. . . The *everything*!'

He was. He was so tightly embroidered into my life – there on my first day at school, there to try and catch me the time I fell out of that tree, there when I followed Mum's coffin out of the church – that even if I could unpick him, he'd still leave a hole in every memory I have.

'I'm not breaking up with you, Lola. You said you wanted time. I'm giving you time.'

'Not time away from *you*!' I swatted at a tear with my hand and sucked in a shaky breath. 'I've never needed you so much! If you leave me now, that's it!'

'Is that an ultimatum?'

My hands balled into fists when the crease between his eyebrows deepened. I honestly thought I was going to punch him. 'You can't just love the girl who likes Taylor Swift and comes to your basketball games in a PAN'S THE MAN T-shirt! You have to love this me, too! The hurt, confused, angry, fucking fucked up me who keeps doing stupid shit and doesn't know why.'

'Lola, I do.'

When his shoulders fell, I finally heard what he was

160

trying to say, and it was like wiping steam from a bathroom mirror after a shower.

It was the first moment of clarity I'd had in months.

'You love me, but you don't like me any more, do you, Pan?'

In the end, that's what broke me. Not Mum dying or Dad marrying Agatha but that I was so far gone that even Pan, the boy who used to climb up trees after me, who would have put me in his car and driven off the edge of the earth if I'd asked, didn't want to follow. That's what I was trying to say earlier about love being fallible. It's brittle. Breakable. But hate, hate is a flame that never goes out. If you're lucky, you only feel the burn of it sometimes, like a cigarette left in an ashtray. But if you're not, it gets hotter and hotter until it eats away everything, until it's all you can feel.

That's all I felt when I walked out of Gare du Nord: hate. A bright, red burn that made my legs shake as I walked back to the apartment. I was hoping it would help, that walking would burn some of it away, but Agatha was the first person I saw and I felt a fresh flare in my stomach.

'Welcome home,' she said when I walked into the kitchen to find her flicking through *Le Monde*. It sounded sincere (if Dad had been there he certainly would have thought so) but I heard it.

The way she said home.

I should have left it, I know, I should have walked back

out of the kitchen, been the bigger person. But I'm not the bigger person, am I? If I was, I wouldn't have done what I did to you. So I took the bait.

'You're enjoying this, aren't you, Agatha?'

She didn't look up from the newspaper. 'Enjoying what, dear?'

'You know what.'

'Do I?'

'Pan broke up with me.'

'It's probably for the best, dear.'

When she turned the page with a small nod, I lost it.

'Don't call me dear! I am not your dear!'

'Very well.'

'What is wrong with you?' I was so stunned I stared across the kitchen at her, the tops of my ears burning. 'Do you have any feelings or have you botoxed them as well?'

'Don't be so dramatic, Lola.'

'Dramatic? You're ruining my life!'

That did sound dramatic and it didn't go unnoticed as Agatha finally lifted her chin to look at me. 'I'm just saying: it's probably for the best that Pandiyan give you some time to deal with this.'

I was about to ask her what it had to do with her when something nudged at me.

'Did you speak to Pan? Did you tell him to break up with me?'

'Of course not.' She sighed as if to say, *You're being hysterical.* 'I merely pointed out that you're only so

164

determined to go home because of him, so if he took himself out of the equation—'

'You bitch!' I hissed, taking a step towards her, but she didn't flinch.

'Maybe so, but I'm looking out for your best interests, Lola.'

'How?'

She tilted her head at me. 'Never make a decision as important as this based on a boy.'

'Are you seriously giving me relationship advice right now? *You?*'

'Well I am *fifty*,' she said pointedly. 'I've done this dozens of times. This too shall pass.'

'Don't patronise me!'

'Lola, dear.' She took her glasses off to look me in the eye for the first time since I'd walked into the kitchen. 'I know it feels like the end of the world now but in a few months Pan will just be that nice boy who used to live next door to you.' She put her glasses back on and looked down at the newspaper. 'Boys are like houses, Lola, you should never settle for the first one you see.'

Even after everything, it had never occurred to me that things could unravel so quickly. I wonder sometimes if I could have stopped it, if I should have tried a little harder, held on a little tighter. The answer is yes – always yes – and I did, I just went about it the wrong way. Fighting is still trying and I chose to fight.

I stayed in my room for the rest of the day, pacing back and forth, back and forth, back and forth, until my father knocked on my door.

He didn't wait to be invited in. '*Viens*, Lola. Coline and Max are here.'

I stopped pacing. 'What?'

'Coline and her husband Max are here for dinner,' he said, one hand on the door handle and the other on his tie as he straightened it. He frowned at my denim shorts. 'Are you ready?'

'Who?'

'Coline, from the hospital.' When it was clear that I had no idea who he was talking about he added, 'She mistook Agatha's chicken consommé for a finger bowl the last time she was here.'

Oh yeah. I liked Coline.

'Will you be joining us for dinner?'

I crossed my arms and tried not to huff. 'No.'

'Fine.'

When he closed the door, I threw myself face down on the bed. I must have landed on my phone because I felt it vibrating against my stomach and was determined to ignore it until I realised that it might be Pan. It was and I was delighted.

'Hello?' I said, breathless. 'Pan? Are you home?'

'I just walked in.'

And his first thought was to ring me.

I felt something in the Universe realign as I rolled onto my back with a grin. 'How was the train? Did you get told off for having your iPod up too loud again?'

'Lola, I know you don't want to talk to me right now.'

'No! I do! I'm so glad you called.' I was smiling so much my cheeks hurt. I knew he wouldn't give up on me. I knew it. 'I'm sorry about earlier. I just—'

'Lola, listen,' he interrupted. 'I need to tell you something.'

My heart stopped.

'What?'

'There's a *For Sale* sign outside your house.'

When I charged into the dining room, Dad was laughing and pouring Coline a glass of red wine. When I roared, 'How could you, Dad?' he was so startled, he spilt some.

'*Merde*,' he said under his breath, dabbing at the stain with a napkin.

It looked like the table was bleeding.

'Dad, how could you?'

'How could I *what*, Lola?'

'Are you selling our house?'

He looked so bewildered that for one sweet second I thought it wasn't true, but then he looked at Agatha and something in me buckled.

'You can't, Dad! You can't sell our house!'

'Lola, please.' He smiled tightly. 'This isn't the time.'

'Unless Coline and Max are interested in moving to Richmond.' Agatha chuckled happily.

When Dad stared at her, I did, too. 'I'll get you back for this, you witch.'

She raised her wine glass with a smooth smile. 'I look forward to it, dear.'

I had to wait a week but it was worth it. I admit: I only went into Agatha's studio to find something to destroy. I wanted to rip something, cut something, scribble over her sketches and throw handfuls of buttons around like confetti. It was childish, I suppose, but then I am a child. I do everything I can not to look like one, but I'm just a child who smokes cigarettes and steals cans of cider from the supermarket so no one notices that I don't have a clue what I'm doing.

I know that now.

That was only six weeks ago but I've learned so much since then. I've grown up. Or at least I feel grown up, sitting here, writing this. Actually, I feel old. I feel like I've made it out the other side of this with scars and shrapnel embedded too deep to reach and I'm stronger for it.

I feel awful saying that, given that we don't know if you'll do the same, if you'll even make it out the other side. But if you do, please know that it wasn't for nothing, what happened to you. You saved me. That sounds pathetic and melodramatic and so fucking selfish, but you did.

I'm a better person because of you, though I recognise that doesn't change what I did.

I honestly hadn't gone into Agatha's studio that day to do anything other than be destructive. But as I was about to sweep my arm across the table and send magazines fluttering off, I saw something poking out from under one of her sketchbooks. I only saw the tiniest hint of red but I stopped. I don't know why, it could have been anything – just some junk mail asking for donations – but I plucked it out from under the sketchbook. I was right, it was a letter from the Red Cross. Dad volunteers for them and always seems to be running a marathon to raise money for them or going to speak at one of their events, so I've seen enough of their letters around our house to recognise the logo. Agatha would never do anything like that, which is what piqued my curiosity, and I was right about that, too.

The letter wasn't addressed to her; it was addressed to Agatha Park, a mailing list error, I assumed, given the address was correct. This would have made her eyebrow arch when she saw it, which I found unreasonably amusing. I was sure then that it was just a generic mail-out and was about to put it back on the desk when my gaze strayed to the first line.

Dear Ms Park, I am writing on behalf of your daughter.

It was as if I'd had the air kicked right out of me and I almost dropped the letter. I should have put it back, but before I could stop myself, I read on. *I am writing on behalf of your daughter, Holly Stapleton, who was adopted in 1996, and would like to make contact with you.*

My eyes lost focus after that.

I should have put it back, I know. I should have replaced the letter under the sketchbook and pretended that I hadn't seen it, but I didn't. I kept it, read it again and again, like I did the first letter Pan ever sent me and I didn't quite believe that anyone could love me that much. I read it until my heart started to beat in the same excited way, because I knew this was it.

This was the proof I needed that Agatha wasn't as perfect as Dad thought she was.

And that's when I got in touch with you.

You know what happened after that, but if you've read this far and you still haven't worked it out, then it was me who contacted the Red Cross, not Agatha. It was remarkably easy, actually, kind of like being set up on a blind date; they made all the arrangements, which helped. It also helped that you lost your phone so we couldn't even exchange numbers, just email addresses.

Jesus. Reading that back is making my hand shake because it's so fucked up. I don't even know what to say, Holly. This is the part I don't want to write down but the one that I have to, because you don't remember this bit, do you? You do, I mean, *you will*, you just can't right now. Things will come back to you, though, like they do with me. You'll open your wardrobe one morning and remember what you were wearing that day or you'll hear a song on the radio and remember listening to it on the Eurostar and how your ears popped when it went through the tunnel.

I talked to Dad and he says it's normal. He'd know, he's the best neurosurgeon in Europe, if the Lariboisière website is to be believed. So don't worry if you can't remember everything right away. That's what our brains do when these things happen. They try to protect us. That's what happened with Mum's funeral. For months after I couldn't remember it. I retained pieces. I was hugged a lot and offered plates of food that I put down a few minutes later only to be handed another one. And I remember Dad, how calm he was, how he shook everyone's hand with a smooth smile, the dark skin under his eyes the only thing that betrayed him. But I couldn't remember his eulogy or who planned the funeral, who picked the hymns and the flowers and the photo they used on the programme. It just kind of happened. One minute I was sitting in that green plastic chair at St Thomas', waiting for someone to tell me that Mum was going to be okay, and the next I was watching a hearse pull up outside our house.

I remember it all now, of course. Every detail, from the way everyone held their breath when they carried the coffin into the church, kind of like when a bride walks down the aisle (even if we cried for different reasons), to the way the heels of my shoes sank into the grass by the grave as though I wanted to leave some bit of me there, even if it was just holes.

You may not want to remember – and I get that – but you will. Until then, I'll try to fill in the gaps. I'm sorry that you're at my mercy here. I know you don't want to be, but you have to be careful who you listen to about that morning. As I said, half of Paris says they were there. One guy even claimed that he stopped one of the bombers. I have no idea why you would want to lie about something like that. I mean, I get that he enjoyed the attention but it can't have been worth it; he didn't even get his allotted fifteen minutes of fame. He went from being a hero to being reviled in the space of a few hours. So you can't believe everything you read. Between the assholes like him and the conspiracy theorists, there are several different versions of what happened that morning. I don't blame you if you don't trust mine, either, but if you've read this far I hope that means you'll continue. If you do, then I promise to tell you everything I know. It's the least I can do.

So these are the facts as I know them. First, it wasn't a terrorist attack. That's what everyone thought, but it wasn't. The car bomb that went off outside Charles de Gaulle Airport and the grenades thrown into the kosher shops and synagogues around Paris two days before were. An Islamic group called the GIA claimed those straight away, but the Paris prosecutor, Maxime Lefèvre, later confirmed that the explosion at Gare du Nord was nothing to do with them.

It was a gas leak. They're still looking into the cause of it so I can't comment on how it happened other than to say that it was just one of those freakish things that happen sometimes. With so many people saying they were there, it's impossible to really know how many people were hurt, but we know that 19 people died and 56 were seriously injured, including you. It feels crude to say this, but given Gare du Nord is the busiest station outside Japan, it could have been much worse. But it was a Sunday and yours was the first train in. Mercifully, it was running late, but it was still close enough to blow out the windows and kill two people.

You were lucky. I know you won't think so but you were. Someone on your carriage had a heart attack and someone else was killed by a falling suitcase, so you were lucky. That's something I keep telling myself, at night, when I can't sleep, or when I ask Dad how you're doing: it could have been worse. It shouldn't have happened at all, I know, but it could have been worse.

As for me, I was outside, my curls wilting in the rain. A woman next to me was the first to say it – *Bombe!* – but I didn't look at her as I took my hands away from my face and stared at the black smoke curling through the roof of the station like a cat's tail.

Are you trying to picture it? Given how often we see these things happen in films and on the news, it wouldn't be hard to, but it wasn't like that. Perhaps it's time – and self-preservation – softening the edges of everything, or maybe this is my brain's way of dealing with it, but whatever you're picturing, it wasn't like that. I mean, it was. It was devastating in every sense of the word, Gare du Nord – quiet, solid Gare du Nord that's always felt like the door in and out of Paris to me – was in pieces, but the silence that followed was more shocking. Dad says the force of the explosion affected my hearing and it probably did, but I can't find the words to describe that silence. It was as though the whole of Paris had stopped to hold its breath.

I guess they did.

Bombe!

This time everyone turned and ran as if we'd been playing a game of statues.

The cab driver told me to get back in the cab and perhaps I should have got in and told him to drive as fast and as far away as possible, but while everyone around me scattered in different directions, I ran towards the station. He called after me, telling me I was mad, and maybe I was, but it's the bravest thing I've ever done. I don't expect you to congratulate me, I'm just saying: it's the bravest thing I've ever done. I'm more the light-the-touch-paper-and-run sort. As a kid I had two tactics when I got into trouble: blame it on Pan's cat or hide the evidence. That's what I did when I was ten and I fell out of a tree in the park. I didn't tell anyone, just went home and hid in bed because Dad had told me several times that I was too old to climb trees so I was sure he'd be livid. I didn't even go downstairs for dinner when Mum called and it was only when I heard her coming up the stairs and I didn't have the strength to hide that I knew something was really wrong. So when she ripped back my duvet to find me clutching my arm and cried out for Dad, I dissolved into tears, sobbing *Sorry* over and over on the way to the hospital.

I know you think I don't care about you. I don't blame you. Between being passed from foster home to foster home and me using you to get back at Agatha, you must feel like no one gives a shit about you, but that's not true. I hadn't even met you and I cared enough to run straight towards a problem for the first time in my life and I need you to know that. I need you to know that I'm sitting in this café right now trying not to cry because I don't think I'm ever going to get a chance to say that to your face.

Maybe that's guilt or regret or maybe I do have a conscience, after all, which is why I'm so desperate to tell you all of this, but I need you to know that I'm the asshole here. I'm the one who should be questioning if anyone loves me, not you. But whatever you think of my motives, that's what I did: I ran towards the station. I didn't get there, though. A policeman stuck his arm out to stop me. It winded me so I couldn't tell him to stop as he tugged me back and told me to stay back in English, no doubt assuming I was a tourist. And I felt like one, my brain frantically trying to find the words to tell him that I had to see. I had to see that it wasn't that bad.

That you were okay.

'Mon amie!' I pointed at the station. 'Mon amie est là!'

He shook his head and held me tighter when I tried to run again, telling me it was too dangerous. That's when I felt the glass under my feet. I say I felt it; it didn't cut me; I felt the crunch of it under my boots, like fresh snow, and looked down. There was a shoe on the pavement, a black loafer, like something my father would wear at the weekend, and I started to shake. When I looked up again, the blur began to take shape. I was surrounded, everyone turned towards the station, watching people pour out. Some were crying, most were screaming, tripping over their sandals and reaching out for someone to steady themselves on as they followed one another like ants. I can see it so clearly now, but at the time it was like standing in the sea and letting a wave crash over me as they ran past, looking for a crack in the crowd.

After that, it became a blur again as everyone on the pavement began to run, too. When the police officer went to help a woman carrying a wailing toddler on her hip, I felt someone shove past me and turned to look back at the café I was standing outside. It was bedlam, people abandoning their shopping bags and knocking over glasses of wine in their haste to get out. The sound of breaking glass made me jump again and it wasn't until I turned back to the station that I realised why they were running. Everything around me was grey – the rain, the smoke, the shards of glass sugaring the road – so that first flash of blood – of red – was like a flare in the middle of a storm.

'Come on!' Someone grabbed my arm. It was a woman who looked so much like my mother that when she tugged me away, I let her. 'This way!' she said, shouting over the commotion as she pulled me to the left. I tried to keep up, my fingers fisting in my leather jacket, struggling to hold onto it as she led me through the knot of people running down rue de Dunkerque. I didn't know what they were saying, all of it a mess of different languages, so I think that's why I heard it, that first siren, because it was the only sound I recognised.

'This way!' I don't think I even looked when she led me across the road. I can't have, because I almost tripped over an abandoned basket of groceries on the pavement outside the supermarket. It was only then, when I remembered stopping in there to buy cigarettes the last time I met my father for dinner, that I realised how close we were to Lariboisière. I looked down the narrow road towards it, the tricolour flying from the flagpole like a lighthouse on the horizon, and my instinct was to run towards it. But then I saw a man in a white coat running up the road towards me. He was swiftly followed by a woman in blue scrubs, her hand pressed to her chest to stop her stethoscope bouncing, and I suddenly couldn't move.

'I have to call my father,' I murmured, but when I let go of her hand to take my phone out of my bag, she shook her head. She said it wouldn't work but I tried anyway, hissing under my breath when it wouldn't connect. So I tried Dad's assistant, Sabine, and when that wouldn't connect, either, I felt the first sting of tears as I thought about you.

Why did you have to lose your phone?

I thought she'd say, *I told you so*, but she didn't say anything, just took my hand again and led me into the café we were standing in front of. Or maybe I followed her. I don't even know any more. Thinking about it now, I should have just run down the road to the hospital. I don't know why I didn't. Clearly, I'm that girl you yell at in horror films who goes back into the house. But panic makes you do the stupidest things, doesn't it? You have no idea how many times I've almost been hit by a car running across the road to catch a bus. Or how many times I've sobbed, sure that I've lost my purse when if I'd just *calmed the fuck down* and looked properly, I would have found it at the bottom of my bag. That's what happened, I guess. The panic swallowed all reason – all logic – as I tried Dad's number over and over, saying a little prayer each time I did.

I didn't even look up, not until I heard the woman say, '*Il y a quelqu'un là?*' and lifted my chin to find the café like a scene from *Titanic*, the tables dotted with half-drunk cups of coffee and uneaten salads as a Benjamin Biolay song played to the empty room. She reached her arm back to warn me about a chair on its side as I followed her. Most of them were, knocked over no doubt when people heard what had happened at the station and ran out. Some had left their sunglasses behind, others their guide books, things they'd probably made sure they had before they left their hotels that morning but were not important enough to grab when they left. There was even a buggy in the corner by the fridge, which was ominously empty, I realised as we approached it.

The woman called out again, asking if anyone was there, her arm back to make sure I was behind her. It was so protective I had to blink away a tear, but I don't know how she thought she was going to protect me; she was smaller than me. The biggest part of her was her hair, which was in twists a bit longer than Mum's were, and was held back with a green scarf that was knotted on top of her head. Still, there was something so solid about her – calm – her voice steady as she asked again if anyone was there. It was a mother's voice. A *It's just a cut* voice. A *Get me the glue and I'll fix it* voice. And that's another reason I stayed with her instead of going to the hospital, I think, because for the first time since Mum had died, I felt safe.

'*Qui est là?*' I nearly dropped my phone as a man, his navy apron stretched tight over his belly, walked out of the door behind the bar. When he saw us, he waved his hands, telling us the café was closed. She ignored him, asking if he was the owner, and he looked at us as if we were batshit, telling us to go home. He was quite right to say this, but she pressed her hand to her chest and carried on. Her name was Ninon, she explained, and she was a doctor. His name was Victor, and he looked as relieved as I felt when she told him not to worry, everything would be okay.

'*Héloïse, ma fille,*' he said when a woman not much older than me emerged through the door with a bunch of keys in her hands. Héloïse stopped and looked at us like he had, the skin between her black eyebrows wrinkling as she asked what we wanted.

'*S'il vous plaît.*' Ninon pressed her hands together and nodded slowly. She had a silver ring on each of her fingers. '*J'ai besoin de votre assistance.*'

'*Mon assistance?*'

I was as confused as Héloïse was as Ninon explained that she wanted to use the café to tend to anyone injured at Gare du Nord. When she looked around at the mess of tables and chairs, I thought she was going to tell Ninon that she was mad, but she shrugged and said, 'Biensûr,' as though it was ridiculous that she was even asking.

When she gestured at her father to help her clear the tables, Ninon turned to me.

'Parlez-vous français?' I nodded, but she wasn't convinced. 'Are you English?'

It took me a moment too long to find the words. 'Oui, mais je parle français.'

'I speak English.'

'Je parle français.' I tried not to sound defensive, but failed as I frowned furiously at her.

'It's okay.' She smiled, her eyes bright. 'I spent three years at Johns Hopkins in Baltimore so I speak English almost as well as I speak French now.'

'Moi aussi. Mon père est français. Il travaille à Lariboisière.'

'Your father works at Lariboisière? Me too,' she said in English, much to my irritation.

I made sure I answered her in French. 'Simon Durand. Il est neurochirurgien.'

She grinned. 'You're Lola?'

'Yes.' I blinked at her. 'How did you know that?'

'He talks about you all the time.'

'He does?' I said under my breath, looking down at my phone again.

'It won't work for a while,' she said.

'Do you think they have a phone here I can use?'

'It isn't just you. None of the phones will work.'

185

'Why not?'

'They'll have scrambled the lines so they can't detonate any more bombs.'

It was as if I'd been winded again as I remembered when this happened in London and how Mum and I had to go to the hospital to make sure Dad was okay.

Then I thought of you and how there was no one calling to make sure you were okay.

I don't know how she knew, but she asked, 'Who were you meeting at Gare du Nord?'

'A friend.'

I knew she was waiting for me to look at her, but I couldn't. Luckily, before she could say anything else she was distracted by something behind me. 'I'll be back.'

I turned to see where she was going, watching through the window as she stopped to let a car pass then ran out to the police officer in the middle of the road directing everyone away from the station. When she pointed towards the café, the officer smiled gratefully, his shirt almost see-through in the rain. Even from there, I could see huge drops spilling off his jaw, his forehead clenched as though his eyebrows could shield him from the downpour as he turned to say something into the radio on his shoulder.

When I watched Ninon dip her head and run back, I couldn't help but think of Dad. It was his day off but I knew he wouldn't stay in the apartment. If he wasn't at the hospital, he'd be at church praying for everyone. He had no idea I was going to Gare du Nord to meet you – no one did

– so he wouldn't have been worried. I still should have told him, though. Then there was you.

You.

'The police are going to direct the walking wounded our way,' Ninon said, suddenly in front of me again. It was like being shoved as the reality of what she was suggesting set in. I looked at Victor as he looked at Héloïse, and as much as I needed to go to the hospital to find Dad – and look for you – I suddenly realised that I couldn't just leave her to it.

'What? You can't treat people *here*,' I said, looking around the café, at the crumbs on the tables and the fridge with its bottles of Orangina and dishes of profiteroles.

'Why not? I had much less to work with in Afghanistan.'

'Afghanistan?' I felt like I needed to sit down.

'We have about ten minutes before people start getting here,' she said, hands on her hips as she looked around. 'Help me get these tables outside. We need all the room we can get.'

I don't respond well to instructions. I rarely wait for the green man before I cross a road and I never take soup out of the microwave and stir it halfway through. (Who does?) So when she walked over to one of the tables I don't know why I didn't just peace out and leave her to it. But as much as I try to fight it, I guess I am my father's daughter, because I didn't even think about it, I just did as I was told, throwing my leather jacket onto the nearest chair and walking over to her.

My hands were shaking so much that it took two attempts to keep my grip on the table. Ninon smiled at me as I helped her carry it towards the door.

'What's your friend's name?'

'Huh?' I gasped, almost tripping on a silk scarf someone had left behind.

'Your friend. What's her name?'

My cheeks stung at the thought of you. I knew what she was doing; she was doing what Dad does when I'm freaking out, trying to keep me talking. That never works, but after keeping you a secret for almost a week, it was strangely comforting to be able to talk about you.

To say your name.

'Holly.'

'What does she look like?'

'Why?' I asked, hoping she would read my defensiveness as frustration as we tried to angle the table out of the narrow door.

'Because she might come in.'

My heart lifted so suddenly I almost dropped my end. 'Do you think?'

'She might. They'll be focused on getting people out, so they'll only be able to take the critical ones in the ambulances. Anyone else will have to walk to the hospital. That's why I'm setting up here, so we can deal with as many of them as we can. Take some of the pressure off Lariboisière.'

'So the police will direct her here?'

'They should,' Ninon said, wincing as she caught her knuckles on the frame of the door. 'Only if she needs treating, though. She might be fine.'

I felt a tickle of hope. 'Do you think she is?'

'She might be.'

'But how do I find her?'

'You wait for the phones to start working again and call her.'

'But she doesn't have a mobile. She lost it.'

'Does she have your number?' When I nodded she stopped to look at me over the table. 'Then she'll find a way.'

'Yeah,' I said, almost shouting over the sound of the rain as we got the table out the door. 'She was in coach four. That's almost the middle. That's good, right? She wasn't in the front.'

'Tell me what she looks like so I know her when I see her.'

Thanks to your phone debacle, I hadn't seen a photo of you, so could only describe you the way you'd described yourself to me. 'She's seventeen and has long blond hair and blue eyes.'

Ninon tilted her head at me. 'That narrows it down.'

'She's wearing a skull scarf.'

'A skull scarf?'

I almost smiled because it did sound like something from a personal ad – *meet me under the clock at Waterloo, I'll be the one with the red carnation* – but half of Paris is blonde with

189

blue eyes, so I told you to wear something distinctive. 'It's blue with pink skulls on it.'

'Blue with pink skulls,' she repeated when we finally put the table down. Rue de Dunkerque was a mess as ambulances and police cars tore towards Gare du Nord. I covered my ears with my hands, but I still heard a helicopter stuttering overhead. Ninon must have too, because she nodded across the road at the pharmacy.

'I know you need to go, but we don't have much time and we need supplies.'

'Okay,' I said, wiping the rain from my cheeks with my fingers, sure that my eyeliner was bleeding down my face. 'Like what?'

'Everything.'

'But what if the pharmacy is shut?'

'Kick the door in,' she said, then whistled at Victor to help her with another table.

I clenched my hands into fists as I ran across the road, my shoulders tensing when the police officer she'd been talking to followed. I thought he was going to tell me to go back to the café, but he said, 'Let me, *mademoiselle*.' I took a step back but when he pounded his fist against the door to the pharmacy, I realised that he must have heard Ninon and me speaking English and was trying to help. Before I could correct him, he yelled, *'Police! Ouvrez!'* That would no doubt be more effective than anything I would have said – in French or English – so I let him get on with it, taking another step back to look at the front of the shop. The lights were off but the green neon PHARMACIE sign was still on, which gave me some hope, but when I stepped forward to peer through the wet glass, the shop was empty.

The door was locked, but the officer tried again. '*Police! Ouvrez!*'

This time there was movement and my heart leapt into my throat as I saw someone in a white coat running towards the door. '*Entrez,*' he said, gesturing at us to come in when he opened it. He was a small man with a scrap of black hair combed carefully over his head. I guess he'd seen what we were doing at the café because when the police officer and I followed him in, I saw that he'd already filled four wire baskets with boxes of bandages and bottles of antiseptic.

'*Qu'est-ce qu'il vous faut?*' he asked, walking back behind the counter. He said it so calmly – *What do you need?* – as though he was asking us what we wanted for lunch, that it made me realise what a mess I was, my hair dripping and my nerves fluttering. He looked immaculate in his white coat. Something about him made me think of Agatha and it surprised me how much better it made me feel, like he knew what he was doing.

'People are amazing,' I told the officer when we ran back out into the rain with a basket in each hand. *Take anything you need*, the pharmacist had said before we left, holding his arm out to the shop. I'm not sure the officer got what I meant, though. The kindness of strangers, I almost added, but I didn't need to because when we got back to the café, I think he understood what I was trying to tell him, his lips parting as he saw the other people who'd arrived to help. There was a guy I'd never seen before helping Victor carry the tables outside while a woman I didn't recognise, either, heaved an armful of blankets and pillows onto one of the booths.

'*Vite!*' Ninon was telling Héloïse, who was frantically mopping the floor with so much bleach I couldn't smell coffee any more. I think Ninon was about to take the mop from her and do it herself when she saw me and the police officer in the doorway and marched over.

'Sit down,' she told me, taking the baskets from me and guiding me into the nearest chair. 'Let me see your leg before you go,' she muttered, holding her hand up when I said it was fine.

'I can't even feel it,' I insisted. 'It looks much worse than it is.'

'Did you bring gloves?' she asked, not waiting for a response and looking through what we'd brought from the pharmacy. 'Stay still,' she hissed when she found a box of them, snapping on a pair and kneeling down to inspect the scrape on my shin.

'It's just a cut.'

'You'll live,' she confirmed, bedside manner forgotten as she reached over my shoulder and grabbed a bottle of antiseptic then nodded at the police officer. '*Y at-il de l'ouate?*' He checked his basket and when he found a bag of cotton wool, he tore into it and handed her some. I yelped as she doused it in antiseptic and cleaned out the scrape with as much vigour as my mother used to, as though it was my punishment for ruining another dress.

'*Ah! Tu es comme un bébé!*' she told me when she was done, handing the officer a roll of bandage and gesturing at him to wind it around my leg before going to check the floor was clean enough.

Sometimes I lose faith in humanity, when everyone on my train carriage pretends not to see the pregnant woman who gets on during rush hour or when one of Dad's friends is vile to a waitress because it makes him feel better about his wife leaving him. So it's kind of funny that on a day when I should have lost my faith in humanity altogether, it was restored as I looked around the café to find that the tables were gone and the other people who'd arrived to help were getting on with it. The man helping Victor was Ali, who owned a newsagent a few doors down and had brought all the bottled water he had, and the woman with the blankets was Carla, who lived upstairs. She was another tiny but surprisingly strong woman who was trying to slide the fridge into the corner by herself while Victor and Ali put the chairs in neat rows so it resembled a waiting room.

The pharmacist (I never did find out his name) came in as Ninon was gathering us around, the briefcase he was holding with the medicine he'd said he'd bring dotted with rain. He held his hand up, either to say hello or to apologise for interrupting, I wasn't sure which, too distracted as Ninon explained what would be happening at Gare du

Nord. Everyone would be prioritised by colour – green, yellow, red or black – depending on their injuries. She'd be dealing with minor injuries (people with green cards) but most of them wouldn't have one because if they could run they would have done so before anyone had a chance to give them a card.

As if on cue, a woman came in. She didn't seem to have a card, but then all I could see was her torn dress and the blood dripping down her neck from the deep gash on her jaw.

I grabbed Ninon's arm. 'Blue with pink skulls.'

'If she comes in I'll tell her you're at Lariboisière.'

She nodded towards the door but I was already running.

I lasted about three minutes in Accident and Emergency before I realised that no one was going to notice me in the pack of people trying to get the attention of one of the nurses. I mean, I may be scrappy, but even I couldn't get through the sliding doors it was so full. So I headed to Dad's office and when neither he nor Sabine were there, I didn't know what to do and drifted back towards Accident and Emergency because I had nowhere else to go. I thought being outside would clear my head, but as I huddled against the wall by the ambulance bay with everyone else trying to avoid the rain, listening as they shuffled and smoked and swapped stories about their loved ones while they waited for news, it made me feel even worse.

There was one guy in particular, who, despite looking nothing like him, made me think of my father. He wasn't smoking, just pacing, back and forth, back and forth, back and forth over the same patch of tarmac, like Dad had at St Thomas' when we were waiting for news about Mum. My father isn't a pacer, he's a fixer. That's what he does – he fixes things – so it didn't occur to me until then how excruciating it must have been, having to stay in the waiting room while someone else operated on Mum. I forget sometimes, when I'm trying to fill the hole she left behind with cider and cigarettes and whatever else I can do to distract myself, that he lost her, too. Sad, isn't it? It should have brought us closer, but it's the thing that separated us, as though there's an appropriate way of handling it and we each think the other is doing it wrong.

Sometimes I wonder what Mum would think. She'd be furious, I'm sure. But grief's a funny thing, isn't it? It's so personal. My loss is different from Dad's loss. I can never understand his and he'll never understand mine, so some days it feels less of a hole and more a *gulf*, and what if this is it? What if the space between us just keeps getting bigger and bigger until we can't see each other any more? Until I learn how to live without him, too.

'*Parlez-vous anglais?*' the pacer said, suddenly in front of me.

I was so startled that I answered in French. '*Oui.*' I shook my head. 'I mean, *yes.*'

'Who are you waiting for?'

That startled me, too, the brutality of it. No polite preamble. No *How's it going?* Or *Have you been here long?* like we were at a bus stop. Just straight to it. *Who are you waiting for?*

'A friend,' I said carefully, blowing at the end of my cigarette so I didn't have to meet his gaze. Not because I didn't know what to say but because I didn't know what I'd come out with, scared that if he asked me more it would all spill out of me – why I was there, what I'd done – and I wouldn't be able to stop. But when I peeked at him from under my eyelashes he was nodding.

'My wife,' he said, slipping his hands into the pockets of his jeans. I thought that was it, but he shook his head. 'I work in advertising. We're pitching to L'Oréal tomorrow so we came early, made a weekend of it. We were in a café having breakfast before she had to get her train.' He stopped to clear his throat. 'She went ahead to print her ticket while I paid the bill.'

I didn't say anything – couldn't say anything – but he didn't wait for a response. 'I didn't think it was that bad.' He laughed, a bitter, brittle laugh that plucked at my nerves as I wondered how long he'd been waiting for someone to stand next to him so he could say it. 'When I got here everyone looked okay. Not *okay*, just cuts and bruises, you know?' I nodded, looking down at the dots of rain on the toes of my DMs. 'It was nearly an hour before the first ambulance got here. They arrived before the ambulances did.' He nodded at the FRANCE 24 truck that was parked across the road in the taxi rank, a woman with a blue and white umbrella standing next to it.

'It's not like at home,' he said with a frown. 'There are different ambulances.'

'That's the fire brigade.' I gestured at the red and yellow one parked near us.

'Oh.' He nodded. 'I guess it's all hands on deck.'

I wanted to say something, tell him that I was sorry, that

it would be okay, but I didn't know if it would be okay. I was like him, waiting. But he wasn't listening anyway as another ambulance rushed through the gates towards us. Everyone stopped, struggling to get a look as the doors opened, each of us unsure what we should be wishing for: that whoever we were there for was in the ambulance or not. I didn't know, either. I looked for a flash of blue and pink and felt lightheaded when I realised it wasn't you. But the relief only lasted a few seconds as I remembered that I still had no idea where you were.

So that's how I ended up in the old part of the hospital, standing in the doorway that leads into the neurosurgery wing, watching the rain drip off the stone arch onto the step under my feet. Hopefully you'll see for yourself, but Lariboisière is a bit strange. I'm sure Dad will tell you the story of why it was built. It's something to do with cholera or something. I don't know. I wasn't listening. It's as old as balls, basically, but very pretty. It looks more like a boarding school than a hospital, actually. There's a courtyard and a lawn and a bell tower. There's even a bandstand. I have no idea why – Dad doesn't even know – but it adds to the charm, I suppose.

Your ward is in the new bit so you can't see any of that where you are. You're probably wondering what the hell I'm on about, but just imagine a square, okay? The courtyard is in the middle and the hospital is built around it so you can walk around the ground floor in a circle. (A square, actually.) Okay. If Dad reads this, he'll kill me dead because I'm not doing it any justice. Lariboisière doesn't look like a hospital, okay? Hospitals are supposed to be white with squeaky lino floors and posters about what to do if someone has a stroke. Lariboisière is pretty much nothing like that (the original part, anyway). It has chequerboard tile floors and window seats so that you can sit and look out at the courtyard. And the chapel is incredible, like an actual church with stained glass windows and a painting behind the altar. I know. Weird. The signs look odd (the whole hospital is split into zones, you're in porte 10, which is in the blue zone, not that you asked); they're too bright – too colourful – like children's drawings stuck to the stone walls. As do the vending machines by the stairs, which hum steadily and give off an orange glow.

But then that's part of its charm, too, how the new bits and the old bits don't even try to make sense of each other. Like Accident and Emergency – it's all glass, but it isn't like the Shard, it isn't trying to make any sort of statement, it's merely propped up against the end of the hospital like a bookend. And it's too small; the waiting room only seats about fifteen people at the best of times so it was *chaos*, the automatic doors permanently open there were so many people in there. And it's kind of shabby. Where the original part of the hospital is big and bright, the floors always immaculate and the lawn always neatly cut, in Accident and Emergency the lino is split and the chairs are cheap plastic things that you can't sit on for more than a few minutes without getting a numb bum. So I usually wait for

Dad in the courtyard when he's running late and I'm bored of making polite conversation with his assistant, Sabine, who asks far too many questions and tells me to sit like a lady.

I ended up there via Dad's office, which was still empty. By then they'd set up a waiting room in the Day Surgery Unit, which was much bigger than Accident and Emergency. It was still full, of course, every seat taken, even the walls lined with people leaning against them, looking like they'd been slapped across the face. After I asked about you I sat next to a guy in a white kufi for a while. He was counting tasbih, his eyes fixed on the wall ahead of him. It was so soothing I might have sat there forever if a woman hadn't limped past looking for a seat. I offered her mine but she wouldn't take it. '*Ça va, merci,*' she said, shaking her head, but she wasn't looking at me, she was looking around at everyone waiting for news. When she saw the guy sitting opposite us, his head in his hands, she looked embarrassed, her cheeks pink when I insisted she sit down. '*Je viens de glisser dans la douche,*' she said sheepishly and in a weird way it made me feel better, that even after something like that, the world kept turning and people kept living, slipping in the shower as if it was any other day.

So I went and stood in the doorway near Dad's office and I was on my third cigarette when I felt my phone buzz in my hand. It was the first time it had worked since the explosion and I almost dropped it. It was a voicemail from Pan, but before I could call him back, I saw Dad's assistant,

Sabine, walking across the courtyard towards me and flicked my cigarette away.

She gasped when she saw me running towards her. '*Lola. Tout va bien?*'

'*Mon père est ici?*'

'*Oui.*'

'*Où est-il?*'

'*Je ne sais pas. C'est le chaos!*'

It didn't look like chaos. She'd just bought a sandwich. I asked if he was in surgery, but when she shrugged as if to say, *How should I know?* I decided to check for myself. I don't know why it hadn't occurred to me to do so before then. I was too scared, I realised as I ran back across the courtyard. I don't think I've ever been so scared. Even the night Mum died because I was so sure that she'd be fine, that my bright, brave mother who had a laugh that could fill a room and seemed to be able to take things out of the oven with her bare hands was unbreakable somehow.

I'd still prayed, though, while Dad paced, because back then I believed in God and hospitals and justice, I suppose. In a world where drunk drivers are the ones to die, not the people they hit. I know now that isn't the case so I don't know why I was saying the Hail Mary to myself. You might be surprised to hear that, given everything I've done, but my father, ever the contradiction, is super religious. I grew up going to church every Sunday, but I hadn't prayed since the night Mum died and it didn't work.

I guess I never forgave God for that, because it was the

first time I'd actually asked him for something. Not to pass an exam or for Beyoncé tickets or for my parents not to catch me when I was sneaking into the house at 1 a.m., but something real. So I don't know why I prayed for you, but I suppose, when stuff like that happens, we need to believe that there's something – or someone – out there bigger than us who can fix the unfixable and I really needed to believe it.

I think I still do.

The operating theatres are on the first floor. I don't know how I remembered that, because on the rare occasions I submit to meeting Dad for dinner, I use the sunshine as an excuse to meet him outside, having learned my lesson the first time I met him in his office and he insisted on giving me a tour of the hospital. I'd sighed and dragged my feet like I used to when we were on holiday and he and Mum would make me schlep around a crumbling church when I'd rather have been on the beach, so I wasn't paying attention.

Mercifully, I recognised someone. 'Coline!'

She stopped and turned to face me. 'Lola.' She tugged off her cap. '*Ça va?*'

'*Oui. Je vais bien,*' I said, stopping to suck in a breath. '*Avez-vous vu mon père?*'

She pointed to the floor. '*Les urgences.*'

'*Merci beaucoup!*' I said over my shoulder as I turned and ran back towards the stairs.

I had no idea how to get to A & E from there, I just

knew it was on the ground floor. So when I got to the bottom of the stairs I was relieved to find signs on the wall – *LES URGENCES* → – grateful to whoever had printed them out and stuck them along the corridor. They were in various languages – *ACCIDENT AND EMERGENCY, URGENCIAS, IZBA PRZYJĘĆ* – but in the end I didn't need them as I followed a nurse clutching an IV bag.

I heard it before I saw it. I don't even know how to describe it. No one was crying or screaming; it was more of a commotion, I suppose. Kind of like rush hour. People were running, phones were ringing and under it all there was something else. Something strained. Wheels, I realised later. The grind of gurneys and wheelchairs and IV stands. And the smell. Blood. The smell of my grandmother's cleaver after she's chopped raw chicken.

It's making me lightheaded just thinking about it.

When I followed the nurse around the corner I stopped as I was confronted by a line of beds on either side of the corridor. I couldn't bring myself to look at the people in them, at their sunken shoulders and ripped, blood-bruised clothes, or at the ones who weren't in beds, just slumped on chairs, heads hanging as they waited for someone to tend to them.

A man in one of the gurneys turned his face towards me as if he knew me, and for a second I thought he did, until he murmured, '*Manon, c'est toi?*'

I stopped, trying not to look at the blossom of blood seeping through the bandage around his head as I asked him if he wanted me to find him a nurse, but when he said it again – '*Manon, c'est toi?*' – I stepped back and continued on down the corridor.

I realised then that going that way meant I avoided the crush of the waiting room, kind of like when Michelle and I used to avoid being ID'd by sneaking in through the beer garden at that pub on the river. When I saw the sign directing friends and relatives back to the Day Surgery Unit, I ignored it and waited by the automatic doors for someone to come out. As soon as they did, I slipped past them into the emergency room. Not that anyone noticed in the mess of people fighting for space, beds shoved wherever they would fit as doctors struggled to navigate around them. There was no one at the desk, the phone ringing and ringing and ringing as a nurse in blue scrubs wrote a name on the whiteboard. I looked for yours, but I couldn't see it, and when she noticed me standing there, she lifted her chin.

'*Puis-je vous aider?*'

'*Je cherche mon père.*' She pointed the marker in her hand towards the double doors, but before she could tell me to go back to the waiting room, I shook my head. '*Non, mon père est médecin, il travaille ici.*'

'*Quel est son nom?*'

'*Simon Durand.*'

'*Ah, Lola.*' She smiled and pointed the marker over my shoulder. '*Il est là-bas.*'

'*Merci.*' I nodded, turning around.

I saw the scarf before I saw Dad.

Blue with pink skulls.

I couldn't help but count your limbs – your fingers, your ears, I would have counted every hair on your head if you'd let me – and my legs almost gave way with relief when I realised that there wasn't a scratch on you apart from a bruise darkening on your temple.

'Holly?'

I'll never forget how you turned to look at me. I saw something flicker across your face and for a second I thought you recognised me, but you smiled at Dad.

'Holly. That's my name. My name is Holly.'

Amnesia. Retrograde Amnesia, to be precise. In the absence of Dad, I just looked it up on my phone. According to Wikipedia it means: *The loss of memory-access to events that occurred, or information that was learned, before an injury.* You couldn't remember anything before the explosion, basically. It's pretty common. Half the people in the emergency room that day didn't know who they were or how they got there. Dad said it was probably a combination of shock and banging your head. So when your CT scan came back normal, he wasn't concerned, especially as you were less disoriented when I got there. You recognised your name and Agatha's and when I told you that she was your mother, you said that's why you were in Paris, to meet her.

I thought Dad would yell at me or at least gasp when he heard who you were – but he was unnervingly quiet, rubbing his jaw with his hand as I told you everything I knew about you until you began to finish my sentences. I could feel him watching – could literally *feel* the anger burning off him – as he took it all in. I couldn't take it, so when a nurse brought over a wheelchair, I offered to take you to the ward to get away from the heat of his glare, but he shook his head.

'I'll take her.'

'Let's all go,' you said, throwing your arms up as if to say, *Ice cream for everyone*.

So we did.

Getting to the lifts was an ordeal, the corridor an assault course of beds and other people in wheelchairs. I'd offered to push you, something Dad didn't fight me on, even when he saw me struggling as I tried to navigate you towards the lifts. When we eventually got to them, me breathless and you delighted at almost being tipped out of the wheelchair three times, the lift took so long to come that you asked if it would be quicker to walk.

'You need to rest,' Dad said, writing something on your chart.

'I hurt my head, not my legs,' you reminded him, but he ignored you and the silence that followed was so awkward that if the lift hadn't come then, I would have carried you up to avoid it.

Dad didn't say a word when he followed us in, just crossed his arms and leaned back against the rail as a nurse wheeled a woman in a bloodstained *J'aime Paris!* T-shirt in after us.

'*Quel étage?*' I asked, pointing at the panel.

The nurse held up three fingers.

You turned to the woman in the wheelchair. 'Hi. I'm Holly, apparently.'

She looked bewildered, but went with it. 'Apparently?'

Her Liverpudlian accent was so thick I felt homesick as I thought of my Economics tutor, Mr Banks. I never thought I'd miss college, but I did. I missed how he writes the score on the whiteboard if Liverpool beat Chelsea and the smell of the marker pens he used. I even missed the miserable chips in the canteen. When I thought about how I was always refusing to get them in favour of a sandwich, then eating all of Pan's, I suddenly felt very far away from home.

'I have amnesia,' you told her with a nod.

'Jean,' she said miserably. 'Broken ankle.'

'You're not on your own, are you?'

'No, my husband's downstairs. He must be going spare. He can't speak a word of French.'

'Have you tried calling him?'

'His phone's dead.'

'I can go and find him, if you like?' I offered and she looked up at me.

'Would you?'

'Of course. I'll go when Holly's settled. Do you have a photo?'

I hate lifts. Actually, that isn't true, I just hate the ones in hospitals. Perhaps I've watched too many horror films set in abandoned psychiatric units, but they freak me out. The one we were in was especially old and *huge*, big enough for a gurney, but when Jean took her phone out of the pocket and I saw that the case was pink diamanté, it was enough to make me smile.

'Here.' She handed it to me. 'His name's Al.'

They looked so happy with their cheeks pressed together, the Eiffel Tower behind them, almost gold against the blue, blue sky, that I couldn't help but think of Pan.

'I'll let him know that you're okay.'

'Thank you, sweetheart.' She swept her thumb fondly over the screen.

'Were you coming in or going home?' you asked, tucking your hair behind your ears.

'Going home,' she said quietly, looking down at her phone again.

You smiled and nudged her with your elbow. 'At least you get to stay a bit longer. There are worse places to be stuck with your husband than Paris.'

To my surprise, she smiled back then waved as I pushed your wheelchair towards the doors when the lift stopped on the second floor and they slid open.

'Bye, Holly.'

'Take care, Jean,' you grinned, like you were old friends.

You were still grinning when I wheeled you onto the ward. Dad wanted you on one of his so that he could keep an eye on you. The bay you were in was supposed to be women only, but as the hospital needed every bed, it was a motley mix of women and men of all ages. You were the youngest and by some happy accident you ended up in the bed by the window with two of the oldest – a woman on your left and a man opposite you. The woman looked so fragile that I couldn't look at her, her skin so thin – onionskin thin – that I could probably have counted each of her veins. Her head was tipped back on the pillow, her eyes closed and her mouth open as a monitor beeped steadily next to her, and I wondered how long she'd been there – how long she'd *be* there – as I helped you out of the wheelchair. The man opposite you was much more sprightly, though. He looked like my Uncle George, his brown eyes bright as you sat on the edge of the bed.

'*Le décors s'est amélioré tout d'un coup*,' he grinned.

You asked me what he'd said and when I told you that he'd said that his view had just improved, you laughed. 'Tell him mine, too.'

I did and he laughed, big and bright.

'I see you've met Grant,' my father said when he returned with a nurse, a toothpick-thin woman who didn't introduce herself and didn't smile back at you when she handed you a gown.

You wrinkled your nose at it. 'Does this mean I'm staying?'

'Just overnight.' Dad gestured at me to close the curtain. 'We'll leave you to get changed.'

When we got back out into the corridor, I thumbed over my shoulder. 'I might as well go downstairs and find Jean's husband while Holly sorts herself out.'

Dad raised an eyebrow at me. 'I think we need to talk, don't you, Lola?'

I thought he'd take me to his office but he led me down the corridor into what I guessed was the staff room. It looked like the café when Ninon and I first got there. There were cold cups of coffee and abandoned Tupperware boxes of salad on the table, and the television, which was mounted to the wall in the corner, was on France 24. My breath caught in my throat as I saw the reporter standing outside Gare du Nord, or as near as she could get due to the perimeter of ambulances, but as I was reading the ticker along the bottom of the screen Dad turned it off.

'Are you going to tell me what's going on?'

I had to take a deep breath, but then I told him everything. Even about pretending to be Agatha, which I still hadn't confessed to you. He was very, very quiet and when I finished, he crossed his arms.

'I'm so sorry that you had to find out about Holly like this, Dad.'

'I know about Holly.'

I looked up at him with a frown. 'You do?'

'Of course I do. Agatha and I are married. Do you think she'd keep something like this from me?' He shook his head and laughed sourly. 'Actually, I think you do.'

'I'm sorry, Dad.'

'Stop saying sorry,' he snapped and it was enough to make me flinch. 'Do you even know what you've done? It was up to Agatha to get in touch with Holly when she was ready.'

'I know.'

'*Do you?* I don't think you do, Lola. I don't think you have *any idea* how difficult this has been for Agatha. For both of us. The funny thing is we were worried about *you*. You already think that I'm trying to replace your mother, and we didn't want you to think that I was replacing you as well.'

'Dad—'

He didn't let me finish. 'What were you thinking?' He still didn't raise his voice and that was worse, as though it would hurt too much to do so. 'Do you really hate Agatha that much?'

When I didn't respond, just looked down at my boots, he said, 'Answer me, Lola. Do you know what you've done? Not just to Agatha but to that poor girl. She could have died today and for what? Because you want to stay in London?'

It was like being punched repeatedly in the stomach.

'How *awful* for you, Lola, being forced to move to Paris. Meanwhile, I have a girl your age in a coma who I can't identify because no one is looking for her.'

I looked up sheepishly. I've never seen my father so angry. *Ever.* He was actually shaking. When he shook his head and sighed I was sure he was going to walk out, but he took his phone out of his pocket.

'Who are you calling?'

I half expected him to say the police.

'Agatha.'

My heart stopped. 'Dad, you can't!'

'Holly is her daughter. She deserves to know.'

'Not like this! Not over the phone. I'll go to the apartment now and tell her.'

When he turned away from me, I covered my face with my hands to stop myself crying. Not because I didn't want him to feel sorry for me, but because I knew it would piss him off even more. He hates it when I cry. He doesn't know what to do and asks me why I'm doing it, as if there has to be a reason for crying. One you can put into words, anyway. When I heard him say Agatha's name, my heart started beating so hard I couldn't hear anything else over the sound of it in my ears. Not until he said, 'I'll see you soon,' and the sudden surge of panic made me lightheaded.

Before I could say anything, his pager went off.

'Stay with Holly until Agatha gets here. I'm needed back in A and E.'

Then he was gone. He didn't even look at me when he left, the room noticeably warmer after he'd gone.

When I got back to your bed, you weren't in it; you were standing by Grant's bed while he showed you a card trick. '*Et voilà!*' he said and you clapped, thrilled.

'*Holly! Venez vous mettre au lit. Vous devriez vous reposer,*' the miserable nurse said. I don't know if you understood, but her tone was enough to make you scurry off.

'*À bientôt, Grant,*' you said over your shoulder as you jumped back into bed.

'How are you feeling?' I asked.

'Look at this.' You tried to fan the deck of cards you were holding with one hand, but promptly dropped them all into your lap. 'Oh.'

'Holly, listen.' It sounded hissier than I intended, but it was enough to make you stop playing with the cards and look up. 'I have to tell you something.'

'Is it about pizza? Because I am *starving*.'

'I'll get you something to eat in a sec, but this is important.' I dragged the chair over and sat down, not trusting my legs not to betray me.

'Don't forget about Jean's husband.'

'I won't, just listen. Agatha's coming.'

You were quiet for a second or two then nodded. 'I'm sure that when I've pictured this moment, I wasn't wearing a backless hospital gown. It's like a stress dream when you have to sit an exam naked.'

I didn't know what to say. Actually I did, but you weren't listening as you held up a card.

'Is this your card?'

'I didn't pick a card, Holly.'

'Dude, I have amnesia. How am I supposed to remember that?' You threw your head back and laughed. 'My first amnesia joke!'

'Holly,' I said, putting my hand on your arm. 'I have to tell you something.'

'Tell me. Tell me.'

'It's about Agatha.'

'Oh, what do you think I should call her? Mum or Agatha?'

'That's the thing,' I said, but when I couldn't catch my breath, you carried on.

215

'The French for mum is *maman*, right? That's what Grant says. What's the French for Snap?'

'Holly—'

'I'm listening. I'm just saying: can't we play Snap, too?'

'Agatha doesn't know about you,' I said, then covered my mouth with my hand. I wished I didn't have to spit it out like that, but you weren't letting me say it.

You chuckled, though. 'You just said that she's on her way here.'

'No. I mean, *yes* she is but she didn't know you were here.'

You tried to shuffle the cards and dropped them again. 'What *here*? In the hospital?'

'No,' I put my hand over yours before you could pick them up, '*here*, in Paris.'

The corners of your mouth fell. 'But you said that's why I was here, to meet her.'

'Technically you are.'

'Huh?' you asked, rightly confused.

'I lied, Holly.'

I heard myself say it and it was like when I spoke to Pan the night Mum died. I'd sent him home, telling him that she'd be fine, and when she wasn't, I had to call him. My voice sounded the same, kind of hollow – kind of sorry – like I knew I'd said something to turn the world inside out.

'Lied about what?' you asked and you sounded tiny, like a kid. You looked like one, too, swaddled in the dressing gown, blond hair everywhere and your eyes wide.

'About Agatha,' I said, putting my elbows on the bed and pressing my hands to my face so I wouldn't have to look at you. 'I pretended to be her and invited you to come here.'

'Why would you do that?'

'Because I'm an asshole.' I don't know what I expected you to say to that, but when you didn't say anything, I made myself sit up and look at you, even if you didn't want to look at me. 'Because Agatha and I don't get on,' I admitted, pathetic as it sounded. 'I was trying to hurt her.'

'So she doesn't want to meet me?'

'Holly—' I started to say, but when I stopped to bite my bottom lip you shook your head.

'I think you should go.'

But as you said it, I heard something and my heart thumped. 'She's here.'

I don't know how I knew it was her (I must be like a cat, I sense evil), but as I stood up and turned to look at the door to the ward, I knew it was her in the corridor. I'd know that sound anywhere, the clack, clack, clack of her heels. She didn't run, didn't hurry. She didn't even miss a step.

'Je cherche Holly Stapleton.'

You said later that it sounded like she was ordering a coffee, but I knew her well enough to hear the way she said your name, to spot that moment's hesitation before she said it, as though she was trying to translate it into French and wasn't sure if it was the right word. So when I saw that she'd buttoned her mac up wrong, I had to look away

217

because I knew her well enough to see that, too: she was so flustered she hadn't even noticed she'd done it.

Not that you'd know it from the way she lifted her chin to look at the nurse when she asked who she was. 'Agatha Abbot,' she said with no hesitation this time and I guess you heard her, too, because you sat a little straighter. I can't imagine how you felt. Even thinking about it now I could cry, how you adjusted your dressing gown and tried to smooth your hair down with your palms when we heard the nurse say, *'Elle est là-bas, près de la fenêtre,'* followed by the snap of Agatha's heels.

Then there she was, at the end of your bed.

We both looked up at once, but you were the first to speak.

'Hello, Agatha.'

She didn't respond, just looked at me then at you with the precision of a sniper.

'It's nice to meet you,' you added when the silence went on a moment too long.

'Hello,' she said with that I *know* smile she gives everyone who says that to her. But that's all she said. She didn't agree that it was nice to meet you, she didn't even say your name, just pressed her palms together with a look that almost made me reach for your hand.

Mercifully, my father appeared.

'Agatha, I'm so sorry that you had to find out like this.'

She didn't flinch, just turned to let him kiss her on both cheeks. 'Is she okay?'

'Nothing serious. Just a bang on the head. Her memory should come back in a few days.'

Agatha nodded, then turned to look at you again. 'Do you need anything?'

You shook your head.

'Let Simon know if you do.'

And with that she was gone.

For a moment I thought she'd gone to get something, perhaps to berate the nurse for not bringing you any water or to insist that you have a private room, but when Dad went after her, I followed. She was halfway down the corridor when I got out there. Something told me to stay in the doorway as he ran after her, but I was still close enough to hear her turn to him when he reached her and say, 'I don't know who that girl is, Simon, but she is *not* my daughter.'

So that was it. Thanks to me, that's how Agatha met her daughter.

I think about it a lot, about what you must have imagined when you were a kid or on your first night in another foster home. You don't have to tell me about it, but I bet you pictured every detail from what you were wearing to the first thing she said to you and now I've ruined it. How do I even say sorry for that? I'm flicking through the pages, looking at my scruffy writing and asking myself why I'm bothering to do this. I could write until this notebook is full and I still couldn't take back what I've done. But I think this is about more than that now. More than me apologising or trying to understand why I did it. I think you want to know what happened and, as I'm one of the few people who knows, I can at least do that for you. So I'll keep going.

When Agatha left, I didn't know what to do. I don't know for sure if you heard what she said but I think you did, because when I went back you were pretending to be asleep. I didn't want to leave you but I'd humiliated you enough so I left, figuring that you probably didn't want me to see you crying, too. But I couldn't leave you on your own, so I sat on one of the window seats in the corridor and looked out at the rain, Paris back to its delicate, dreamy self. I have no idea how long I was sitting out there, but it was a while, because when Dad got back, it was dark.

'Why aren't you with Holly?'

I sat up and blinked a few times as though he'd woken me up. 'She's sleeping.'

'Wake her up. We need to take her back to the apartment.'

'Back to the apartment? Why?' I stood up to face him. 'I thought you said she had to stay in overnight?'

'She should.' He tugged off his surgical cap and scrubbed his fingers through his hair so it was sticking up. 'But we need the beds. On top of all this, there was just a pile up on the A3.'

When Dad told you that you had to come back to the apartment with us, you'd think he'd punched you. You actually sounded winded when you said, 'Okay,' and kicked the sheet back. I know I'd only known you a few hours, but the change in you was painful. You didn't look at us, didn't smile or make a joke about not wanting to leave Grant; you just got dressed and met us in the corridor. I heard you saying goodbye to everyone before you came out. I don't know how you knew their names, but even the miserable nurse hugged you goodbye. She works with Dad and I don't know her name. He's been at Lariboisière for *months* and the only people I know are Sabine and Coline, so hearing you only served to remind me what a miserable cow I am.

Needless to say, the ride to Agatha's apartment was painful. The roads were still chaos so after almost twenty minutes of trying in vain to find a cab in the rain, Dad gave up and borrowed Sabine's car, a prim little Citröen that reeked of Gauloises. Understandably, you insisted on sitting in the front, but didn't say a word after that, not even when Dad opened his window and asked if it bothered you. You just shook your head and it felt like someone was kneading my stomach like dough, because I'd broken you. Even after the explosion you were this bright, giggly thing and there you were, hunched as though I'd turned a switch off.

I didn't take my eyes off you the entire journey, looking for some sign of life, some spark in your eyes or warmth in your cheeks, but there was nothing. As we drove along rue du Faubourg Poissonnière, you let your temple fall against the glass and I wondered if you'd done the same thing on the Eurostar. If you'd looked out at the green blur of the Kent countryside while you replayed the daydream about meeting Agatha in your head. I had to look away as I thought about it, about how excited you must have been – how scared, how nervous – and I'm so sorry. I know what it's like to lose a mother but at least I had seventeen years with mine.

You had less than a minute with Agatha.

When we got back to the apartment, she came out of

her studio to greet us, chin up, ready to strike, like a cobra, but when she saw that you were with us, she stopped.

'We need the beds,' Dad explained before she could say anything.

Agatha smiled smoothly. 'She's had a head injury,' she said in her *Your daughter's drunk on champagne and embarrassing me, Simon* voice. 'Shouldn't she be at the hospital?'

Holly, I wanted to yell. *Her name is Holly.*

Dad looked at you and winked. 'Who better to keep an eye on her than me?'

'True.' Agatha's smile got noticeably tighter. 'But aren't you needed there, Simon? I just heard about the accident on the A3 on the news. It sounds terrible.'

'Yes, but Lola's offered to look after Holly until I get back.'

'What could go wrong?' she said with a head tilt that said you'd be dead within the hour.

Dad ignored her. 'Holly needs to rest. We should get her into bed.'

'Of course.' Agatha turned her face. 'Josette.'

Josette was at her side before she'd finished saying her name. '*Oui, madame?*'

'Make up the bedroom opposite Lola's. We have a guest.'

She only speaks to Josette in French, so I know that was for your benefit. I think you did, too, because I felt you tense when she said guest.

'It's all right.' I waved my hand at Agatha. 'I can do it.'

224

'Oh so helpful, Lola,' she sang as I walked towards the spiral staircase.

I had to stop myself running up the stairs, but you took your time, following me into the room opposite mine a few moments later, your hands in your pockets. You didn't look at me or at the room, seemingly unfazed as you shuffled on the spot, no doubt waiting for me to leave. That was the first time I noticed what you were wearing, the pristine parquet floor and white bed sheets in sharp contrast to the frayed cuffs of your jeans. Then I saw the rip in your T-shirt and while, with hindsight, it probably happened while you were at Gare du Nord, it occurred to me that you might only be staying because you had no other option.

'If you want to get out of here, I understand. I can find you a hotel. I have like, two hundred euros.'

You didn't say anything, though, just tugged your scarf off and threw it on the bed.

'Can I get you anything, then? I can get you some towels if you fancy a shower?'

'Yeah.' You nodded at that. 'A shower would be nice, actually.'

'Okay,' I said, relieved to be able to do something useful, but as I turned to leave, Josette walked in with a stack under one arm and a pile of clean sheets under the other.

'Bonsoir, Holly,' she said, handing you the towels.

'Josette,' I hissed as she headed for the bed, 'Holly doesn't speak French.'

'Je suis française,' she said, humming 'La Marseillaise' as

she peeled the case off one of the pillows. '*Je parle le français.*'

'*Où est la salle de bain, Josette?*' you said suddenly and we turned to look at you. 'What?' You shrugged. 'Did you think I'd come here without knowing how to ask where the bathroom is?'

'*Par là.*' Josette pointed to the door in the corner of the room and when you disappeared into it, she shook her head at me and tutted. 'She doesn't like you.'

I stomped out, muttering about her only speaking French as I headed across the hall to my room to find something for you to wear. I stopped and looked despairingly at the clothes tumbling out of my suitcase onto the floor then walked over to the wardrobe.

'*Agatha aimerait te voir dans le salon,*' Josette said, suddenly in the doorway.

'*Moi?*' I asked, fingers curling around the coat hanger in my hand. But Josette just tilted her head at me as if to say, *Yes, you* and gestured at me to follow her.

I knew it was coming but I didn't expect it to be so formal, for Agatha to summon me to the salon like Tony Soprano, so when I got to the bottom of the stairs, the temptation to turn and run towards the front door was unbearable. She was waiting for me on one of the two armchairs by the fireplace, tea set up on the small table between them. I say *armchairs*, they're more like dollhouse furniture, tightly upholstered things with fragile wooden legs that were miserably uncomfortable, especially with Agatha next to me, her legs crossed neatly.

'Tea?' she asked when I'd stopped fidgeting.

'Yes, please.' I didn't actually want any, but I thought refusing might piss her off more.

Thankfully, Josette poured; my hands were shaking so much I dread to think what damage I would have done if I had. She handed us each a cup and saucer then retreated from the room as I held mine with both hands in case Agatha heard them rattle when she turned to me.

'Your father's gone back to the hospital,' she said, taking a small sip. I heard the unsaid, *So there's no one here to save you*, and focused on not dropping my cup.

'I thought this would be a good time to talk,' she said, putting hers back on the saucer. 'I think it's time to wave the white flag, don't you, Lola?'

'Yes.' I turned to put my cup and saucer on the table and braced myself.

'Today, someone was seriously hurt because of this,' she gestured at the space between us, '*this*, whatever it is that made you do this. So,' she stopped to take another sip of tea, 'I'll speak to your father. You clearly don't want to be here, Lola, and I won't make you stay, especially if it provokes you to do something like this again. So,' she put her cup down, 'you'll go back to London, your father will find you a suitable counsellor and we'll go from there.'

'Thank you,' I said warily, startled at how reasonable she was being.

'As for Holly,' I swear her cup and saucer shivered when she said your name, just for a second, I heard it, 'she'll head back to London as soon as she's well enough.'

There it is, I thought.

I knew it was too good to be true.

I should have shut up, but I couldn't help myself. 'But what if she wants to stay in Paris?'

'Then she can stay.' Agatha shrugged gracefully. 'It's nothing to do with me.'

'Stay *here*, I mean. With you. I—'

She raised her hand to stop me. 'Lola, please do not confuse my calmness with forgiveness.' I felt my whole body sag as though she'd stuck a pin in me. 'What you did today was appalling. Not only have you humiliated me, which I assume was your intention, but you've put me in an impossible situation I need not be in.'

'Agatha, I'm sorry.'

'Lola,' she closed her eyes and exhaled slowly through her nose, 'you want so much to be grown up, to be an adult. Well,' she opened her eyes again and lifted her right shoulder, 'this is your first lesson as an adult: not everything can be fixed with an *I'm sorry* and a hug. Sometimes you break things and they stay broken and there's absolutely nothing you can do about it.'

I didn't bother to stop the tear that rolled down my cheek. 'I don't know what to say.'

'There's nothing to say, Lola. It's done.'

She called for Josette to clear the cups.

You stayed in your room for the rest of the evening. I did too, neither of us responding when Josette called us for dinner. She eventually bustled in with a tray and I'm guessing she did the same to you because I heard her telling you to eat otherwise you wouldn't get better. I waited for Agatha to come up and dispense some similar advice, at least say something – anything – but she didn't. I lay there and waited for the clack of her heels until 2 a.m., but there was nothing.

I guess I fell asleep because I woke with a start. I thought it was the rain, which was even heavier and throwing itself against the windows so hard it sounded like rice at a wedding. But then I heard Dad's voice. He wasn't shouting, but he wasn't making an effort to be quiet, either, which was unlike him, so it was enough to get me out of bed. I crept over to the door and opened it carefully, not sure where he was. I checked that he wasn't in the hall and stepped out. I heard him again but it took me a moment to work out that he was at the bottom of the staircase. My instinct was to check if he was okay but I heard Agatha's voice and stopped.

'How long will she be here, Simon?'

'As long as she needs to be.'

The muscles in my shoulders clenched. He's used that tone enough times with me that I knew he was losing his patience. It was the first time I'd heard him like that with Agatha, though.

'Impossible,' she said curtly. 'I'll tell Sylvie to find her somewhere to stay.'

'Agatha, she's not a puppy who needs rehousing.'

'The Plaza is hardly a kennel, Simon.' I could imagine the look he gave her because she said, 'What? She should be grateful I'm not putting her up in a Holiday Inn given that *I'm the one* footing the bill. I should send her back to whatever council estate in Croydon she crawled out of.'

I managed to cover my mouth with my hand before they heard me gasp.

Dad didn't try to muffle his, though. 'Agatha.'

'What?'

'She's your daughter.'

'No, she isn't.'

'Agatha, please.'

'She doesn't look anything like me, Simon.'

'She does.'

'She doesn't. Don't you think I'd know my own daughter if I saw her?'

'How? You haven't seen her since the day she was born.'

'I just know, okay? I look at her and I don't feel a thing.'

'It's the shock, *chérie*. You just need to give it time.'

'Don't patronise me, Simon.'

'I'm not.' I heard Dad sigh. 'I'm just saying: I'm not surprised that you're rattled.'

'I am not rattled. I'm perfectly calm.'

'It's okay to be rattled. I would be, too, if I was confronted with my fully grown daughter.'

'Do you think this is the first time this has happened, Simon?'

'That what's happened?'

'That a long-lost relative has just shown up out of the blue, desperate to be reunited.'

'She's not a long-lost relative, Agatha, she's your daughter.'

'Something I am yet to see any evidence of.'

'Let's do a DNA test, then. Resolve this once and for all.'

'Fine. But she's still not staying here.'

'You're being paranoid. The poor girl didn't even know who you were until she got here.' I had to stop myself cheering. 'On her birth certificate you're Agatha *Park*.'

'I don't know what gave you the impression that this is open for discussion, Simon, because it really isn't. She's not staying and that's that.'

I heard the clack of her heels then Dad said, 'Where are you going?'

'To hide the silverware.'

I was so stunned that I stood just there, listening to the sound of her footsteps fade. You're probably wondering why

I was so surprised, given my feelings towards her, but I was genuinely astonished. I knew Agatha was vile, but I had no idea she could be so nasty. Cutting comments about what I'm wearing are one thing, but that, that was *cruel* and I'm sorry. I felt awful that I'd ruined the fantasy of who your real mother was, the gentle, kind woman who was going to rescue you from a life of bouncing from one foster home to the next.

I hoped you hadn't heard, but when Dad started walking up the stairs and I turned to run back into my room, I saw you in your doorway. 'Holly,' I breathed, but you closed the door.

I don't know how given that I kept replaying Dad and Agatha's conversation over and over in my head, but I must have fallen asleep again. The rain woke me this time. I can't have slept for long because every bit of me ached as I hauled myself out of bed. I knew I would, but it was still a shock when I started to cry in the shower. Not the tears themselves, but the force of them, big, breathless sobs that made my knees weak. But I felt better when I stopped – stronger – as though a fever had run its course and I was able to focus on how to fix what I'd done.

I thought a walk would help. With hindsight, a walk in the stinging rain doesn't sound very appealing, but that's how desperate I was to get out of the apartment. I was rooting through my suitcase for something clean to wear when I heard the pipes creak. I didn't know who was up but whoever it was got ready faster than I did, because as I was tugging on a pair of socks, I heard footsteps in the hall. I tensed when they stopped, sure the knock was on my door, but you answered. I was surprised to hear Dad's voice given how late he'd got back, but if he was exhausted he didn't sound it as he told you that he had to return to the hospital.

I waited for the sound of his shoes on the staircase and when the front door closed, I grabbed my bag, sure that if I could just get out, everything would be okay. I couldn't think in the apartment. I don't know how somewhere so huge can feel so small. I was aware of every wall, every door, could hear the pipes and the floorboards and the clock in the salon that ticked between each tap of Josette's knife as she cut up fruit for breakfast. Perhaps I was the only one who could hear those things, like a dripping tap, but I had to get out because I couldn't keep hiding in my room hoping that Agatha would weep and tell you how glad she was to see you.

I went to the café first and sat outside under the dripping red awning, watching the rain while I chain-smoked and drank coffee until the ache in my stomach began to match the one in my chest. Usually Laurent would have told me off, made me a crêpe and insisted that I eat it, but he didn't say a thing, just kept refilling my cup with an uneasy frown.

When the rain eased to a drizzle, I wandered around for a while. Saint-Germain isn't the sort of place you wander around, though, especially when you're mixed and wearing a MODELS SUCK hoodie (which I'd bought to wind Agatha up), so I only went into a few shops, picking things up and putting them back down again. That's how I ended up in Carrefour, because it was the first place I'd been in for more than five minutes before the shop assistant began to follow me around. By then it was pissing down again, so I spent more time in there than I normally would have, studying the yogurts with the sort of concentration usually reserved for reading an exam paper.

I was heading to the till with one when I heard someone say my name. The supermarket was bustling with tourists buying croissants and bananas for breakfast so it took a moment to see who was calling me. Then, all of a sudden, a woman emerged from one of the aisles, the bottles of wine in her basket banging together as she waved frantically. 'Lola!' she sang with a grand wave.

I went rigid, my gaze flicking over to the exit, calculating the steps between me and it, but it was too late; she was in front of me.

'Lola! What are you doing here?'

'Sue,' I said, my fingers curling around the yogurt pot in my hand. 'How nice to see you.'

It wasn't at all. If my father was there he would have pushed me towards her and run.

'Why aren't you in Carcassonne?' she asked, smoothing the back of her neat grey bob with her hand as she caught her breath. Mercifully, she didn't give me the chance to answer, just began babbling about how she was in Paris to buy an outfit for her niece's wedding, and for once, I was content to let her prattle on, my stomach tensing as I realised that I hadn't seen her since—

'I haven't seen you since last summer!' she said, finishing the thought. It made my stomach lurch this time, so suddenly that I don't know how I didn't throw up on her sandals. 'We keep meaning to come back and say hello, but we've just been so busy with the new house. It was a wreck when we bought it. Utter mess. I mean, how do people live like that? There wasn't even a shower when we moved in.'

I stopped listening, something I'd learned to do with Sue.

I don't remember ever meeting her, she was just *there*, as much a part of my summers in Carcassonne as my grandmother's cassoulet and falling asleep on the canal boat Dad rents every year. Sue and her husband – the eternally patient Andy – used to rent the house next door every year. We always knew when she'd arrived because the birds would flee from the trees and my grandparents' dog would retreat to the mountains and spend the rest of the summer there, only coming back for food.

Clearly he was the smartest one of the lot of us.

I would threaten to do the same, my mother vowing to come with me, equally annoyed by the fact that Sue was always *there*. She and Andy would 'pop in' as we were preparing supper, then stay long after I'd gone to bed, guzzling wine and passing around photographs of their dinner with the captain on the QE2. And even if she wasn't there, you could still hear her, Sue's laugh loud enough to pierce through even the deepest afternoon nap.

I hated her. Hated how she didn't know a word of French but would complain about the foreigners who moved to England and refused to assimilate. ('Not you,

236

Alicia,' she'd say, pointing her wine glass at Mum. 'At least you've learned how to speak English.') And I hated how she said my name ('Lolaaaaaaaa!' as though there were fourteen A's in it) and how she sang Figaro when she watered her window boxes and how she ended every anecdote with, 'Isn't that right, Andy?' I don't think I've ever heard him speak, he just nods and drinks his wine while Sue moves on to her next story. I never believed in soulmates until I met them, but some force must have brought them together, because I've never known two people who balance each other out so perfectly.

Mercifully, they bought a place in Labastide-Esparbairenque last year. Why there I don't know; it's about thirty kilometres from Carcassonne and barely a village. It only has a population of thirty-five, but Sue wanted to live somewhere remote and it doesn't get more remote than a house carved out of the side of a mountain. Bless that poor village, though. I bet it didn't know what hit it. Neither did I, because after not seeing Sue for so long I'd forgotten how loud she was.

And tactile.

'Oh,' I gasped when she hugged me, the wine bottles in her basket banging together again as she pulled me to her and squeezed so hard I don't know how she didn't leave bruises.

'Look at you!' she cooed, finally letting go. 'Gorgeous as always!' When she stepped back I watched her gaze flit from my nose stud down to my MODELS SUCK hoodie and saw a flicker of disapproval before she caught herself and smiled brightly. 'And so *with it!*'

With it.

I considered the logistics of killing myself with a fig yogurt and smiled back.

'What are you doing here, Lola? Why aren't you with your grandparents?'

'They're in Toronto.'

'With Louis and the kids?'

I nodded, praying this would prompt her to go off on one about her grandchildren, but she just wrinkled her nose at me and smiled.

'How is Louis?'

'Fine.'

'And Georgette and Rosie?'

'Fine.'

'How's your father?'

'Fine.'

I felt my bottom lip tremble and bit down on it as my heart started to thud. Not thud, *gallop*, like a startled horse jumping a fence. I knew what she was going to say and the threat of it was enough to make my legs shake as I took a step back.

'Sue, I have to—' I started to say but not quick enough to stop her.

'How's your mum?'

It was kind of like that moment of silence after the explosion at Gare du Nord, like three explosions, actually, that seemed to go off all at once and made the floor shift beneath my feet. I couldn't move, except I must have because I remember my toes curling in my boots and the thin plastic of the yogurt pot giving as I squeezed my hand around it. But it felt like I couldn't move, like I was holding my breath as I was waiting for it to hit me, knock me clean off my feet.

I couldn't say it. I'd never needed to. Everyone knew. My friends, my teachers, even the woman in the corner shop who always smiled at me when she gave me my change. I know that smile. I think you do, too, don't you? The *poor thing* smile. The *she's so brave* smile. The *I'm glad it wasn't me* smile.

I haven't even told Laurent, but I think he knows. He looks at me sometimes, when he's persuaded me to play the piano or he's brought me a *chocolat viennois* for no reason. I'll smile when I catch him looking at me and he'll frown, and it's the way the tourists frown when they first see the *Mona Lisa* at the Louvre, like they know she isn't happy. I don't know how he knows. I guess I must smell of grief, like flowers dying in a vase. But if I do, then Sue didn't notice as she pointed her finger at me.

'Oh, what was that cheese your mum likes?'

Likes.

It had been a while since anyone had referred to my mother in the present tense and I don't know how my legs didn't give way. It was like recovering from a punch.

'Manchego!' Sue grinned, thrilled with herself. 'That's it! Do they sell it here?'

The last time I'd felt this way was at the hospital when the surgeon and his team had ushered Dad, Nan and me into the office by the relatives' room, the one with photos of someone's kid pinned to the noticeboard. I'd heard the words so many times on TV – *despite our best efforts there was nothing we could do* – that it was like I wasn't there, like I was watching an episode of *Casualty* and waiting for Dad to tut and say, 'That never happens in hospitals!' That's how it felt as I stood there watching Sue's bob flick back and forth as she looked around the supermarket.

'I want to do those things she used to make. What were those cheese things?'

She looked at me, waiting for me to tell her, and I stared. I know I'm a selfish, entitled brat sometimes but even *I* wouldn't be so oblivious. Surely she could see I was in agony. Why couldn't she see? I wanted to grab her by the shirt and shake her, put her hand to my chest and make her feel the bang of my heart so she'd shut the fuck up about fucking cheese.

'The cheese things, Lola,' she said, rolling her eyes as if to say, *Come on.*

'She's dead!' I hissed, so loud I startled someone heading to the till with a carton of juice.

'What?' Sue laughed. She actually laughed. 'Oh, don't be silly, Lola.'

'She's dead.'

I didn't hiss this time, but it sounded just as unnatural.

Sue blinked at me. 'What?'

I couldn't say it again, just shook my head until she started shaking hers, too.

'No.'

I watched her deflate and it was as if she had a puncture, her shoulders sagging and her eyelids dipping as the spark in her eyes went out.

I never want to do that to someone again.

'When?'

'Christmas Eve.'

'Christmas Eve,' she repeated, chewing on her bottom lip as she no doubt tried to remember where she'd been, if she'd been making Andy take the camp bed out of the loft and hanging the grandkids' stockings on the mantelpiece, their names sewn onto each one. 'How?'

'Drunk driver.'

She shook her head again. 'No.'

I nodded carefully, sure that every bone in my body would come loose if I did it harder.

She didn't say anything and that was more unsettling than if she'd burst into tears, because I'd never seen Sue so quiet – so still – but when I was brave enough to lift my chin to look her in the eye, I saw the way she was frowning and I knew it was coming, the speech everyone's been giving me since it happened, the one about how wonderful Mum was and what a loss it was.

What a tragedy.

But Sue didn't say a thing for once, just put her basket down and hugged me. I tried to pull away, but as soon as my cheek touched the cool fabric of her shirt I smelt her perfume and thought of those summers with my grandparents, Dad at the stove, tending to a spitting pan and telling Mum, '*this* is how you cook a steak, Alicia,' while she ignored him.

It hit me then: we'd never have a summer like that again. We'd go back to Carcassonne, of course, but it wouldn't be like that. Dad would bring Agatha. The thought made my heart clench like a fist. Agatha on Mum's side of the bed, a copy of *Vogue* on the bedside table instead of a Dorothy Koomson novel. Agatha on the patio, sipping wine. Agatha sitting across from me at dinner, complimenting my grandmother's cassoulet but not finishing it.

It was wrong. She wouldn't push me into the pool when I was being stroppy or laugh at Dad's sunburnt nose. If I had known last summer was our last I would have taken more photos, spent more time with Mum rather than dozing in the hammock with Pan. But I didn't know.

I didn't know.

I cried then, huge, ugly, *wracking* sobs in the middle of Carrefour as Sue held me like she was trying to hold me together with her arms, like I might come apart at the seams if she let go. I might have. It felt that way as I cried for what I'd done and what I hadn't done and what I'd never do again, babbled into her chest, all the things I wanted to say to Mum – to Dad, to you – and couldn't. And of all the people to listen – to make me feel safe again

– it was Sue. Funny, isn't it? But it just goes to show: people are never as awful as you think they are, are they?

You'd think I'd know that better than anyone.

I was on my third eclair when my father found me. 'Fermes ta bouche, Lola,' he said as he sat opposite me at the table. Our knees touched and it made me think of home, of dinner with him and Mum, of Eartha Kitt and the sticky bottle of Aunt May's pepper sauce that was always on the table. The weird thing is, that's all I'd been thinking about since I'd left Sue – home. She'd wiped my cheeks with her thumbs then kissed me on the forehead and said that everything would be okay and it made me cry again because it was exactly what Mum would have done. She'd have been furious with me, of course – for what I did to you – but that was the thing with my mother, she might have lost her temper much quicker than my father, but when she said what she had to say it was done. She didn't bring it up three weeks later when I'd forgotten to take something out of the freezer for dinner. It was like the rain showers in Barbados: quick and fierce then over as suddenly as it began. So if she was there, she would have been pissed off, of course, but then she would have calmed down and asked me what I was going to do to fix it.

Except she wasn't there. That's how I ended up in

Angelina's, because it was the only place in the city that reminded me of her. Actually, everything reminded me of her – the rain, the mangoes at Marché Raspail, the bright rolls of silk in Agatha's studio – but it was the only place we'd been to together. I was so besotted with their eclairs that every time we were in the city we'd go while Dad spoke at whatever medical conference had brought him to Paris. It was our place, I suppose. It would always be our place even though we'd only been there a few times. We spoke of it fondly, usually with a wistful smile as we passed the bakery at the top of our road. 'I'm having two Mont Blancs next time,' Mum would say when she looked at the iced buns. She vowed to have two *every time* we went, but always admitted defeat midway through the first one.

I'd ordered one but didn't eat it, just looked at it sitting proudly on the white plate as I ate an eclair. Pan didn't know – about the Mont Blancs, that this was our place – and pointed at them in the window the first time we went there. 'Looks like a brain,' he'd said, smiling to himself. I smiled, too, and looked at one, at the spaghetti of chestnut vermicelli that covered the dome of cream and meringue. It did look like a brain. Only Pan would see something like that.

When I bit into my first eclair, I expected to have some sort of Proustian epiphany. I thought it would all come flooding back to me – the first time I had one when I was five that snowy day in February – but it tasted different, sweeter than I remembered. So I ordered another, and

246

another, but nothing happened and I don't know why I'd thought it would. It was just an eclair, they aren't magic, they can't make everything better, and it made me cry again.

I think you get that, don't you? What it is to miss someone, not just the space they used to take up in your life, but the way they made you feel when you were with them. I realised then that I'd never feel that again, even at home. It's just a house now. Dad still hasn't sold it, what with everything that has happened, but I know that it won't be ours much longer. Soon it will be some other family's home, a family who'll laugh and fight and laugh, like we did.

Until then it's just a house with all of our furniture in it, but even that looks different, the armchair closer to the television so my grandmother can see it and her tchotchkes dotted around the place, a growing collection of crystal animals that I'm not allowed to touch. Even the crucifix in the hallway has moved and now hangs over the fireplace next to a framed photo of Mum that I can't look at. And it smells different, of my grandmother's perfume and food – of *cooking*, actually, like a house should smell. Salt fish and cou cou and macaroni pie bubbling in the oven.

When I left for Paris it didn't occur to me that I'd never go back there. Home wasn't somewhere I'd given much thought to before, other than to complain that we weren't living in London or Paris or New York or wherever I'd rather have been that week. Richmond was just *Richmond*, another of those prim Surrey towns that had a Waitrose and a weekly farmers' market and a last train from London that left an hour before you wanted to go home. Perhaps that's why I like being by the Seine so much, because it reminds me of those afternoons I spent lying by the river with Pan, waving at the boats as they passed and throwing the crusts from my sandwich at the ducks. Back when all I had to worry about was my History coursework and sneaking into Brixton Academy to see Vampire Weekend on a Saturday night.

I'll have to go back at some point, of course, to pack my stuff and quit my job at the hospice, say goodbye to Mrs Morris who likes me to read *Cider with Rosie* to her and doesn't mind when I skip over the part with Lizzy Berkeley. But I won't live there any more, will I? That's what I was thinking about before Dad got there, about the clothes in my laundry hamper, the jeans I forgot to wash and the unicorn T-shirt I spilt ketchup down from the hot dog I snuck into the cinema when Pan took me to see *Psycho* the night before I left for Paris. Stupid things, I suppose. Stuff I didn't mind leaving behind but suddenly missed with an unreasonable ache.

But it's not the same house I grew up in, where my mother used to leave banana skins on the arm of the sofa but told me off if I didn't put my mug in the dishwasher. The house with the back door that sticks in the summer and the uneven step in the garden I always trip up on and the Justin Bieber stickers that I've tried – and failed – to peel off the front of my wardrobe. It will never be that house again, so maybe it's best that my father is selling it.

I think that's the first thing we've agreed on since Mum died.

'Dad,' I said through a mouthful of eclair.

'Fermes ta bouche,' he said again, fighting a smile as I stared across the table at him.

I did as I was told, swallowing hard and putting the rest of the eclair I was holding on my plate.

'What are you doing here?'

He crossed his legs and smoothed his tie with his hand. 'Sue called me at the hospital.'

'Oh.'

My gaze dipped back down to the eclair, the muscles in my shoulders tensing as I waited for him to have a go at me again, like he had the day before when he found out about Holly, but he didn't say anything and that was worse, like he didn't know what to say to me any more.

'Aren't you supposed to be in surgery or something?'

'No. I'm supposed to be here.'

I lifted my chin to look at him again, holding my breath as he pushed the plate with the Mont Blanc on it away from him so it sat between us on the table.

'Holly's going to be fine, Lola. Her MRI and CAT scan came back clear and her memory will return in a few days.' He tried to meet my gaze but I couldn't look at him. 'This isn't your fault, Lola.'

Something in me finally buckled.

'Yes, it is,' I said with a heave and a sob.

'No, it isn't,' he said with a tender sigh. 'What you did was awful, Lola. But what I did was just as bad.'

'You didn't do anything, Dad.'

'That's the point: I didn't do anything.'

'You didn't know, Dad,' I sobbed. Actually it was somewhere between a sob and a hiccup. I sounded four years old. 'How could you have stopped me?'

'Lola, listen.' He took the handkerchief out of the breast pocket of his suit jacket and handed it to me. I wiped my cheeks, looking at the black smears so I wouldn't have to look at him. 'I'm just as much to blame for this as you are.'

'You're not.'

'I am. I've known for a long time that you weren't okay. But you kept telling me that you were fine and I wanted so much to believe that you were.' He sat back in his chair and exhaled through his nose. 'I've been so focused on myself, on doing what I needed to do to get out of bed in the morning, that I forgot about you and I'll never forgive myself for that.'

'Dad—'

'Let me finish. I need to say this.' He sucked in a breath and I felt a prickle of panic across the back of my neck. 'I did meet Agatha before your mother died.'

I knew it.

The waiter approached our table before I could say it.

Dad smiled like nothing had happened. *'Deux cafés, s'il*

vous plaît,' he said, holding up two fingers. When the waiter nodded and headed back towards the kitchen, Dad looked at me, clearly waiting for me to smile back. When I didn't, the corners of his mouth fell. 'We met at a Paris V fundraiser last year,' he said, his voice a little lower. 'But I didn't see her again until after your mother died.'

I didn't believe him.

It must have been obvious because when I sat back in my chair and crossed my arms, his handkerchief balled in my fist, he sat forward.

'She marched into my office my first day at Lariboisière. She had a tumour, a high-grade glioma in the thalamus, which was inoperable.'

It was as though he'd slapped me across the face. My eyes lost focus for a moment as the words collided in my head. He always does this, switches to surgeon mode when he's explaining things like this. Perhaps it's easier to say words like *inoperable* than it is to say the one he has to.

Cancer.

'The thalamus,' he explained, lowering his chin to tap the top of his head with his finger, 'is pretty much in the centre of the brain so Agatha couldn't find a surgeon willing to remove it.'

'They wouldn't even try?' I asked, unsure how someone could be lucid enough to walk into his office and tell him that yet still be dying.

It didn't make any sense.

'The problem was, the thalamus is one of the areas of

251

the brain associated with critical function and getting to it would have involved removing a considerable amount of healthy brain tissue.' I must have looked confused because he said, 'No surgeon would touch her, basically, because even if they could reach the tumour it would have caused significant neurologic injury.'

I didn't know what *significant neurologic injury* would be, but knew it was bad.

'So she came to you?'

'Remember when I went to San Diego?' I nodded. 'I went to observe a surgery treating an inoperable brain tumour with an MRI-guided laser. Agatha read about it while she was looking into surgeons and insisted I do it on her.'

'Had you done it before?'

'Not at all.' He sat back again as the waiter returned and put the coffees on the table between us. 'I'd only *observed* another surgeon doing it. I hadn't actually done it myself and I told her that much, suggesting she persist with radiotherapy.'

I suddenly thought of Agatha's short hair.

'Did she?' I asked, reaching my hand up to touch my own.

He tilted his head at me as he reached for his cup. 'Of course she didn't.'

I caught myself smiling fondly as I rolled my eyes.

'She wouldn't listen and said,' he sat a little straighter, '"Most people would be content with that, Professor

Durand. They'd shave their heads and get a tattoo and go to Disneyland.'"

I could just hear her saying it – *go to Disneyland* – with a disgusted sigh.

If I could have, I would have laughed.

'She said that she and I weren't most people, though,' he went on. 'That we were special, that we had to believe we were special to do the jobs we do when we could have been accountants or worked for the council or something, a nine-to-five with twenty-eight days' holiday and a pension.' He looked down at the Mont Blanc which was beginning to sweat under the lights in the tearoom. 'She said that we'd given up so much to be at the point we were at, that we wouldn't have done it if we didn't believe we were special, that we can do things most people can't.'

I realised what he was trying to say. 'Is that when she told you about Holly?'

He didn't look at me, just nodded.

'What did she say?'

'That she didn't do it for nothing, that she didn't give her up to die like that.'

I couldn't speak as a thorn of pain sank into my throat.

'"I don't want to die, Professor Durand."' He looked up at me then. 'I'd never heard anyone put it so simply. My patients tell me about all the things they haven't done, about their kids and wives and the boats they're restoring. But no one had ever said that, that they didn't want to die.'

I didn't know what to say. Thankfully, the waiter came

over to ask if we needed anything, which was a polite way of telling us to hurry up. The tearoom was heaving, as always, and he was clearly irked that we seemed in no hurry to leave. I hadn't even touched my coffee.

'*Non, merci,*' Dad said so firmly, the waiter took the hint and left us alone.

'I thought about your mother when she said it, about how I couldn't fix her,' Dad said when the waiter sauntered off. 'That's what I do: I fix people, and I couldn't fix your mother, so I fixed Agatha instead. I gave her a second chance and she gave me one, too.'

He nodded quickly, as if to convince himself that it had been the right thing to do, but when the skin between his eyebrows creased, I didn't think, just reached my hand across the table and squeezed his. He looked down at it – at my small hand covering his – clearly startled, but then he smiled and turned his hand over to thread his fingers through mine.

'So no, Lola,' he shook his head, 'I don't love Agatha like I love your mother. I can't. She was my first love. You understand that now, don't you? After Pan.' He lifted his eyelashes to look at me when he said *after*. It hurt like hell, but I knew what he was saying and nodded. 'I miss her every day. I miss her awful cooking and the banana skins she left everywhere and her laugh that used to make me laugh, too. I even miss how she interrupted me—'

'God, that was annoying, wasn't it?'

He chuckled lightly. 'I could never love Agatha like I

loved your mother, just like Agatha could never love me like she loved her first husband.'

'Agatha was married before?'

When I gasped he rubbed his lips together.

He'd obviously said too much.

'Not quite.'

'She's divorced?'

'No.'

'Wait. So they're still together?'

He shook his head and I blinked at him. 'But,' I started to say, then stopped when he avoided my gaze and looked down at the Mont Blanc again. 'Shit.'

He nodded.

'When did he die?'

'A long time ago.'

'How?'

I didn't think he was going to tell me, but he pinched the bridge of his nose and said, 'He jumped in front of a train the morning of their wedding.'

'What?' I gasped again. 'He killed himself? Why?'

'He didn't leave a note.'

Dad wouldn't look at me and it took a moment to realise why.

'Holly's father?' I said carefully, as though the words were made of glass.

He nodded.

'*That's* why she's freaking out about seeing Holly.'

He nodded again. 'It must have been like seeing a ghost.'

By the time we got back to the apartment I felt wrung out. All I wanted to do was get back into bed and not get out again, but as I was passing your door, it opened.

I was so startled, I took a step back.

'Hey,' I said with a stupid wave.

You leaned against the doorframe. 'Where've you been?'

'I needed some air.'

'So do I.'

I nodded down the hall towards Agatha's room. 'There's a balcony in—'

'I want to go *out* out, Lola.'

'I—' I started to say then stopped when you walked out into the hall to face me.

'I have to get out of here, Lola.' You lowered your voice. 'I can't breathe.'

I raised my eyebrows as if to say, *I get that*. 'Aren't you supposed to be resting, though?'

'All I've done since I got here last night is rest. I haven't left my room.'

'I don't know if going out in this rain is such a good idea, Holly.'

'Lola, please.' You rolled your eyes. 'Like you give a shit about my well-being.'

I deserved that, but it still stung as you walked past me into my room.

'I need to borrow something. Josette took my clothes to wash and I can't wear these.' You gestured at the pineapple print pyjamas I'd lent you.

'Sure. Take whatever you want.'

Take it all.

Need a kidney?

'Holy shit,' you muttered when you opened the wardrobe. 'Look at this.'

'They're not mine.' I nodded at my suitcase on the floor. '*They're* mine.'

You looked down at it then back up at the rail of clothes. 'So who do these belong to?'

'Me, I suppose, but I don't want them. Have at it.'

'Why don't you want them?'

'Not my style.'

'But look at this leather jacket! This is like three grand.'

'Is it?'

'Oh God, I'm sweating! Is this Saint Laurent?'

'Yves Saint Laurent?'

You turned to glare at me, about to tell me off, when you were distracted by one of the handbags I'd slung at the bottom of the wardrobe. You bent down to pick it up then turned to face me again, holding it up like a fisherman with his prize catch. 'Is this an *Agatha Abbot*?'

258

'Yep.'

'These are like a grand each, Lola, and you have one in every colour!'

'Take it.'

I'd rather carry a plastic bag than one of Agatha's handbags.

You considered it, then threw it back in the wardrobe and closed the doors. 'Can you believe I used to have a fake one of those?' You walked over to my suitcase. 'I got it off eBay.' You chuckled bitterly and bent down to pick a pair of jeans from my mound of clothes. I looked away as you wriggled out of your pyjama bottoms and tugged them on.

'Can I borrow this?' You didn't wait for me to respond, snatching the black hoodie off my bed and putting it on. It was Pan's. He'd forgotten it and I'd been sleeping in it since he left but I didn't stop you, even though I was trying to conserve the smell. 'Got any socks?'

'Somewhere,' I said, shrugging off my bag and walking over to you. You sat on the edge of the bed and watched as I kneeled down and picked through my suitcase. I couldn't find a matching pair, but you didn't seem bothered when I handed you odd ones.

'Let me get my trainers and we'll go.'

You told me that you were hungry. By then it was almost three o'clock and all the cafés on Boulevard Saint-Germain were heaving with tourists so I offered to take you to my café. You seemed intrigued by the *my* but it was still awkward as hell. When I offered to share my umbrella, you dipped your head and tugged your hood up. You'd be soaked through by the time we got there, which was exactly what you needed – to get pneumonia on top of everything else – but we only got as far as the corner before you stopped and pointed at Les Deux Magots.

'I know this café.'

I stopped too. 'You do?'

'I've been here before.'

'Are you sure? It's pretty famous. Ernest Hemingway used to come here.'

'Yeah.' You nodded, but you weren't looking at me, you were looking at the people sitting outside under the green and white awning that was shivering in the wind. 'I know I have.'

Before I could stop you, you ran across the road. I called after you, but you didn't stop. You didn't even look, just headed straight for the café and stood in front of it. I apologised to the waiter when you began darting between the tables as though you'd lost something, but he just said, 'C'est bien' with a lazy shrug and told us to sit anywhere that was free.

I was going to insist we sit inside but you stopped at an empty table by the window. I wondered what you were doing, the tip of your tongue poking out from the corner of your mouth as you ran your hand over it. So did everyone else, each of them looking up from their salads and croque-monsieurs to frown at you as you slipped your hand under the table.

'I knew it!' you squealed. 'Come here!'

When I got to you, you had tears in your eyes, but before I could ask if you were okay, you grabbed my hand and put it under the table. I winced when I touched a lump of dry chewing gum then gasped when you took my finger and traced the heart carved into the wood.

'Did you do that, Holly?'

'I must have!'

'How do you know?'

'How did I know it was there?' You grinned, your face pure sunshine. And with that, I felt something fall between us as you smiled at me like you did when we met at the hospital. I thought you were going to hug me and I think you might have if the waiter hadn't interrupted, coming over to wipe the table and ask us if we were going to sit there.

'*Oui.*' I held up two fingers. '*Deux menus, s'il vous plaît. Merci.*'

'Are you swearing at him?' you asked, feigning shock as you sat down.

'I asked for two menus.'

'Yeah, yeah.' And just like that you were back to the Holly I'd met the day before, bouncing in your chair then grinning at the waiter when he brought the menus.

'*Je vais vous apporter un cendrier,*' he said when I took my cigarettes out of my bag.

'*Merci.*'

'What did he say?' you asked, leaning across the table.

261

'He's bringing me an ashtray.'

You frowned when I offered you a cigarette. 'Do I smoke?' you asked, then took one. I lit it for you but as soon as I had, I knew you didn't. Sure enough, a second later you started coughing, your cheeks red as you handed it back to me. 'You really are trying to kill me, aren't you, Lola?'

I think you were joking, but it still made my stomach knot as I took it back.

'What you getting?' You pouted at the menu. 'I don't even know what I like.'

'What do you fancy?'

'That's the point, Lola: I can't remember, can I? Do I like *saumon fumé* or *jambon* or *Comté*?' You frowned. 'What's *Comté*?'

'Cheese.'

'Cheese,' you repeated then looked at me, eyes wide. 'What if I'm a veggie?'

'It's like the cigarette. You don't know until you try,' I said, and I shouldn't have, because knowing my luck, you were a strict vegan who was about to chow down on a ham sandwich.

'Maybe I should just get one of everything. Try them all and see what I like. Bloody hell.' You gaped at the menu. 'Five euros fifty for a coffee? Maybe not.'

'*Bienvenue à Paris*.' I shrugged and took a long drag on my cigarette.

'He's coming,' you hissed when the waiter started walking towards us. 'Order for me.'

I kept it simple. '*Deux sandwiches Comté et deux cafés, s'il vous plaît.*'

'You're so French,' you said, jiggling your shoulders as he walked away.

'Half French.'

'What's the other half?'

'Bajan.'

'Are your parents divorced?'

My gaze dipped as I tapped my cigarette on the edge of the ashtray. 'No.'

'So they're still together?'

'No.'

You looked confused. 'But,' you started to say, tilting your head at me, then stopped when I avoided your gaze, tapping my cigarette on the edge of the ashtray again. 'Oh. I'm sorry.'

I nodded, blinking away a tear.

'When did she die?'

'Christmas Eve.'

'Just gone?' I knew you were working it out in your head. 'It's August, right?'

'Actually, today's the first of September.'

'And your dad's married already? Damn. How long have they been married?'

'Almost four months.'

'Four months? Shut up!' You stared at me. 'That would fuck me up, too.'

I shrugged and took another pull on my cigarette.

263

'Do you reckon he cheated on your mum with Agatha?'

It almost knocked me clean off my chair, but I managed to shake my head.

Yesterday I would have said otherwise but after what Dad had just told me, I knew he hadn't.

'What was she like, your mum? Sorry,' you said when I turned to tap my cigarette on the ashtray again. 'I know I'm asking lots of questions, but I can't remember anything so I have nothing to contribute. Unless you want to hear the story about Grant's abscess.'

'No.' I raised my eyebrows. 'You're all right.'

'Was your mum a doctor, too?'

'A speech therapist.'

'What's that?'

'She helped people who have trouble talking.'

'Like a stammer?'

'Yeah.' I stopped to smile at the waiter as he brought our coffee and sandwiches. 'But also when people have strokes and cancer and stuff.'

'Cool.' You nodded, taking a sip of coffee. As soon as you tasted it, you scrunched your face up and I turned to get the waiter's attention. '*Excusez-moi. Un thé au lait, s'il vous plaît.*'

'Darjeeling?'

I nodded and turned back to find you wiping your tongue with a napkin.

'That tastes like ass.'

'Well, we can cross coffee off the list of things to try.'

'How can you drink that?' You pretended to heave.

'I grew up with it.'

'Was your dad born here?'

'Carcassonne, in the South. But he went to uni here.'

You were quiet for a moment and as I listened to the rain tapping on the awning over our heads, I wondered if you were thinking about your dad. I felt awful. Did you know what happened to him? That he killed himself? I thought you must have because you looked so sad, but then your shoulders lifted when you saw the waiter approaching our table with your tea.

'Much better,' you said with a sigh after you took a tentative sip.

'So we know you like tea. How about cheese?'

'It isn't what I expected.'

'The sandwich?'

'No. The apartment. I thought it would be all white, like an art gallery.'

I watched you bite into your sandwich. 'It's inspired by Coco Chanel's apartment.'

'She isn't what I was expecting, either.'

'Who? Agatha?'

'She's old.'

'Don't tell her that.'

You raised your eyebrows as if to say, *I wouldn't dare*, then asked, 'How old is she?'

'Forty, I think,' I said, stirring a sugar cube into my coffee.

You went quiet again as you calculated the dates. 'So she was twenty-three when she had me.'

I'd never thought about it.

'I thought she was like, fifteen,' you said, taking another bite of your sandwich. 'She was twenty-three when she started at Chanel.'

'How did you know that?'

Even I didn't know that.

You lifted your shoulder then let it drop. 'I couldn't sleep so I read her *Vogues*.'

I smiled. 'Did you put them back in the wrong order?'

'Of course.'

'Good.'

'That must be why she had me adopted, right?' I could feel your leg bouncing under the table as I took another drag on my cigarette. 'She couldn't pass up a job at Chanel, could she?'

I guess not.

'It's kind of fucked up, isn't it?' You laughed suddenly, and I could see you looking over my shoulder at Agatha's building. 'She wouldn't have any of this if she'd kept me.'

I couldn't look at you and stared at the bubbles on the surface of my coffee.

'I mean, I don't blame her. She wouldn't be Agatha Abbot if she'd stayed Agatha Park.'

For the first time since I'd met her, I felt an urge to defend Agatha, to tell you to cut her some slack and ignore her bravado because she was just as fucked up as the rest of us, but I couldn't. That was something she had to tell you herself.

'Have you discussed it?'

I knew you hadn't, so I don't know why I asked. I guess I hoped that Agatha had at least tried.

'Nope. But I heard all I needed to last night.'

I looked down at my coffee again.

'Why does she think I'm lying, Lola?'

'She's in shock.' I took a final drag on my cigarette and stubbed it out. 'Give her time.'

'Why?' When I looked up, you shrugged. 'If she doesn't want me here, I'll go.'

'You can't go.'

'Come on. She's not going to change her mind, is she, Lola? She seems pretty convinced that I'm pretending to be her daughter to con her out of – what? Money? A handbag?'

'Just let her calm down.'

'Why should I?' You stopped to sip your tea. 'And why should I do a DNA test?'

'You don't have to do anything you don't want to, Holly.'

'Well, I'm not. As soon as your dad lets me, I'm going.'

I pinched the bridge of my nose and sighed. 'Jesus. This is a mess.'

'*She's* a mess. But at least your dad's cool.'

I looked up with a smile. 'Thanks.'

'I said *he* was cool, not you.'

'Yeah, but I have his DNA so I'm part cool.'

'What does that say about me?' You wrinkled your nose at me. 'Seriously, though. He is cool. We talked for ages at the hospital yesterday. He made me feel loads better.' You tore another chunk of bread and squeezed it between your fingers. 'This amnesia thing is so weird. Like, I can remember how to walk and talk but I can't remember my name. What is that?'

'I looked it up. It's because that stuff is stored in another part of your brain.'

'That's what he said.'

We winked theatrically at each other.

'It's just weird.' You popped the squashed piece of bread in your mouth.

'It must be so frustrating. Have you remembered anything else?'

'No. Just what you told me.'

'Nothing at all?'

'Nothing. It's like trying to remember the words to a song, you know? It's *there*. When you told me my name, I recognised it, and when you told me about Agatha, I knew what you were talking about. It's like it's on the tip of my tongue but I can't get there on my own.' You stopped to swallow. 'Your dad says there are still loads of people from Gare du Nord they haven't identified.'

'Really?'

'Yeah. They didn't have ID on them so until someone claims them, they have no idea who they are. Apparently, there's a girl our age in a coma. Imagine. Why isn't anyone looking for her?' You shook your head. 'And some guy who thinks he's Henry IV. If you hadn't come to the hospital to find me that could be me. I'd be just wandering around Paris right now, thinking I'm Henry IV.'

'It's not forever, though.'

'That's the thing.' You reached for your cup again and pointed it at me. 'Am I going to wake up one morning and realise that I'm a hairdresser or an electrician or a ninja assassin?'

'A ninja assassin?'

'What if it all comes back to me at once, Lola, and I can't take it and freak out like Arnold Schwarzenegger in *Total Recall*?'

'What did Dad say?'

'He said that your head can't explode.'

'He'd know.'

'I hope I am a ninja assassin, but I bet I work in a petrol station or something.'

I felt so bad that I pushed my plate towards you. 'Do you want my sandwich?'

You took it. 'God, I'm so cheap.'

'Don't worry. I know it'll take more than a sandwich.'

'Forget it. I have,' you said, then laughed. 'Hey! My first amnesia joke!'

It was actually your second, but you were so pleased with yourself that I didn't have the heart to tell you. I excused myself and went inside to use the toilet. The café was full and there was a queue forming by the door, so when I was done and went back outside to find a guy standing by our table, I thought he was asking if we were finished, but he was shouting and jabbing at his temple with his finger. 'What is wrong with you?'

That's the trouble with sitting outside: if it isn't the thieves who pretend to be lost while they snatch your phone off the table or the ones who ask you to sign a petition while someone else steals your bag, it's beggars or men trying to chat you up, or just the good old-fashioned Bible bashers who think you need Jesus. I didn't know which this guy was but I didn't bother to ask, just walked over to our table and held my hand up. 'Go away. She's not interested.'

'She's fucking mad! *Folle!*' he spat, jabbing his temple with his finger again, then charged off, the glass door to the café almost breaking as he stormed inside.

I rolled my eyes and sat down. 'Are you okay?'

'No,' you murmured, then fainted.

Okay. If I thought I was scared the day before, it was nothing compared to sitting in Accident and Emergency watching you puke your guts up. Granted it was much calmer, the beds back in neat rows and the names written on the whiteboard with less haste, but there was still a steady hum of uneasiness. There always is in A & E. The doctors and nurses move more urgently than they do anywhere else. Not frantically, but they get to the phone quicker and shut the curtains with a swift swish that puts my teeth on edge. Plus, I could hear a baby crying, which didn't help, the sound grating on my nerves as I told you that Dad would be there soon. And he was, striding in wearing scrubs flanked by two interns who didn't look much older than me. They kept their distance, clutching notepads, as he stood at the foot of your bed.

'What happened?'

'I'm so sorry, Dad. We just went out for a coffee.'

'How long did she black out for?'

'Less than a minute.'

'How long has she been vomiting?'

'As soon as she came round. It's probably something she

271

ate but you always say that vomiting after a head injury isn't a good thing so I called an ambulance.'

'Hello?' you said, making the word sound about two minutes long. 'I am here, you know. Despite your daughter's best efforts, Simon.'

I thought he'd be mortified, but he laughed.

'Glad to hear it, Holly. Do you have a headache?'

You shook your head. 'But I'm never eating Comté again.'

'Maybe she's lactose intolerant, Dad? What if she is and she can't remember?' I said as the doctor who'd examined you when we'd got there approached the bed.

'*Renseignez-moi,*' Dad said to him, putting his hands on his hips. I didn't understand most of it – the medical terminology would have gone over my head in English as well – but Dad didn't look concerned as the doctor filled him in while the interns took notes.

'*Je les poursuivrai moi-même,*' he told the doctor then turned to you with a smile. 'Don't worry, Holly. I'm sure this is nothing to do with what happened yesterday but we'll give you another CAT scan just in case. In the meantime, I'm going to chase your bloods myself.' One of the interns tensed. I'm guessing he was supposed to do that. 'We're still so backed up from yesterday that we haven't got the results back from the blood we took from you then.'

When the doctor thanked Dad and went to tend to another patient, Dad gestured at one of the nurses and pointed at your bed.

'What's he saying?' you whispered.

Before I could answer, he closed your chart and looked up. 'I'm telling them to make sure that you're nil by mouth in case we need to operate.'

'Operate?' we said in unison.

'It's just a precaution.'

You looked horrified. I thought you were scared, but you said, 'So I can't have pizza?'

I frowned. 'I swear you just puked up two sandwiches, Holly.'

'Now there's more room, innit.'

'How do you even know you like pizza when you didn't know if you liked coffee?'

'I just know it in my bones, Lola.'

'No pizza.' Dad pointed the chart at you. 'And don't drink anything, either.'

'Until when? I'm so thirsty.'

'I know. Just until we know what's going on.'

'Kill me now,' you said, throwing your head back on the pillow.

'That's the spirit. Now tell me, Holly, what have you eaten so far today?'

You held up two fingers. 'Just two sandwiches but I puked them back up.'

'Okay.' He squeezed your foot with his hand. 'I'll be back.'

'Are you swearing at my father?' I asked, feigning shock as he walked away.

You turned your fingers and stuck them up. 'As if! He's the only one of you lot I like.'

I laughed, stepping back to let the nurse stand by your bed.

'Sanura.' You scowled at her and clutched your arm. 'Are you going to poke me again? I can't take it.' You held up your hand to show me the cannula. 'Tell her, Lola. No more needles.'

'*Plus de piqûres, Sanura!*' I wagged my finger at her.

'*Plus de piqûres,*' she promised, and held up a sample bottle with a smile.

You looked at it, then at me, and I tried not to laugh again as I backed away from the bed, offering to give you some privacy. I heard you complaining to Sanura as I headed out into the corridor and I did laugh then, when I heard you ask how you were meant to aim for the bottle.

Out there it was much cooler than it had been the day before. It wasn't quiet, all the seats taken, but at least I could walk towards the automatic doors this time. When I stepped through them, I glanced across at the ambulance bay, half-expecting to see the huddle of people I'd left there yesterday. It was empty, of course, but I check every time I go to the hospital now. I think I always will because those are the things that keep me up at night. Not just what I did to you but what I saw. The guy on the gurney who thought I was Manon and the guy pacing outside, waiting for his wife. We'll probably never see each other again, but from now on when we can't sleep or we've drunk too much or we're just sad for no reason, we'll think back to that day, and that guy who was pacing outside will wonder if I ever found my friend as I wonder if he found his wife, and we'll always be connected. Our lives forever meeting at that one, painful point.

I didn't know how long you'd be, so I wandered around the grounds for a while, reading old texts from Pan. I almost called him – I'd almost called him dozens of times since he'd left – but I couldn't bear to tell him what I'd done, so when it started raining, I headed inside. I expected you to be demanding pizza, but when I got back to your bed, Dad was there and you were crying.

'What's wrong? What is it? What happened?'

When you didn't answer, I took your hand and squeezed it until you looked at me.

'Holly, what's wrong?'

'Lola, I'm pregnant.'

You didn't want to go back to the apartment and Dad didn't fight you on it. If anything, he seemed relieved. Probably because at the hospital he could keep an eye on you, but I'm pretty sure it was also because it meant he didn't have to tell Agatha that you were pregnant.

I didn't blame him. Even I was trying to brace myself for her reaction, which would be apocalyptic, I was sure, and no doubt she would claim this as further proof that you only got in touch because you needed money. So I offered to pay for a hotel room, but Dad wouldn't hear of it. I don't know how, given that the hospital was full after what had happened at Gare du Nord, but he found you a private room. Then it was my turn to be relieved, because as much as I couldn't bear the thought of you alone in hospital, at least you wouldn't be alone in a hotel, eating a room service burger in bed.

The room was small but it had a TV and it was near the nurses' station. You seemed content enough, especially when Dad got you a fancy nightgown, which wasn't actually that fancy, but it had a back, which you were thrilled about until you looked up at him, your gaze narrowing.

'Who died in this, Simon?'

He laughed. 'No one. They're for the private patients,' he explained. 'We have loads of them because they always bring their own.'

You didn't seem convinced but put it on anyway because, as you said, your options were limited, so if it was a choice between having your arse hanging out or a dead woman's nightie, the latter was preferable.

If only just.

When a nurse came in, pushing an ultrasound machine with the same bored look that Dad gets when he's at the supermarket, I hovered by your bed for a moment or two, unsure if you wanted me to stay or not. In the end it was the nurse who asked me to leave, but when I went to, you grabbed my wrist. 'You are coming back, aren't you?' you asked with a worried frown, and I was so pleased that you wanted me to that I smiled. 'Can you come back with pizza?'

Only you could think of pizza at a time like that. Mind you, it was comforting to have something practical to do. Dad and the nurses knew what to do. They took your temperature and tested your blood pressure and scribbled in your chart while I tried not to get in their way. Plus, going and getting you a pizza had the added bonus of thoroughly pissing off the miserable nurse from the day before (Alix, apparently, but she'll always be the miserable nurse to me), who told me off when she saw me walking back onto the ward with the box. 'Ce n'est pas un hôtel,

278

Lola,' she told me with a disgusted sigh, then sighed again when I offered her some.

When I got to your room, the nurse with the ultrasound machine was gone and you were trying to turn on the television with the thing that adjusts the bed. 'It's broken,' you pouted, then pressed something that made the back of the bed go up so suddenly, you nearly shot clear across the room. You were laughing so much when I ran over to rescue you and then so excited about the prospect of pizza that I didn't get a chance to ask how the scan went, and when you started ranting that olives on pizza were heresy, I took the hint, figuring you didn't want to talk about it.

I suppose it should have been weird after everything that had happened, but you just had this way of forgetting stuff. Okay. Bad choice of words given the amnesia, but you know what I mean. So it wasn't weird. It was the opposite of weird.

Normal, I guess.

It had been a while since anything felt normal.

You have the attention span of a two-year-old, though, so by the time Dad came to check on you, you were fidgeting with boredom, having exhausted all the television channels, and killing the battery on my phone playing Techno Castle. So you asked him about coma girl, who you'd become a bit obsessed with, which is understandable given that if you'd been sitting in a different carriage, that could have been you. Dad wouldn't tell you anything, only that she still hadn't been identified, reminding you that it was a hospital, not a zoo, when you asked if you could see her.

So we watched a French translation of *Toy Story 3*, which you were hugely amused by, howling every time someone said Buzz, even though it happened every thirty seconds. 'Booooz,' you said, then slapped your leg, and every time you did, I looked at you, unable to believe that this tiny girl who loved *Toy Story 3* so much was going to have a baby.

I didn't say that, though, happy to humour you in pretending that nothing was wrong as I watched you pick the discs of pepperoni off the leftover pizza and eat them. I even slept there, in a chair next to your bed, despite Dad insisting that he'd get a nurse to find a roll-up bed. *'Ce n'est pas un hôtel, Papa,'* I told him with a smile, but when I woke up the next morning, I regretted it.

'Oh God, I'm dying,' I groaned when I tried to move my neck.

You didn't seem worried, though. 'You snore.'

I opened my eyes to find you sitting on the bed eating a cold slice of pizza.

'What?'

'You snore.'

'No, I don't.'

'You snore worse than my dog.'

I stopped trying to sit up and stared at you. 'You have a dog?'

It took you a second but when you realised what I was saying, you gasped.

'Lola, I have a dog!'

'You're remembering stuff!'

'I have a dog,' you said to yourself, then laughed.

'Yes!' I said, clambering out of the chair to tell a nurse to page Dad.

When I got back, you were grinning.

'You're my trigger,' you told me, biting the tip off another slice of pizza.

'Your what?'

'Your dad says I need a trigger, like a song, that will trigger my memory.'

'Like the heart under the table at Les Deux Magots yesterday?'

'Exactly! Your snoring must have reminded me that I have a dog.'

I smiled, oddly proud of myself.

'That's what we should do today. Find some stuff to trigger my memory.'

'Oh, that's a good idea.'

'What's a good idea?' Dad asked, sweeping in suddenly and making me jump.

'Face tattoos.' You pointed the pizza crust at him then threw it in the box.

He stopped mid-step.

'She's joking, Dad,' I said, closing the box and taking it out of your lap.

'Ask me why I'm joking, though, Simon.'

He crossed his arms and smiled. 'Why are you joking, Holly?'

'Because I remembered that I have a dog!'

'You did? What's his name?'

'Um, slow your roll, Simon,' you told him as he took the chart from the end of the bed and opened it. 'One thing at a time.'

'What made you remember that?'

'Lola's snoring.'

'Bad, isn't it?'

'I do not snore!'

They ignored me.

'She's gonna take me around Paris today, see if it will trigger anything else.'

He nodded, hooking the chart back on the end of your bed. 'That's a good idea, actually.'

'Don't say it like that!'

'Like what?'

'*Actually*, like you're surprised that I had a good idea.'

'Holly,' he said with a solemn sigh, crossing his arms again. 'Remember last night when you thought that banging your head again would reset your brain?'

'Oh, what do you know?' you huffed, kicking back the sheet.

When you were discharged, we headed straight for Les Deux Magots, figuring that it must have meant something to you if you carved a heart into that table. If the waiter thought we were mad for insisting on only sitting there then waiting for it to be free, he didn't say anything, no doubt used to the varied proclivities of the people who go in there. I never thought I was particularly difficult, but thinking about it now, I refuse to sit on the tables closest to the street and I also have a weird aversion to booths, for some reason. Probably due to some childhood trauma at a Pizza Hut. But I'm nothing compared to Agatha, who won't sit by the window ('I'd just like to eat in peace without people gawping at me') or the kitchen or the toilet.

There's basically one table she'll sit at and God help you if it's not free.

We only had to wait fifteen minutes, but it was long enough for you to be starving, so when our croque-madames arrived, you inhaled yours, then mine, then ordered an eclair.

'Don't say it,' you warned when the waiter brought it.

'Say what?'

'That I'm eating for two.'

I held my hands up and shook my head as if to say, *I wouldn't dare.*

'I don't want to talk about it,' you warned, biting the end off the eclair.

I nodded.

'I don't.'

I nodded again.

'Lola!' You stopped to swallow. 'How can I be pregnant and not know?'

'I—'

You didn't let me finish, leaning across the table. 'There is a baby in me,' you pointed at your stomach then lowered your voice like it could hear you, 'a *baby.*'

'I know.'

'Whose is it?'

'I don't know.'

You sat back again. 'How can I not know who it belongs to?'

'You do,' I said, softly, 'you just can't remember.'

'Am I in love?'

'You might be.'

'Is that why I drew a heart under this table?' You looked down at it and lowered your voice again as though you thought the table could hear you as well. 'Do you think we came here together?'

'You might have. Have you called home? Maybe he's looking for you.'

The corners of her mouth drooped. 'Your dad did.'

'What happened?'

'Nothing.'

I didn't push it as you bit another hunk off the eclair, but when you swallowed it, you shrugged. 'Turns out I don't have a home,' you said, touching the bruise on your temple with your finger. 'That's what social services told your dad yesterday while you were out getting the pizza.'

'Social services?'

'They're the ones who reported me missing.'

'Not your adoptive parents?'

'They died when I was fourteen, apparently.'

I couldn't catch my breath. 'What?'

'Motorcycle accident.'

'Does Agatha know?'

'No, and don't tell her, either.' You pointed the eclair at me with a fierce frown. 'It will only convince her that I'm after her money.'

'But what about your new parents?'

I felt so stupid saying *new parents*, like they were a car you'd traded in. And I felt even more stupid when you said, 'I don't have new parents. No one wants to adopt a fourteen-year-old. According to social services I'm in a children's home called Gravel Hill.' You laughed, but I couldn't. 'It sounds like something from a horror film.'

'Did they know? About the baby?'

You shook your head. 'I'm only six weeks pregnant, though. Maybe I didn't tell them.'

'You must have friends there. Maybe you told one of them.'

'Maybe.'

'Do you want to call the home and see?'

'I guess.'

I could tell that you didn't want to talk about it any more so didn't push it. I thought that was it, but you said, 'I've been thinking.' You stopped to lick a smear of chocolate off your thumb. 'What if she's right?'

'Who?'

'Agatha.'

'Right about what?'

'I can't even remember my name, Lola. What if I did come here to con her?'

'Then don't.'

You looked up at me and I shrugged. I couldn't think of another way to say it.

'Who knows why you wanted to meet her, Holly. Maybe it was because you were sick of living in a children's home and you hoped she could help. Or maybe it was because you found out you were pregnant and you needed your mother. I know I would.' You looked down at your empty plate. 'You can't change that, so all that matters is what you do from here on out. Prove her wrong.'

'I guess.'

When you bit down on your lip, I reached for my cigarettes. 'Take it from me,' I told you, stopping to light one. I inhaled then turned to blow the smoke away from you. 'The worst thing you can do is become the person she thinks you are.'

As we were leaving the café, it occurred to me that I had no idea where to start. Finding the table at Les Deux Magots was a fluke. It's a big city; you could have gone *anywhere*. So we started with the obvious places, the places everyone goes when they come to Paris. We started with the Eiffel Tower. It had just rained so the sky was pigeon feather grey and raindrops dripped on us as we walked under it. You recognised it, of course (I'd have found it weirder if you didn't, to be honest), but after circling it a few times, it didn't seem to register any deeper than something most people have seen dozens of times, whether they've been to Paris or not.

So we took the Metro to Musée d'Orsay. It was rush hour so I thought you might have been a little overwhelmed by it, but the only thing you were fazed by was the turnstiles when we got off. You didn't even seem to mind how crammed the carriage was, but it wasn't until we were getting off and I saw your gaze darting around at the sea of people that practically carried us off the train and up the stairs that I realised how much it must have reminded you of what happened at Gare du Nord. I felt awful when we finally made it up to the top of the stairs and out into the open, but if you were upset, you didn't say, just shrugged and told me that you were fine as we followed the stream of people across the bridge towards the Louvre.

It was a Tuesday so the museum was shut, but it was still teeming. Mostly with couples and friends meeting after work, but I could see a harassed woman trying to corral a group of kids in matching green jumpers onto a coach, but they were clearly more interested in chasing one another around and walking along the edge of the fountain. 'I hope one of them falls in,' you muttered, reading my mind, and I laughed so much I almost bumped into the woman in front of us who stopped suddenly as she was approached by a guy selling gold plastic Eiffel Towers.

As soon as we'd righted ourselves and walked around her, we were approached by another guy. They're as ubiquitous (thanks, Agatha!) as the tourists, and very persuasive. Pan had bought three when he was here, but when I told the guy that we weren't interested, he realised I was French and moved on to another couple.

'Look familiar?' I asked when we passed Pavillon Mollien and the museum came into view. You nodded, looking around with a curious frown, but I suppose it would have, the palace another of those places that has been in so many films that you feel like you know it whether you've been there or not. But when most people think of the Louvre, they think of the grand grounds and the statues and the Mona Lisa, so some are startled by the brilliant glass pyramid in the middle of it all, cutting up through the courtyard like it had been underground all along.

Looking at it made me think of the hospital, of A & E and how they'd propped it up against the end of the building. At the Louvre the glass works, though, a diamond in the middle of the magnificent, marzipan coloured palace with its columns and arches and smooth slate roof.

The spoilt little sister who gets all of the attention now.

We walked through the gardens, towards the Paul truck, because you have to eat every ten minutes, I've learned. I asked again if anything looked familiar while we waited in line. You said it did, but you weren't sure if it was because you'd been there or if you'd seen it somewhere else. I didn't push you because that's what I meant when I said that you've got to be careful who you listen to about what happened at Gare du Nord. I don't know how much of it you're going to remember, but it's easy to hear someone else's version of events and assume they are your own.

Too easy.

As we were walking away with our *chocolats chauds*, you reached out to steady yourself, then stopped. I thought you were going to faint again, but you smiled.

'I tripped.' You pointed at the gravel. 'I remember: I tripped here.'

'Are you sure?'

'Yes! I tripped and spilled my hot chocolate.'

'How do you know?'

You weren't listening as you started feeling your chin.

'Here!' You reached for my hand. 'Feel!'

I frowned as my fingers grazed a wrinkle of skin. 'Is that a scar?'

'Yes! From tripping here!'

You were delighted, almost spilling your hot chocolate again as you looked down at the ground and grinned. 'Hello, ground! Do you remember my chin?'

'It worked, Holly!' I said when you looked up. 'You're remembering stuff!'

I was so excited that I had to fight the urge to hug you.

'I am!'

You twirled then walked with me through the Carrousel garden towards the Ferris wheel. There was something about it, about the way you smiled and walked with me – like you knew where we were going – that made me want to twirl, too.

'You're going to remember, aren't you?' I said, breathless. 'I can feel it.'

'Me too, Lola.' You bit down on your bottom lip. 'I just need one more thing.'

So we kept walking.

We didn't think about where we were going, just wandered. Eventually we strayed off the path and into the Tuileries garden, which was still wet with rain, statues speckled with it and the air so damp I knew that it was about to start again. Sure enough, when we got back onto the path, I felt it. It wasn't enough to need an umbrella, but just enough to make everything dimmer. That's the best word to describe Paris in September, like summer, but dimmer. It's still warm and the trees are full, but they're not as green, as though someone has turned down the brightness.

As we approached the basin you stopped. I thought you were looking at the people sitting on the benches around it, undeterred by the drizzle, but you pointed.

'What's this called? This fountain?'

'It's a basin, technically.'

'Does it have a name?'

'*Grand Bassin Octagonal.*'

When you frowned I realised that wasn't what you were thinking.

'It looks different.' You squinted at it. 'Has it always looked like this?'

'Since the seventeenth century. The French don't like change.'

'Okay.' Your frown deepened. 'Maybe I don't know it, then.'

We started walking, veering towards the left of the basin. We were near another food truck so when you stopped, I thought you were hungry again, but you turned and looked back at the basin.

'Has it always had water in it?'

'Always.'

'Oh.'

We started walking again, but I stopped this time.

'They drained it in July.'

'Drained it?' You stopped walking as well. 'Why?'

'Because of the heatwave. People were swimming in it.'

'I knew it.' You spun on your heels to face it again, the gravel crunching.

'How?' I asked before my brain registered. 'Were you here in July, Holly?'

That clearly hadn't occurred to you because you blinked. 'I must have been.'

'Why were you here in July?'

You stared at the basin as though the answer was about to emerge from the water. It didn't, of course, but suddenly, something nudged at me.

'Holly, how far along are you?'

I turned to you just as you turned to me. 'Six weeks.'

'Holly, did you get pregnant here?'

When I pointed at the ground you started to shake your head then stopped. 'It's September second, right?' You worked it out on your fingers. 'The dates add up.'

'Maybe you came here with the father.'

'Maybe the father *lives here*.'

I almost shoved you when I made the connection. 'Holly, the dude!'

'What dude?'

'The dude who was yelling at you at Les Deux Magots yesterday!'

You gasped and pressed your hands to your face. 'The dude!'

The dude was called André and he worked part-time at the café. The manager didn't recognise Holly so told us to come back the next day when André would be working. I'm guessing a lot of girls asked after him, because he wouldn't take my number, not until one of the bus boys went past with a stack of clean plates. He nodded at Holly as he passed and when he did, I pointed at you, asking if he knew you. *'Oui,'* he nodded again, if more warily this time. *'C'est la petite amie d'André.'*

'I'm André's girl,' you said as we left the café. 'I'm someone's girl.'

I was so stunned it didn't occur to me to be nervous about going back to the apartment, not until Agatha sauntered out of the salon as we walked in, a book between her fingers.

'Oh.' She looked disappointed. 'You're back.'

I felt the pinch of it so I don't know how you felt.

'Well,' she said, putting her glasses on and looking down at the book. 'It's Josette's day off so you'll have to fend for yourselves. Simon and I are going out.'

Normally, I would have gone off, but for the first time I saw how thin she was, all sharp lines and jutting bones, her skin the colour of dandelion fluff. I couldn't help but think of what Dad had told me at Angelina's and something in me softened.

'I think Holly and I should come with you.'

I didn't even know that I was going to say it until I heard the words coming out of my mouth and the shock of it made the tops of my ears burn.

Agatha looked up at me, an eyebrow arched. 'Excuse me?'

'I think Holly and I should come with you and Dad.'

'To supper?'

When I nodded, she chuckled to herself.

'There's plenty of food in the house, Lola. I'm sure even you are capable of making toast.'

Don't hit a woman with cancer.

Never hit a woman with cancer.

I called after her as she turned to walk away, 'We can't keep avoiding this.'

She stopped and turned smoothly on the balls of her feet. 'Avoiding what?'

'This.' I gestured at the space between us. 'We need to talk.'

She looked genuinely bewildered. 'About what, dear?'

'About your daughter.'

I felt you tense next to me.

'*Chérie*, are you ready?' Dad asked as he opened the

front door. He smiled when he saw Holly and me standing in the hall. 'Oh you're back, girls.'

'Yes,' Agatha said tightly. 'And they want to talk.'

'Talk?'

'They've built quite an alliance, it seems.'

Dad threw his keys on the side table by the door. 'That's an excellent idea.'

As much as I'd rather have done it at a restaurant – with witnesses – Agatha insisted on ordering in. Of course she ordered the one thing pregnant women can't eat – sushi – so Dad made you an omelette. I haven't seen him do that for years, but he hadn't lost his touch, grating cheese and chopping hunks of ham while Agatha hovered in the kitchen like a wasp, sipping red wine and frowning at how much cheese he was using.

We ate in the dining room, so it felt a little like the last supper as you stabbed at your omelette with your fork while Dad and Agatha sat opposite us, delicately eating sushi. She led the conversation, talking about everything but you. About the rain and how much she missed the summer, the hideous heatwave forgotten as she reminisced over how beautiful Paris looked in the sun, like it was gilded with gold. But by the time Dad poured her third glass of wine, she'd run out of steam. She sighed and pushed her plate away, which was her way of saying, *Let's talk*.

'Okay.' I stopped to take a breath. 'Let me start by saying that this is a mess.'

'And whose fault is that, Lola?' she said before I could finish.

'Mine.' I held my hands up. If she was satisfied with that, she didn't look it as her jaw tightened, but she let me finish. 'It's three hundred per cent my fault, I admit that. Which is why you should be taking it out on me, not Holly. I'm the bad guy.'

Agatha looked indignant. 'I'm not taking it out on anyone.'

'Okay.' I could see where it was going and made a time out sign with my hands. 'I'm not having a go at you. I'm just saying: can we please just draw a line under the whole thing and start again?'

She shook her head swiftly. 'I don't think we can, Lola.'

'Me neither,' you said, speaking for the first time since we'd got home.

It surprised us all, even Agatha, who hesitated before she took a sip of wine.

'Well, we have to,' I said, 'because there's another child about to come into this fucked up family and we owe it to him or her not to fuck them up, too.'

Agatha didn't just hesitate this time, she flinched, her eyebrows shooting up.

'You're pregnant, Lola?'

You raised your hand gingerly. 'No. I am.'

Agatha turned to Dad, who closed his eyes and pinched the bridge of his nose.

'Well,' she put her wine glass down, 'that explains why you couldn't wait until you were eighteen to get in touch. How much do you need?'

'Agatha,' Dad and I said in unison.

'Oh please. You're not buying this little girl lost routine, are you? She knows exactly what she's doing. I heard you yesterday. "Is this Saint Laurent?" You can't remember your name but you knew how much everything in Lola's wardrobe cost.' How did you remember that you'd bought a fake AA bag from eBay, I suddenly thought, but dismissed it as Dad shrugged.

'Maybe she just likes fashion.' The look she gave Dad stopped him from finishing the thought. So he changed tack. 'Agatha, be reasonable. Holly had no idea who you were until she got here on Sunday. She thought you were Agatha Park. How could she possibly know that you're so wealthy?'

'Is that so?' Agatha said, but she didn't look at him, she looked at you and when she did, I heard you suck in a breath. 'So why were you at Les Deux Magots?'

'Just now?' you asked and you'd never looked so young, like a little girl.

'Whenever you carved that heart under the table. If you didn't know who I was, how did you end up in the café *opposite* my apartment?'

Dad interjected. 'Is that what you're basing this on? Les Deux Magots is one of the most famous cafés in Paris, Agatha. It's a tourist trap.'

I could tell he was losing his temper, but I was the one who lost it first. 'And she was shagging the waiter there!'

'Lola!' you barked, turning in your chair towards me.

'I'm sorry,' I couldn't look at you, 'but why aren't you defending yourself, Holly? She's being a total bitch!'

'Lola,' Dad hissed.

I didn't apologise this time, which didn't go unnoted by Agatha, who watched me cross my arms and sit back in my chair with a huff, then turned to face you.

'So you think this waiter is the baby's father?'

You shrugged meekly. 'I don't know.'

'You don't know who the father of your child is?'

'I don't *remember*,' you corrected, with a little more force.

'How far along are you?'

When you didn't answer, just looked down at your half-eaten omelette and started fiddling with the strings on your hoodie (Pan's hoodie), I told her.

'Six weeks. We think she got pregnant when she was here in July.'

Agatha's eyebrows lifted again. 'Why were you in Paris in July?'

'She doesn't remember, does she?' I snapped.

'In the café opposite my apartment, no less,' she went on as if I hadn't spoken.

Dad sighed and poured himself another glass of wine. 'It's just a coincidence.'

'An extraordinary one,' she said, waiting for him to do

298

the same for her. She didn't even look at him, just held her glass up like he was a waiter. So he put the bottle down between them and when he snatched his glass, I'd never loved him more.

If Agatha was perturbed, she didn't seem it as she reached for the bottle. 'So tell me.' She refilled her glass. 'How is it that you have a dog in a children's home?'

My jaw clenched. 'So you did know that she was in care?'

'Speaking of which, how are you planning to raise a child in care? You'll get a council flat, I suppose.' She sipped her wine. 'At least you'll be among friends.'

'Agatha,' Dad said through gritted teeth.

'What? It's a good thing. She'll need help when the baby comes.'

You stood up then. 'I don't need this.'

Agatha tilted her head from side to side as if to say, *I told you so.*

You must have seen her do it because you stopped and turned to look at her.

'No, Agatha. I have no idea how I'm going to raise this child. And I have no idea why I came here, either. But if it was for money it's probably because I thought that suffering the humiliation of asking a stranger for a handout was worth it if it meant this baby has what he or she needs.' You were holding on so tightly to the chair you were standing behind that your knuckles were white. 'I know why I came back today, though. I came back because I wanted to see

299

what kind of woman gives up a baby, and now I know.' You let go of the chair to point at your chest. 'Not me.'

You went back to London the next day. Agatha took it as proof that she was right, especially when you refused to take a DNA test. Not that it would have made a difference either way, because the truth is, there's nothing you could have said or done to convince her otherwise. So I know why you didn't want to take the test. It wasn't because you were scared that she was right; it's because whether you were her daughter or not you were never going to see her again.

I don't blame you, I'm just sorry for the part I played in all of this. Perhaps if I hadn't interfered and had let Agatha get in touch when she was ready, she would have been more welcoming, more ready to deal with it. Or maybe she would never have got in touch and she would have remained the mother you dreamt about your first night in another foster home, the one who was going to rescue you.

Take you away from it all.

So I didn't know what to say when we said goodbye at the airport. You didn't even have any luggage, just the clothes I'd given you to wear and the emergency passport we'd got that morning at the British embassy. You wouldn't take the €200 I tried to give you, so I slipped it into the back pocket of your jeans when we hugged goodbye. Not because I felt guilty or I thought it could possibly compensate for what I'd done, but because that was what

300

was left from the money I'd drawn out of my account after I'd bought your Eurostar ticket. It was supposed to be for getting out, and you were getting out.

It wasn't until I was in the cab back to the city that I realised that I hadn't thought about running away again since that day with Pan. It hadn't even occurred to me when I waved you off that I wanted to go, too, so when my phone rang and I saw that it was Pan, I smiled.

'Hello, stranger.'

'Thank God,' he said, letting go of a breath. 'I've been so worried.'

My smile widened then, because as soon as I heard his voice we fell back into it – it, whatever we are. But as I listened to him telling me off for not calling him back after what had happened at Gare du Nord, I felt something in me sag.

Something was different.

We were different.

I was different.

It was as though the day I got in touch with you I crossed a line I couldn't go back across, so Pan was on one side and I was on the other, and the space between us didn't feel like space any more; it felt like the whole world. I'm sure I don't need to tell you how easy it is to lose people. I don't mean like Mum, but the people you thought would always be there, the ones in your photos who know your secrets and were the first ones you called when you had good news.

A few missed calls and they're gone.

Sad, isn't it?

You don't just lose them, though, do you? You lose a bit of yourself, too. Like Pan. I'll never love anyone as much as I loved him, in that way that made me dizzy sometimes and made me punch Tim Eliot in the stomach when we were twelve because he took the piss out of Pan's hair.

But how can Pan love me when I don't even love me? I don't like what I've become – what all of this has turned me into – so how can I expect him to?

In books and films love is enough, but that's not how it works. I got it then, what Dad was trying to say about loving Mum. I'll never love anyone as much as I loved Pan, in the same unreasonable, unreachable, uncontainable way that you love someone the first time because you're not scared that you're being too clingy or too crazy, when you just let them see it all because it doesn't occur to you that they don't want to. Or maybe it's that I'll never *let* myself love anyone like that, because I never want to feel like that again. I thought of Agatha then and felt another stab of sympathy. Pan and I breaking up was painful enough, but I don't know what I would have done if he'd killed himself and I didn't know why. The thought brought tears to my eyes and while I don't think I'll ever make my peace with the way she is, I understood how she became like that. Why she doesn't trust anyone.

Why she's so careful with her heart.

I will be, too, because I know too much now. I know love isn't enough, that you can love someone with every bit of yourself and still fuck it up beyond repair. And that's okay because sometimes they're your one but you're not their one, which is kind of cruel, but what can you do?

'Sorry,' I said when Pan was done telling me off. 'Things are a mess.'

'Your dad said.'

My shoulders tensed. 'What did he say?'

'Just that there was a lot going on.'

I let go of a breath and rubbed my forehead with my hand. 'Yeah.'

'What happened?'

'Pan, I can't.' I moved my hand over my eyes. 'Not now. Not on the phone.'

'When?'

'Soon.'

'Sorry.' I heard him exhale. 'It's just that it's been three days.'

Had it only been three days?

It felt like a month.

'I've been so worried about you, Lo. Everyone's talking about it.'

'Here, too.'

'I can't believe that asshole lied about stopping one of the bombers. Who does that?' When I didn't agree, he waited a second or two then asked if I was okay, and for the first time since I'd got to Paris, he felt very far away.

'I was just thinking,' I said, looking out the window at the VW ad on the side of a bus, 'about all those people who were supposed to be at Gare du Nord that morning but weren't, you know? All those people who missed their train or couldn't decide what to wear.' He didn't say anything, but I knew he was nodding. 'Dad says it's luck, but what if it's nothing to do with luck?'

'What do you mean?'

'What if it doesn't matter?'

'If what doesn't matter, Lola?'

'What we do or don't do. What if, at any given time, we're exactly where we need to be?'

He was quiet for a moment, then said, 'You're not coming home, are you?'

Even though he couldn't see me, I nodded.

'I think I'm where I need to be, Pan.'

Dad was surprised when he walked out of his office to find me walking in.

'Lola, what's wrong? Did something happen with Holly's flight?'

'No, I just dropped her off at the airport and wondered if you fancied dinner.'

He blinked at me. 'Dinner?'

'Yeah. We can try that Thai place you were telling me about.'

'Yes. Of course,' he said, clearly flustered as he turned to Sabine. '*Annules mon rendez-vous de six heures.*'

I don't know what meeting he'd asked her to cancel, but she looked surprised. I thought she was going to say something, but the phone rang and we slipped out while she answered it. We didn't get far, though, because a few moments later we heard her calling him and stopped. I thought she was going to remind him that the meeting was important, but she frowned. '*Professeur Durand. C'est la police.*'

Agatha was right.

I keep referring to her as *you* – as Holly – but she wasn't, was she?

But you know that.

Her name's Nicola Ferris, the police confirmed it.

She doesn't live in a children's home, either. She has a rather nice life, actually, living in Dorset with her parents, her brother and her dog, Max. She even has a pony. Can you believe it? A fucking pony.

Her parents were on a cruise when the explosion at Gare du Nord happened. Nicola was supposed to be camping with friends so they weren't worried when they saw the news. It wasn't until they stopped off in Antigua and called home to find that she hadn't returned and wasn't answering her phone that they knew something was wrong and told the police.

So while Agatha was right about that, Nicola hadn't been trying to con her. She was heading to Paris to tell André she was pregnant and just happened to be sitting next to you on the Eurostar. You might even remember her. She does, she remembers it all now, how nervous you were about meeting Agatha, how you lent her your scarf when she was cold. So when I turned up at the hospital, babbling about you, Nicola recognised the story and thought she was Holly Stapleton.

As for you, I've been calling you coma girl for so long that this feels strange, too, referring to you as Holly, but that's who you are. The first time we came to see you, I thought Agatha would do the same thing she did with Nicola, that she'd walk out and tell Dad he was wrong, but she looked at you, lifted her chin and said, 'Simon, get her off this ghastly ward.'

I think sometimes about the way my mother would have reacted, how she would have wept and kissed your cheek. But Agatha shows her affection in different ways, I know now. She insisted that you be moved to a private room, somewhere with a view of the rooftops where the sun tumbles in in the afternoon. And she brings clean pillow-cases every day, which she changes herself, and flowers, freesias and lavender and lily of the valley, things you'll be able to smell.

Between them and the scented candles the nurses blow out as soon as she leaves, they've had quite enough of her. Plus, she's always bringing someone in to chant over you or wave incense. She's tried everything from reiki to acupuncture, none of which she'd be allowed to do if she wasn't married to Dad. But the funny thing is, he's the one thing she *hasn't* questioned, so it's kind of weird to see Agatha who, despite her herbalist and psychic and bioenergeticist, only truly believes in the restorative power of a well-cut suit, putting all of her faith in Dad.

He says you're doing really well, by the way. You've been moving your fingers when the nurse changed your cannula and yesterday you opened your eyes when she said your name. Today we're going to see if you'll squeeze his hand.

I guess this is it, then. There's nothing left to say.

Except maybe one more thing . . . I'm so sorry, Holly.

Heart-Shaped Bruise

Tanya Byrne

When Archway Young Offenders Institution is closed down a notebook is found in one of the rooms.

I have to start by saying that this isn't an apology. I'm not sorry. I'm not.

This is that notebook.

They say I'm civil and everyone believed it. Including you.

But you don't know.

Its pages reveal the dark and troubled mind of Emily Koll, Archway's most notorious inmate.

Sometimes I wonder if I'll ever shake off my mistakes or if I'll just carry them around with me forever like a bunch of red balloons.

'Raw and gripping with a wholly unexpected final twist' *Guardian*

'A compulsive and moving novel' *Stylist*

978 0 7553 9606 1

headline

Follow Me Down

Tanya Byrne

First Love. Last lie.

When Adamma Okomma has to leave her glossy high school in New York for a dusty English boarding school, she thinks it's the end of the world – or the end of her social life, at least.

Then she meets the wicked-witted Scarlett Chiltern, who shows her all of Crofton College's darkest corners and Adamma realises that there's much more to her new school than tartan skirts and hockey sticks.

She and Scarlett become inseparable, but when they fall for the same guy, the battle lines are firmly drawn.

Adamma gets the guy but loses her best friend. Then, when Scarlett runs away, Adamma finds herself caught up in something far more sinister than a messy love triangle. Adamma always knew that Scarlett had her secrets, but some secrets are too big to keep and this one will change all of their lives forever.

Praise for Tanya Byrne:

'Intriguing and compelling – a very accomplished debut' Sophie Hannah

'Byrne is a talented writer with attitude and a fresh, original voice' *Daily Mail*

'Reminiscent of *The Catcher in the Rye*, this psychological jigsaw of a novel will appeal to your dark side' *Glamour*

978 0 7553 9309 1

headline

Boy21

Matthew Quick

It's never been easy for Finley, particularly at home. But two things keep him going: his place on the basketball team and his girlfriend, Erin – the light in even the darkest of his days.

Then Russ arrives. He answers only to Boy21, claims to be from outer space, and also has a past he wants to escape. He's one of the best high-school basketball players in the country and threatens to steal Finley's starting position.

Against all the odds, Russ and Finley become friends. Russ could change everything for Finley, both for better and for worse. But sometimes the person you least expect can give you the courage to face what's gone before . . . and work out where you're going next.

Praise for Matthew Quick:

'Beautiful . . . a first-rate work of art' *New York Times*

'Transfixed me from the opening line to the last' Annabel Pitcher

'Dark and intense yet funny: compelling stuff' *Fabulous*

978 1 4722 1290 0

headline

Hello, Goodbye, and Everything In Between

Jennifer E. Smith

One night. A life-changing decision. And a list . . .

Of course Clare made a list. She creates lists for everything. That's just how she is.

But tonight is Clare and Aidan's last night before college and this list will decide their future, together or apart.

It takes them on a rollercoaster ride through their past – from the first hello in science class to the first conversation at a pizza joint, their first kiss at the beach and their first dance in a darkened gymnasium – all the way up to tonight.

A night of laughs, fresh hurts, last-minute kisses and an inevitable goodbye.

But will it be goodbye forever or goodbye for now?

Praise for Jennifer E. Smith:

'That whole fresh, dizzy, gorgeousness of first love is there . . . Highly recommended!' Carmen Reid

'Packed with fun and romance, this uplifting *You've Got Mail*-style story is totally charming' *Closer*

'A sweet story of summer love with all its myriad complications' *Sunday Express*

978 1 4722 2103 2

headline